“Meet Calico, Bones, Jimmy, Cozy, N[illegible] named Sal and Rufus who all meet up at the Venus Motel somewhere in the desert outside of Paradise, Arizona. The lives of this colorful cast of characters become intertwined by—and ultimately turned upside down by—a “magic” box that makes things disappear . . . forever. *Venus Sings the Blues* is delightful, unforgettable, and quirky, another brilliant work by one of today’s finest storytellers. Keep ’em coming, Buck Storm!”

ANN TATLOCK, award-winning novelist, editor, and children’s book author

“Tears of joy met me on the pages of this book as I traced the path from brokenness to redemption in each character. The reminder that our past doesn’t have to dictate how our story ends is eclipsed only by the lesson that love cannot be earned. People can change, and the words contained here can be part of that process. Enjoy!”

ROBERT CASE, senior pastor, Calvary Chapel Eastside

Praise for Buck Storm

“I’ve never read a phrase from Buck Storm that wasn’t time well spent—and worth reading again. A topflight storyteller, Storm pits his protagonist—an eccentric, homeless widower—against a powerful and wealthy small-town businessman. The engaging story has readers quickly joining the cast of funky supporting characters on the streets of Paradise, Arizona, grooving on creative plot twists and wondering if this hero-and-villain drama can ever be resolved.”

RANDALL MURPHREE, editor of the *AFA Journal*

“Lives change in unexpected and hilarious ways in this novel about love, forgiveness, and Elvis’s ghost. Populated with quirky, memorable characters, Buck Storm’s novel spins a laugh-out-loud tale perfect for a lazy day. . . . But don’t be surprised if, after all the laughter, there’s some water in your eyes by the end of the story.”

THE BANNER

by Buck Storm

The Beautiful Ashes of Gomez Gomez

The Sound the Sun Makes

Venus Sings the Blues

VENUS SINGS THE BLUES

BUCK STORM

Venus Sings the Blues

Published by Kregel Publications, a division of Kregel Inc., 2450 Oak Industrial Dr. NE, Grand Rapids, MI 49505. www.kregel.com.

Lyrics from "Goodbye from Venus" by Buck Storm, 2018.

Library of Congress Cataloging-in-Publication Data
Names: Storm, Buck, author.
Title: Venus sings the blues / Buck Storm.
Description: Grand Rapids, MI : Kregel Publications, [2022]
Identifiers: LCCN 2022011581 (print) | LCCN 2022011582 (ebook) | ISBN 9780825446870 (print) | ISBN 9780825468834 (Kindle) | ISBN 9780825477317 (epub)
Classification: LCC PS3619.T69274 V46 2022 (print) | LCC PS3619.T69274 (ebook) | DDC 813/.6--dc23
LC record available at https://lccn.loc.gov/2022011581
LC ebook record available at https://lccn.loc.gov/2022011582

ISBN 978-0-8254-4687-0, print
ISBN 978-0-8254-7731-7, epub
ISBN 978-0-8254-6883-4, Kindle

Printed in the United States of America
22 23 24 25 26 27 28 29 30 31 / 5 4 3 2 1

When I was fifteen, I made a trade for a 1972 Honda CB 360 with a faded orange gas tank and a seat cover made from an old piece of carpet. It was beautiful. In the span of a single, small-town Arizona afternoon, I became invincible.

I'm not saying the story you're about to read is mine exactly, but who knows, maybe it's yours.

To all you dreamers out there working hard to get your bikes running, maybe they will, maybe they won't. But know this—whether you jump over Evel Knievel's Snake River Canyon and wheelie over the sun, or never get past the corner Circle K convenience store, you are magnificently, perfectly, and endlessly loved.

The road is only beginning.

Hit the gas, kid. This is for you.

Past the edge of town
Out where the world ends
The desert gives the sky
Nothing but silence
There's an old motel
The sign is a shimmering Venus
Even though she smiles
Her eyes are sad . . .
—"Goodbye from Venus"

CHAPTER ONE

It was one of those wide Arizona afternoons. The quiet kind, where tall piles of pillowy clouds pull their shadows across the valley floor, everything sand and sage and sunlight and sharp angles. Where the sky is so deep it feels endless, and hawks dip and circle on the updrafts and never get tired.

Bones was sweeping yesterday's stardust off the sidewalk when the biker rolled out of the desert and into the parking lot of the Venus Motel. That's how life works sometimes. One second all is calm all is bright, and the next the gods or angels or aliens or whatever insert something like this guy with a rattle of pipes and a cloud of dissipating dust. Someone fresh from blasting through the cosmos, sun-streaked hair and muttonchops swept straight back from the lightyears and motorcycle wind. Someone with a hunting knife on his belt and a long mustache that curls up on the ends like a cowboy in an old movie. Jeans and boots and muscles like ropes under his tattoos.

Two eyes surveyed Bones. One ocean-blue and bottomless. Another that looked like someone had spilt milk in it. The blue appeared mildly interested at best. The milky one didn't give a rip. Even from where Bones stood, he could smell the bike's engine. Grease and hot metal. It ticked as it cooled. Its rider made no noise at all.

"Hey," Bones said when the quiet got too heavy. Right away he wished he'd thought of something cooler. For some reason, that milky eye did that to a guy.

The rider dug into the pocket of his jeans and pulled out a pack of smokes, then shook one out and stuck it on his bottom lip without lighting it. "You the boss?" His words rolled out thick, like his tongue was coated with honey. Or maybe motor oil.

Bones knew the guy was kidding, but he could spot no humor behind either blue or milk. He played it safe. "Nah. I'm only fifteen, man."

The rider lit the cig, flipped the Zippo shut, and stuck it back into his pocket. Smoke swirled off toward the highway, dipped and ducked. "So? What's fifteen got to do with the price of tea in Bangladesh?" He put the accent on bang.

"I just work here."

That milky eye. "That's cool. Very industrious. You got a name?"

"Bones."

The rider gave a nod as if this were heavy information that required considerable effort to process. "Bones . . . right. That supposed to make you sound dangerous?"

"It's my name, that's all."

"Not much of one, if you ask me. Who gave it to you?"

"I don't know. My mom, probably."

"What kind of mom calls her kid Bones?"

"The kind that left a long time ago. I don't remember her."

Smoke. "Uh-huh. And what? Everybody's supposed to feel sorry for you now?"

"I didn't say that."

"No, I guess you didn't. That's good, at least. You got a last name?"

"Not one I want to say."

More smoke. More milky eye. "After the first one, I don't blame you."

"How about you?"

"How 'bout me what?"

"You got a name?"

"Jimmy La Roux. And if you notice, I don't mind throwing in the last name right off the bat."

"You from Texas?"

Milk. "Why in heaven's name would you think I'm from Texas?"

"I don't know. You talk like you're from Texas."

"I don't talk like I'm from Texas even a little bit. I talk like I'm from God's country. Louisiana, born and raised." Jimmy La Roux said Louisiana with a modicum of reverence. He used three syllables—*Looz-an-na*—as if four would be sacrilege.

He puffed a few more times. Katydids buzzed in the pepper trees behind the motel. Crazy how such little things could be so loud. "Boss in the office?"

Bones leaned his broom against the wall. "She went up to town. You can wait in the lounge. That's where she'll probably be when she gets back. We're short-staffed, so sometimes she checks guests in and out there."

"Short-staffed. Yeah, you are pretty short when I consider." Jimmy La Roux winked, leaned the bike on its kickstand, climbed off, and stretched. "Lounge it is, then, Bones-without-a-last-name." He pulled a few more puffs, snuffed the cigarette out on the palm of his hand, then flicked the butt onto the gravel.

Bones would be the one who'd have to pick up the butt later, but he couldn't care less. That palm-snuff was the coolest stinking thing he'd seen anybody do in his life. He pointed down the sidewalk, keeping his tone cool. "Lounge is down there."

"I did gather that from the sign that says Lounge, but thanks for the heads-up."

Jimmy La Roux unbuckled a leather pack from the Harley's rear fender, then slung it over his shoulder and started off with a long-legged, rolling gait. Bones, still reeling from the cig snuff, left his broom and the stardust where they were and followed.

Bones imagined the Venus Motel looked a lot like it had the day it was built back in 1940. Story was it had been a real gathering spot in its day. A desert-road-trip destination for the family set, and at times even a semi-secret oasis for the hip, connected, and famous. Not to mention the *in*famous. Sunsets on the pool deck, piano music drifting out from the lounge. Rumor had it Sinatra himself had even graced the place.

The lounge especially looked the part. Long, low, and dim. Lots of dark wood. A bar took up half the wall to the right. Behind it, twinkle lights winked around a big mirror and several shelves of bottles, and behind the old-school cash register on the end closest to the door hung a bunch of signed photographs. Some black and white. Some grainy, over-saturated color. They were all autographed. Brigitte Bardot, Ernest Hemingway, Glenn Ford, Angie Dickinson, Dean Martin, Dennis Hopper, and maybe a dozen others. Bones had never actually counted them.

The kitchen door was at the other end of the bar, and across the room a dozen red-leather booths stretched along the wall. Tables took up space on the open floor, and at the far end of the room, an old baby grand piano sat on a low stage above a little dance floor.

Jimmy La Roux paused inside the door and took in the place. He nodded as if the lounge met his approval, then weaved his way through the tables to the stage. He lifted the piano keys' lid, ran his fingers over both black and white, then played a gentle chord.

"You play piano?" Bones said.

"It ain't a fluegelhorn."

"What's a fluegelhorn?"

"Who knows? But this old piano's a beaut."

"I don't know anything about it."

"Didn't ask if you did. I was telling."

The biker played a slow run on the low keys, then started a melody with his right hand on the higher ones.

"What's that?" Bones said.

The milky eye caught the light from the front window. "This, Bones-with-the-lousy-last-name, is what's known as the blues. You know what that is?"

"Yeah. Like Robert Johnson, right?"

The blue eye took him in with newfound appreciation. "You know Johnson's blues?"

"No, but I read a book about him."

"Hmm. Can't read about the blues. That's like reading about how a chocolate cake tastes. Or a good cigarette. Have a seat and open your ears. Here, listen to this."

CHAPTER TWO

Calico Foster pushed her used-to-be-blue-but-had-sun-faded-to-dull-silver Ford Tempo up to its max speed of sixty and rolled down her window. If there was one universal and undisputed fact for those who've experienced it, it was that nothing on earth smells as good as the Arizona desert after a rain. A high-desert storm had rolled through this afternoon, and today was no exception. She breathed deep and let the creosote-saturated wind cool her skin and whip her hair. Most days she was impatient to get back to the motel after a trip into Paradise, but today she wished the commute was longer.

She slowed as she neared the Venus, rolling into the parking lot without using her turn signal—no one out here to warn anyway—and pulled to a stop in front of her apartment on the other side of the office from the lounge. A broom leaned against the wall, but no Bones, of course. Keeping that kid on task was like trying to wrangle an entire herd of cats. She mentally cursed him.

She climbed out and looked west over the wide desert basin. She didn't have a choice. In her experience, the desert didn't ask or suggest; it demanded. Especially this valley. There was a sense of permanence here. Ancient and unchanging. It was perfect. Baptized by wind and sun, washed clean by Mexican moonlight and Gulf storms. She'd never in her life seen anything so beautiful.

Not that she was a stranger to the landscape. She'd spent her life in Arizona, much of it helping out with her father's motel and bar and then running it altogether after he passed. Bob's Place over in One Horse, a tiny crossroads of a town that lived up to its name. But all that seemed like a shadow life now. The dream-reality before her brother disappeared and Detective Early Pines crashed into her world. And then the road trip that changed everything.

Somewhere along the way Pines had become permanent. And so had the Venus. With the money from selling Bob's along with an I'm-sorry-for-my-peccadillo check from her brother, she'd been able to purchase the Venus.

She'd been here for only a little more than a year, but this was home now. The minute she saw the place she knew she'd never leave. She loved the mountains, the valley, the endless sky. And she loved the motel. The place had history, and now she was becoming part of it. It had its ups and downs throughout the decades—at times a prestigious hideaway, other times a roadside dive—but the towering forty-foot Lady Venus sign fronting the highway never failed to offer her sad-eyed, neon smile to the weary traveler.

Calico opened her trunk, then filled her arms to overflowing with supplies and headed for the lounge. A Harley Davidson that hadn't been there when she left leaned on its stand. Hopefully owned by someone who wanted a room.

The lounge door creaked when she pushed it open, slanting sunlight stretching her shadow the length of the room. Juan—mustachioed, black hair slicked, his guayabera crisp and white as always—was wiping down the bar. Bones sat on a barstool drinking what was no doubt a root beer, his favorite. The news was on the TV up in the corner, but the volume was turned down. To Calico's surprise it had been replaced by piano music coming from the darkened stage. Her eyes, adjusting from sun to sudden shadow, could barely make out the form of a man.

"Those sidewalks sweeping themselves out there, Bones?" she said.

"I'm taking a break."

"So I see. More supplies in the car."

"Okay."

"In case you don't know, by that I mean go and get them *out* of the car."

"Yeah, I picked up on that."

Calico joined Juan behind the bar, set two bags of cleaning supplies on the counter, and then poured herself a cup of coffee. "Who's the Liberace?"

Juan's mouth turned down as he gave an I-don't-know shrug. "I just got here a few minutes ago. He was already up there. Says he's waiting for you. All I know is he likes his coffee black."

"He's got a cool Harley," Bones said. "It's parked outside."

"I saw that."

Calico flipped a switch on the wall, and a handful of stage lights came to life. The man looked up. Something was wrong with one of his eyes. And although his rough appearance definitely fit the Harley outside, it seemed at odds with the soft tune coming from the piano.

He smiled a little, eyes going back to the keys. "Well, well, ladies and gentlemen. Let there be light." His voice was low, resonant, and dripping bayou swamp water. Boots as worn as his jeans. Faded black T-shirt. He looked like he was made out of jerky and cigarette smoke and four-letter words.

"You sound pretty good over there," Calico said.

"It ain't hard. It's a nice piano."

"And that's your Harley out there?"

"If it ain't, some hombre back down the road must be plenty mad."

"How are you doing on coffee?"

"I could use a top off, thanks."

"Bones. The supplies. Then finish sweeping," Calico said. She grabbed the coffeepot from the warmer and headed for the biker, then after glancing at Bones, stopped short. "How long are you planning this break to last, exactly?"

Bones lifted the root beer and eyed it. "I'm almost done."

Calico crossed the room and poured.

The man blew over the rim, then took a sip. "I take it you'd be Calico Foster, owner of this establishment?"

"I've been Calico Foster for as long as I can remember and owner of the Venus for a little over a year."

He held out a calloused hand. "I'm Jimmy La Roux."

She shook it. "Nice to meet you."

"By the look on your face, my name doesn't strike a chord. Am I right?"

"Should it?"

"Probably not. But I been through this way a time or three. Done some hours on this very bench."

"You've played here?"

"Something about that lady out on the highway always seems to call me back. You got anybody working currently?"

"As a piano player, you mean? No. Honestly, I haven't even thought about it."

"How about it?"

"Are you talking about a job?"

"Why not? I got nowhere to be for a couple a weeks."

"How about because I can't afford a piano player, for one?"

"How do you know? We haven't even talked money yet."

"You see those supplies I just brought in? I could hardly afford those. We're not exactly the Hilton."

"Don't say that like it's a bad thing. You're the Venus, and it don't get much better than the Venus."

"Trust me, flattery won't get you the job."

"No flattery. Just the truth."

"We could use some music," Juan said. "It's getting too quiet around here. And I'm tired of the same old, same old on the radio."

"Uh-huh. And are you offering to pay him out of your check?" Calico said.

Jimmy poked a single note. "Things really that tight?"

"New place in up town," Juan said. "Big money. Hotel and lounge. Kind of place the tourists up from Phoenix and Tucson like."

"One of them cookie-cutter deals?"

"No," Calico said. "They did it right. Renovated an old downtown building. I can't imagine what it cost. It's nice, actually."

"Tell you what. What if nothing comes out of your pocket? I'll play for tips. Been my experience that some good music brings folks in. Maybe you can make a dent in the competition's business."

"Boss, you're not gonna get a better deal than that," Juan said.

"It's a nice piano," Jimmy added. "Still in tune. Deserves to get played a little."

"I don't know anything about pianos," Calico said.

"Take my word for it."

"Look. I don't even know you. No offense."

"Come on. Let him play," Juan said. "It sounds good."

Jimmy stopped playing and leaned his elbows on the piano lid. "Listen, Calico Foster. I don't bite often, and when I do it ain't very hard. Tips ain't gonna cost you nothing, and like I said, I got a couple a weeks to kill."

"I don't like not paying somebody to work. It doesn't feel right."

"They do say the best things in life are free. Tell you what. You can cover my room if it'll make you feel better."

"That might make me feel worse."

"Won't know till you try."

"You're a real salesman."

"That's absolutely not true. I'm probably the worst salesman you'll ever meet."

"Do you actually play the piano for a living?"

"On my good days. You want a resume?"

"You don't look like a musician."

"What about those ZZ Top dudes?" Juan said. "They're musicians."

Juan had a point. "I mean you don't look like a lounge piano player."

Jimmy smiled a little and shuffled through a jazz lick. He *was* good. Maybe not Thelonious Monk good, but the guy was certainly no slouch. "No? What's a piano man supposed to look like?"

"I don't know. Piano-y."

"Like what? Nat King Cole?"

"Thelonious Monk was more in my mind."

"You know Monk?"

"My dad had a big record collection. He loved jazz."

"Monk always wore a hat. I'm not much of a hat man."

"You know what I mean."

"I'll get the job done. You don't like it or it don't work out for some reason, I'll leave anytime, no questions asked." He leaned back, looked around the room. "Man, this place has always had a vibe, you know? Ain't no place up in town ever gonna have a vibe like this. So what do you say?"

"Say yes," Juan said.

"Oh fine. But I take you at your word. If it doesn't work, I'll let you know and off you go down the road. I've done this a long time, and you'll find I'm not the roll-over type, even if I am a woman."

"I can already tell that."

"Also, my fiancé is a local police detective. A huge and very protective one."

"That's very true," Juan said. "Guy's an animal."

Jimmy smiled again and nodded. "Warning received. Sounds like I got the gig, then."

"On a trial basis." She couldn't let him forget that part.

"Trial basis and the boyfriend's a cop. Received and understood."

"Fiancé." She turned and walked back to the bar. "Let's see if you do actually get some people to come out."

"We have ourselves an agreement. Now, you're the boss. What do you want to hear?"

"We'll most likely get a handful for dinner later. No point playing to an empty room right now."

"Ain't empty. You're here. Your man over there is here."

"Juan," Juan called. "Juan Rojas."

"See? Juan's here. Bones with the hateful last name is here." Jimmy pressed a key, the note drifting up like smoke. "I'm here. Not to mention a place like the Venus has enough haunts and memories to constitute a packed house without us."

He started in on a song, slow and moody. Only lower notes at first, then bringing in more of the higher keys one or two at a time.

"You're a blues man," Calico said.

Jimmy kept playing with his left hand. With his right he picked up his coffee cup, sipped, then set it back down. "Most days. But I got my sunny moments."

"I'll throw in a room," Calico said. "It's not like we have a shortage at the moment. But no smoking, and don't put the bike inside."

"He's housebroke. Probably a whole lot more than me."

"No bikes in the rooms."

"I can live with that."

Jimmy's bad eye gleamed in the light, and he started in on a song in earnest.

CHAPTER THREE

Bones sipped his second root beer. This was no problem, because after the first one he'd gone invisible. He could sit here for hours, and no one would ever notice.

Most people didn't know invisibility was a practiced skill. It took time and patience. For Bones, it all started at a ranch owned by one of his dad's poker buddies, watching the two men split a bottle of rye whiskey and take potshots at prairie dogs with a .22 pistol.

The whole thing had made Bones a little sick. His dad must have picked up on this, because at one point he'd passed Bones the gun. When Bones refused to shoot, the man had beaten him hard enough his ears rang. He could still see the blood from his nose pooling in the dirt beneath him, feel the rough earth against his body while his dad sucked in a hard breath above him. One last kick, then, "Listen to me, kid. You can either be a prairie dog in this life or you can be the guy with the gun. What you feel like now? That's prairie dog, you hear me? I hope you learned a lesson today. And you're welcome."

Bones *had* learned a lesson. Maybe not the one his dad intended to teach but one he'd never forgotten. *Never ever poke your head out of a hole when the other guys have .22s and pointy-toed boots.*

A second unexpected and vastly more important lesson had come to him several weeks later. That particular part of the rancher's pasture had collapsed into a useless pit from all the unseen digging, and it came to him then with a rush. Live rounds flying or not, invisible ones weren't without power. In fact, maybe being invisible could get you further than pistols or muscle. So Bones had practiced keeping his head down, becoming an expert in the art of anonymity. Even at school. It wasn't hard. He was small for his age. Nondescript. It was easy to simply become background static. White noise. And once he'd mastered the skill, he'd caved in a few pastures of his own.

Jimmy La Roux fascinated him. Bones had a feeling about the guy, and when he had a feeling, he paid attention. Then again, if he was honest with himself, he'd have to admit maybe he simply felt like spying. Maybe he was bored. It definitely wouldn't be the first time.

Either way, he went invisible so he could stick around the lounge. Stardust could wait. Supplies could wait. Calico could wait.

Jimmy stopped his song long enough to lean down and pull a dented and tarnished rectangular metal box from his pack. He set it on the piano.

"That's quite a tip jar," Calico said from behind the bar.

"This thing? Nah. It ain't for tips."

"What is it, then?"

Jimmy smiled. "What's it look like?"

"An old metal box."

"You got it."

"If it's not for tips, what's it for?"

"I pull it out from time to time. This here just might put a dent in that competition of yours up in town."

"I thought that's what your piano playing was for."

"Little music won't hurt, but between you and me and the lamppost, there's always another good player right down the street. This old box of mine'll get the pedal to the floor a little quicker."

"I don't get it."

"Come on over and let me show you something."

Calico joined him.

Jimmy pushed his empty coffee cup toward her. "Here. Put this in the box."

"Why?"

"Just do it. It ain't gonna explode. It's an old box, not a grenade."

Calico lifted the lid, studied the inside of the box for a second, then put the cup in.

"Good. Now close 'er up."

She did.

"Now open it."

She did. Then stared. "It's gone."

"Gone like it was never there in the first place," Jimmy said.

"You have a magic box?"

"Nope. No such thing as a magic box."

"You know what I mean. A trick box, or whatever they're called. So what's next? You make the cup come back? Or it appears someplace else?"

"Nope. It's done. Something goes into the box, it's gone for good. End of story."

"That's it?"

"That's it."

"A trick box will bring people into my lounge?"

"You'd be surprised."

"My uncle used to pull coins from our ears. I hate to burst your bubble, but I don't think a box with a fake bottom will impress anybody all that much."

"That's all right. Only thing on the line is my tips, right?"

"I suppose that's true. But I'd like to think this place has a little class, you know? Mystique. It has history. A lot of famous people used to come out here." She pointed to the photos behind the bar. "I'm not sure I want to be the owner who brought in cheap tricks for kids."

"Making something disappear forever is cheap?"

"Yes, it is. Again, no offense. Maybe you could stick to the piano. Plus you owe me a coffee cup."

"Second thoughts?"

"I'm a direct person, Jimmy. I don't want antics. I have a certain standard. Maybe it's only in my head, but there it is."

Jimmy nodded as he played. "Standards are important. Let me ask you a question. If you could drop something in that box, anything at all, and then it would be gone from this world forever, what would it be?"

"I have no idea, and I think you're changing the subject."

"I'm not. The subject is the box. Anything. Think about it. Like it was never there."

"But it wouldn't really be gone. It would be wherever you put it. Like my uncle's quarters."

Jimmy stabbed a couple of blue-note jazz chords. "Where's the cup?"

"Wherever you put it."

He stopped playing, and the milky eye came up. He pulled out a cig and stuck it on his lip. "I'll tell you what. Give me tonight. If the class meter goes down, the box goes away. Like you said, it'll be only a handful of people."

"No smoking inside, ever. One night. And you better be good."

Jimmy winked the blue eye. "That's one thing I never promise."

CHAPTER FOUR

"THE THING IS," DON SAID around an orange-lipped mouth full of Cheetos, "everybody wants a piece of you. It never ends."

Cozy looked up from her sudoku. He had NASCAR on the television, the volume too loud as usual. "What do you expect? It's a lot of money."

"Charity this, charity that. How about the *Don Jenkins* charity? How about that one? They act like I don't need the money myself." Don was sprawled on the couch in his boxers and a stained tank top. His toenails needed a trim. Or maybe a go-round with a power grinder.

Early evening sun poured in through the window as Cozy stirred a pot of tomato soup on the kitchen stove. She could see—and despite the TV hear—Don fine from there. The trailer had what the real estate lady called an open floor plan back when they bought it. Cozy remembered thinking how sophisticated that sounded at the time.

"I think you mean the Don and *Cozy* Jenkins charity," she said.

"Negative. Three people bought the ticket—me, myself, and I. My money. We've been over this."

"Yeah, we have been over it. You bought the ticket with marital funds. It's *ours*."

"So you keep saying, *chica*."

"What I keep saying is that the money's half mine."

"But it's not half yours because I bought the ticket."

"Google says different, Don."

"Google can kiss my sweet hind end."

"Like I said, it's an issue of marital funds."

Don tossed the Cheetos bag on the floor. "It's an issue of you starting to chap my hide. Any funds we have are *my* funds. I'm the only one working, as I recall. What do you even do all day?" He propped himself up on his elbows. "Hey, are you listening? Come pick up this Cheetos bag. You know I can't abide messes."

"Pick up your own bag."

He was getting mad. She could tell. Good. She picked up her sudoku from the counter, snapped her gum, and wrote a number in a box. "And by the way, I do tons of stuff."

"Tons of stuff, yeah. Name one thing."

"What do *you* do except go down to the Pick-a-Part and flirt with Tanya?"

"I'm working, not flirting. I got a business to run."

"Give me a break. You play with cars all day."

"Play with . . . Do you have any idea what goes into putting a stock car together? Not to mention a crew and a trailer and rig? No, you don't, because all you do is sing into the mirror and play that stupid crossword."

She put the sudoku down. "It's not crossword. And I think I do have an idea. I think I got myself a real good idea when we went through your sprint-car phase. I got an even better idea with that ridiculous monster truck of yours. Cars are *all* you ever talk about, so I think after ten years of being married to you, by now I'm practically an expert on all things that have a motor and suck money out of our pockets."

Don ran his fingers through his hair. It was thick when they'd met. Black and thick. Old-school rockabilly. Now it was thinning, and he was constantly rubbing his head like he thought that would bring the curls back. He scratched at his bare armpit. "I'm just saying six million won't go far. I'll need every thin dime of that."

"Six and a half million."

"Whatever."

"Which is really three and a quarter to you because half of it is mine."

He sighed. "Not in this life."

"Take it up with the internet."

He took a swig of Diet Pepsi—he'd decided he needed to watch his weight—and shook his head. "Let me ask you a question. What would someone like you even do with three million dollars?"

"I'll tell you exactly. First, I'd buy one of those houses across the road and get out of a stupid trailer for once in my life."

Don laughed. "Get out of a trailer? You? Cozy, you were born in a trailer, and you'll die in a trailer. And when you do they'll dig a huge hole and bury you in that trailer. That's one thing you can put down in ink."

"Say what you want. I'm getting my money."

He sat up. "Tell you what. When I win my first big race, maybe we'll talk about a house." His mad was fading, and he was getting that look in his eyes like he always did when he thought he'd come out on top. "Hey, did I tell you how hot you're looking today?"

"Gross."

He crunched a Cheeto, grinning as he chewed with his mouth open.

The soup was bubbling, so she turned off the burner. "Anyway, you already won *the* big one. You won the Mega. You don't need to win a race to buy a house."

"You get to tag along, so why are you whining?"

"I've been tagging along behind you for years. For what? I want my money, and I want my house."

"You don't like this trailer, maybe you should just leave. You thought about that?"

"Every minute of every day."

"Yeah, right." He licked at the orange spit collected in the corners of his mouth and laid back down on the couch again, his hand behind his head. "The money's going to the team, end of subject. Come on over here."

"Stop. Get a sponsor. That's what you did before."

"Yeah, for dirt-track stuff. But Bob's Texaco and Burger Heaven won't fund my way to the big leagues. Six and a half million won't even do that, but it's a start."

"Three and a quarter."

He looked at the TV and stuck three fingers in the waistband of his boxers. "We're not talking about this anymore. Once we get on the circuit, we'll be set for life."

"I have dreams too, Don."

He slapped his forehead, yelling at the television. "No! Take him on the inside! Ugh, what an idiot!"

"Did you hear me?"

"Yeah, I heard you."

"What did I say?"

"How should I know?"

"I said I have dreams too."

He still didn't look at her. "What dreams?"

"You know exactly what dreams."

"No, Cozy, I don't know what dreams because you talk constantly and never actually say anything. I swear, I can't keep any of your babbling straight. You gonna pick up that bag?"

"You know I want to sing. I'm gonna make a recording. They got a place down in Tucson that'll do it all for you. All you have to do is show up."

He crunched his Diet Pepsi can and then threw it in her direction. She picked it up and dropped it into the trash. She could take only so much mess. "Did you hear me, Don? Are you even listening?"

He looked at her now. "You want to sing into a microphone in Tucson. I heard. So what?"

"I could do it."

"You'd embarrass me, is what you'd do."

"It has nothing to do with you. You don't know anything about it."

"I got ears, don't I? I been listening to you howl for years. Trust me, Cozy, let it go. Get me another Pepsi."

"Get your own Pepsi."

"I'm serious. Don't make me tell you again."

"You know what you are? Emotionally abusive. That's what they call people like you."

"Uh-huh. What do they call ear abuse? Because if that was a crime, they'd lock you up and throw away the key."

"You grin like you just won some presidential debate when you really sound like a seventh grader making fun of a girl he has a crush on. You got a crush on me, Don?"

"Yeah, come over here."

Cozy picked up her sudoku.

Don was wiping Cheetos goop off his mouth with the hem of his shirt. "Girl, any crush I had on you died a slow death ten years ago. Where'd you hear about all that emotional abuse crap? On *Dr. Phil*?"

"Everybody's heard of emotional abuse. You do it all the time, and I'm sick of it."

"If you're abused, call the cops."

"I don't want the cops. I want three and a quarter million and a house across the street and a recording of me singing."

"I'm gonna win more than we've ever dreamed of."

"*We've* never dreamed that. You have. And you've been saying the same thing for the last decade."

"It takes money to make money. Haven't you ever heard that? Now I got me some money, so I'm gonna make a whole lot more."

"Yeah? Print it on a T-shirt."

"A better car, and nobody'll stop me. I'm unbeatable with the right car. Facts are facts. You can't argue with facts."

"Yeah, facts are facts. And the fact is, with your race record, you might as well flush that money down the toilet."

"I'll tell you what I'm *not* wasting money on. I'm not wasting it on some stucco McMansion so you can play rich girl. You might as well get that out of your head right now."

"And I'm not wasting money on a truck and trailer and stupid car so you can run around and lose races. So you get *that* out of *your* head."

"It's not your choice."

She walked over, picked up the remote, and switched off the television. "I told you. Google says different. I'm serious about that."

They stared at each other, the clock on the kitchen stove banging railroad spikes.

"Give me the clicker, Cozy."

"No."

"Give me the clicker."

"No."

"Give it to me."

"No."

He grinned. "You know how I like it when you get mad. Come over here and sit down."

"Take me seriously, Don."

"I can't. Come here."

"I'd honestly rather die."

He was still grinning. "I hate you a little more all the time. Have I told you that?"

She tossed the remote onto his Cheetos-fingered chest and went back to her soup. "Only every day, Don. Only every day."

CHAPTER FIVE

Calico leaned against the lounge doorway and watched Bones sweep, little puffs of dust coming up from the broom. Maybe today he'd finish the job.

The kid was too smart for his own good, that was the problem. One of his problems, anyway. They seemed to be legion. He had the mouth to go with the brain too. At least he did when he talked at all. Dirty blond, shaggy hair. Holes in his Levi's, bony knees poking through. A Ramones T-shirt a size too small that looked like it hadn't been washed in . . . well, ever. How did a kid that age know about the Ramones? They were even before her time. He had clean clothes available—she'd seen to that—but he seemed to make a point of ignoring them.

"Hey," she called when he was almost to the far end of the walk. "Don't forget the pool."

He gave a thumbs-up without turning around.

He'd had a hard time. She should be gentler. And she *wanted* to be gentler. But every time she opened her mouth, the wrong thing seemed to come out. It was like a vicious cycle. The more frustrated she became with her own inadequacy, the more she seemed to point it at him, and that only fueled her feelings.

The nearly empty parking lot didn't help her mood. A newer-model Dodge pickup and a Land Rover sat parked outside the only two rooms with paying guests. The Dodge had some kind of state insignia on the side she hadn't noticed when it came in. The Land Rover looked like it had been beaten with bats, turned sideways, and rolled down a mountain. The couple it belonged to looked like the kind who wanted it that way. Road-less-traveled adventure types.

Both rooms would be empty by tomorrow morning.

Jimmy La Roux's Harley was acting housebroken in front of room fourteen. What had she been thinking yesterday? He played fine, but come on. The guy looked like a convict. Not at all what she dreamed for the Venus. And the weird box that made things disappear? It all sounded like the beginning of a real-life crime drama straight from Bizarro World.

On top of that, she'd been semi-bluffing when she mentioned having a fiancé for protection. Not that Pines didn't exist, or that he wasn't huge, or that he wasn't a police detective. His location at the moment was the problem. The department had loaned him out to some little town up in the mountains without a detective of their own. Someone was killing cattle up there, and he'd had his hands full with the case. He'd be there for at least several more days, but she didn't really know how long he'd need.

At least Jimmy hadn't done the box thing last night. She'd made up her mind to revisit the decision to let him be her motel's entertainment, but she had to admit she'd enjoyed the music. With only a handful of patrons, he'd played quietly, and no one had complained about the way he looked.

A couple more guests were scheduled to arrive within the next two days. One even wanted a room for an indefinite amount of time. But a few booked rooms here and there wouldn't even cover the electric bill.

It wasn't about losing the place. She'd paid cash for it, so at least no bank was breathing down her neck. But her savings were down to the bottom of the barrel. And anyway, business was business. Black meant good, red bad, and her books were starting to look like a page out of a King James Gospel. The lounge usually brought in a few ranchers for dinner or beers, occasionally a back-road wanderer or two, but nothing she could count on.

"Ride the horse as long as it's still walking," her dad had always said.

And she would. She'd never abandon the Venus. It needed her like she needed it.

She looked down the sidewalk at the motel's turquoise doors and whitewashed brick. Bones was nearly to the end, but he'd be a few more minutes. She crossed the parking lot and made her way to the far end of the pool, then leaned her arms against the fence, looking west across the valley and the darkening sky beyond. The Venus might struggle a little, but nothing could stop an Arizona sunset.

Her phone chirped in her pocket, and she pulled it out. "It's about time. I want you to know I'm very close to being bored to death, and I blame you."

"How's the sunset?"

"Come home and see."

"I would if I could."

"I'm kidding, Pines. I know you have to work. I'm a big girl." She could picture him on the other end of the satellite. Detective Early Pines was less than a quarter Navajo but looked more. Dark hair to his shoulders. Nose angled a bit to the left. Scar running up his cheek from the left side of his mouth. What was the expression? A face only a mother could love? Make that a mother and Calico Foster. "Sounds like a lot of people there. Where are you?"

"Some barbecue place. Guy's gotta eat."

"A barbecue restaurant sounds ironic considering you're there to investigate dead cows."

"Kinda does. Come to think of it, maybe I should get paid for eating. I could call it research."

"Just remember to leave some food for the rest of the town. I know you. How's the sunset there?"

"Not great—and behind a mountain so it's pretty much gone."

Calico glanced at the bottle in her hand. "Hey, guess what I'm drinking right now?"

"I have no idea."

"That's why I said to guess. You really are dim sometimes, Pines."

"When are we getting married?"

"Guess what I'm drinking."

"Mexican Coke."

"How did you know?"

"Because that's what I drink and you miss me. When are we getting married?"

"I'm drinking a Mexican Coke because it's cold and tastes good. Don't give yourself so much credit." She sipped.

"I say we do it in October. And I hope you haven't made a pros-and-cons list about a date."

"Don't bash my lists, Pines. They're very helpful."

"So you keep saying. I'd like to burn that notebook of yours."

"That's just mean."

"No, it's just love. You're probably writing in it right now."

"Wrong. It's under the counter in the lounge. But pros-and-cons lists are a logical way to approach decision-making. At least, they help me."

"I don't even want to know what the cons are on the Early Pines list."

"I don't have an Early Pines list."

Thin music in the background. Old country. "No? Never?" Pines said.

"All right. There was an Early Pines list at one time. A long time ago. But you're one entity that defies logic."

"Is that code for way too many cons are on that list but you love me anyway?"

"October's in two months."

"So?"

"It's right around the corner."

"So?"

"So now that I'm hooked on Mexican Cokes, I might need some time to lose weight so I can fit into a wedding dress. That takes time."

"You're perfect."

"Not if I keep drinking these."

"Buy a bigger dress."

"We'll talk about it when you get back."

"We've done too much talking about it already. Let's quit talking and do."

"Maybe. It rained last night."

"Did it?"

"It still smells good out here."

"You have a great knack for changing the subject."

"Pines . . ."

"Yeah?"

Calico turned and looked back at the motel, where Bones was still sweeping. "Did anyone call yet? About Bones? Did they find a place for him?"

He was quiet for a few seconds. "What's he done now?"

"Nothing, he's just . . . you know."

"He's just Bones."

"I don't want to sound mean, but you know how he is."

"The thing is I don't know if they *will* find a place. They've already kind of run through all the available foster families in town. I don't want them to ship him somewhere else. He's been through enough."

"I know what he's been through, but if there's no other choice . . ."

Pines was silent on the other end of the phone.

"What?" she said.

"I'm thinking maybe he can come to my place when I get back."

"Your place? To stay?"

"Yeah, my place. Why not?"

"As in you might take him in permanently?"

"He's fifteen. It's not that permanent. In less than three years he'll be eighteen."

"And you were planning on telling me about this when? Because you're talking about my life too."

"I know that. It's just—"

"One breath you want to get married, and in the next you're taking in a troubled teenager? Don't you think this is maybe something we should decide together?"

"You're the one who sounds like she doesn't want to get married."

"That's not true. But if we don't talk about things, we'll never make this work. This is big, Pines."

"You're mad."

"Yes, I am mad. You're very observant. Must be why you made detective."

"Look. I'm sorry. I should have talked to you about it when I brought him to you, but I had to get up here, and nothing's set in stone. I just don't know what else to do with him. And I feel responsible for the kid."

She sighed. "I know you do. And that's something I love about you. But it's us now, not just you. Don't you get that?"

"Of course I do."

"And it's not that I don't feel sorry for him."

"I know he can be an acquired taste."

"It's not even that."

"What, then?"

The sun touched the distant mountains, a hot coal on the horizon line. "It's that I'm not his mom, all right? I'm not cut out for it. He needs someone better at this than me."

"I'm not asking you to be his mom. Right now all I'm asking is for you to give him a place to stay until I get back. After that, we'll figure it out."

"What's he supposed to do out at your place in the desert all day? School doesn't start for a while."

"I'll bring him to the Venus in the mornings so he can work for you the rest of the summer. Once he's sixteen he can ride his bike, if he ever gets the thing running."

"I'm happy to give him a job, especially since I lost Denise. And I'm happy to pay him. He seems to appreciate that part, at least. But there's a difference between having an employee and raising a kid. I'm not good with teenagers, Pines. In fact, I'm pretty horrible."

"You're being way too hard on yourself."

"Says you, not even here to see me try and fail."

"If it happens at all, it won't be forever. And we'll talk about it first. We'll talk as much as you want."

She wanted to talk now. "If you think it's easy, it's not. He's stubborn. I try to get him to dress at least clean if not nice, and look at him. He works when he wants. When he doesn't want, he's holed up in the shop messing with that bike of his. That's another thing. I have a perfectly good guest room in my apartment with an actual bed in it, but he insists on staying out there with the snakes and bugs and who knows what else. Why?"

"I don't know. He's independent. It's what he's learned, what he knows. Look at his dad. The man basically ignored him his whole life."

Calico sighed. "He needs real help."

"He doesn't trust very easy, that's all. You can't blame the kid."

"I don't blame him, Pines. I blame you."

"You're still mad."

"I don't know what I am. This is all way beyond me. Bones is disconnected. He's *out there*. You know it, and I know it."

"We'll figure it out when I get back, all right? Together. I promise. Can you hang in there until then?"

Calico shook her head, ignoring the fact he couldn't see her. "It's not a matter of hanging in there. Of course I can hang in there. Ugh, I sound like some kind of monster. I'm as bad as Don Jenkins."

"Never compare yourself to Don Jenkins. You're helping, not tossing a kid out on his ear."

"It's hard to believe people would foster a child for the money and then kick him out the day they win the lottery."

"People foster for the money all the time."

Calico toyed with the rim of the Coke bottle. "I'm sorry, okay? But you're a detective, not Family Services. You're not an expert on these things."

"I'll talk to him about his clothes. I'll clean him up."

"You're a good man, Pines. And I actually love the way you want to protect him. It's me, that's all. I'm not right for this."

"I promise we'll figure it out."

"Find him a place."
"They just called my number."
"Go eat."
"Enjoy the sunset."
"Sure. Enjoy the dead cows."

CHAPTER SIX

Bones stayed visible but kept one eye on Calico out by the pool as he swept. She'd be wanting privacy. That's why she'd gone out there. Not that he cared. He could practically hear the conversation in his mind anyway. She was talking to Early. He could tell by her face. She always got both more peaceful and more conflicted when she talked to him.

He could also tell they were talking about him. She'd looked over several times, and it was all over her body language. People were such open books. Her—*I don't know what to do with him. He's weird.* Him—*Just hang in there until I get back. I'll figure something out.* Yeah, well, maybe Bones was weird, but he was himself. And besides, Early or no Early, she wouldn't have to worry about him much longer. As soon as the bike ran, he'd blow.

He imagined a job at the Venus Motel was a little like working on a cruise with hardly any passengers on the ship. Only a few people came and went. Stayed only a night or two. But then there was the handful of people you were around all the time, the crew. These were the ones you had to be able to at least tolerate. He was decent at tolerating, but that's about as far as it went. He could handle people okay as long as they kept their distance, which usually wasn't a problem. He'd met very few humans who had any interest in getting close to him.

Calico was all right, and the Venus was better than the Jenkins trailer. No mystery that Don Jenkins had only been in the foster game for a little extra cash. Bones was just one in a string of kids there.

The guy hadn't liked him from the first minute, and the feeling was mutual. Don thought fosters should be seen and not heard, period. Said it from the get-go.

Whatever. Bones didn't need to be heard *or* seen when it came to a dude like that. Don was cars. He talked about cars, dreamed about cars, smelled like cars. If he got cut, he'd probably bleed oil, his blood type 30 weight. He had a good-sized shop out back of the trailer where he worked on everything with a motor. It would have been a cool place if the guy wasn't such a jerk. Bones had been told he wasn't allowed in there immediately upon arrival. Which, of course, made it the first place he wanted to go and the first place he went. Don never locked the door, so it wasn't hard. But even if it had been hard, that wouldn't have stopped Bones.

He'd checked the tools, gone through papers, briefly scanned a stack of dirty magazines he'd found in a hidden cubby behind Don's workbench. In the end, Bones categorized the man, placing him in the what-you-see-is-what-you-get file. Don was one of the ordinaries. One of the unidimensionals.

When Bones thought about Cozy, which was almost never, he mostly thought of soup. He'd never seen a person so into soup. She had cans and cans of every kind of it stuffed into the kitchen cupboards of their mobile home. Cozy would definitely survive an apocalypse if it ever came down to stored sustenance. Bones had never particularly cared for soup, and after his brief months in that place, where there plain old wasn't any choice, he liked it even less.

Then came the day Don walked into the double-wide with his winning Mega ticket, waved it at Bones, and said, "Out ya go, Bones, you little weirdo." Early had come then. Bones thought Early might knock off Don's head, even hoped he would, but he hadn't. Just packed up Bones's stuff into the back of his pickup and driven him out to the Venus. Fine with Bones, as it turned out. There was very little soup at the Venus.

Calico was beautiful, for sure. Tall. Nearly six feet. Long dark hair and eyes to match. And she could be friendly enough. But she was definitely uncomfortable around him. Maybe because he was kind of different from other kids, or maybe because she was uncomfortable around kids in general. She was also completely preoccupied with running the motel. Whatever. Bones didn't care. He didn't need her attention. Besides, he wasn't a kid.

He didn't mind the cook, Juan. He put roasted serrano peppers on Bones's burgers, which was cool because Bones dug hot stuff. Denise, the lady who up until last week had cleaned the rooms and sometimes helped out in the lounge, Bones could do without. She stole shampoo and smelled like burnt toast. Anyway, she'd quit the job because of so-called tendinitis, so she was a nonissue. Or would have been a nonissue if Calico hadn't informed Bones he'd have to help clean rooms on top of other jobs she'd assigned him, at least until she found someone else. *If* she found someone else.

And now there was Jimmy La Roux. Jimmy was a whole different animal. Not a long-term stayer, but he'd be entertaining to watch for a couple of weeks. Jimmy rode a Harley and put cigs out on his palm. He played piano and had a freaky milky eye and a box that made stuff disappear. Jimmy was decidedly *not* unidimensional.

Bones waited for Calico to slide her phone back into the pocket of her jeans before he headed out to clean the pool. She watched him approach, distance and maybe a twinge of guilt in her smile. "Heya. I was thinking the pool can wait. It's not like anybody's using it tonight."

"I can clean it. It's cool."

She smiled for real now. "Are you saying you actually want to work?"

"I don't know. Nothing else to do."

"Okay. It's up to you. Just make sure you head over to the lounge and get some food when you're done. No holing up in the shop without eating." She was doing her pretending-to-care thing. It sometimes came out after she talked to Early.

"Yeah, cool. I'll probably hang and watch Jimmy play anyway."

"Okay. Tell Juan I'll be in my apartment. He can call me if he needs help." She started off but then stopped and turned. "Hey."

"Yeah?"

"Are you all right out there in that shop? Everything good?"

"I'm cool."

"Because there's always my extra room." Definitely post-Early guilt. Must have been quite the phone call.

"I like it out there," he said.

"Yeah, okay. See you tomorrow."

"Yeah."

Bones watched her go, then cleaned the pool and swept the deck. He liked the pool deck this time of night, after sunset. Quiet but a heavy quiet. Pregnant with the weight of galaxies. He'd read that phrase in a book one time. Liked the way it sounded so he'd filed it away. Up in the hills, coyotes yipped. Wind rustled the sage. At length, he put the brushes and brooms away and made his way across the parking lot, scraping his tennis shoes extra hard on the gravel for no other reason but that he felt like it. He was Bones. He did what he wanted.

Nobody was behind the bar in the lounge, but Juan was singing in Spanish in the kitchen. Bones poked his head through the swinging door.

"Dinnertime?" Juan was short and fat and had the blackest eyes Bones had ever seen.

"Calico told me to come in and eat."

"Let me guess. The Bones special, cheeseburger with extra onions and serrano peppers."

"That's what I was thinking."

Juan shook his head. "You have the same thing every day. Time to expand your horizons. You can eat menudo tonight. I make the best menudo this side of Nogales. The other side too."

"What's menudo?"

"You never had menudo?"

"No."

"It's like a Mexican stew made with *el mondongo*."

"Like soup?"

"Yes, like soup."

Bones gave an involuntary shudder. "You got anything that's not soup to expand my horizons? What's el mondongo?"

"Tripe."

"What's tripe?"

"Cow stomach."

"Seriously?"

"You got something against cow stomach?"

"Shouldn't everybody?"

"Not me."

"Why would anybody eat a cow's stomach?"

"Because it's delicious."

"No way, man."

"Way, man."

"How about if I have a burrito or something?"

"A tripe burrito?"

"Seriously, I'm not eating a cow's stomach, man."

Juan laughed. "I think we can swing a burrito."

"Extra hot?"

"It'll light up your world, boy."

"Cool."

Minutes later, burrito on a plate, Bones returned to the lounge and took a seat at the end of the bar by the wall. A talk show was on the TV, but the volume was down as usual. So he read a travel pamphlet about some caves in New Mexico.

A third of the way through the burrito, Juan came out of the kitchen and started wiping beer glasses with a bar towel. Two-thirds through, Jimmy came in and walked up to the stage. He took a seat at the piano, lifted the lid covering the keys, and started playing.

"He's pretty good, eh?" Juan said.

"I guess so. I don't really know much about piano music."

"That's jazz, amigo. Old school. Makes you *feel*. You feel it?"

"I don't know. I guess."

"You guess?"

"I don't know, man. It's just music."

"Just music. Ain't no such thing as *just* music. That's like saying there's *just* the moon. Or there's *just* love. You gotta *feel*, man."

"I'll try."

Juan laughed. "Okay, you try. Let me know if you want anything else, eh?"

Bones nodded the affirmative, and Juan continued with the glasses.

Burrito gone, Bones gave it a minute or two, then went invisible. He moved deeper into the lounge and slid into a booth near the stage. Jimmy never even looked up, but Bones knew he wouldn't. Bones could stay here all night, invisible as air.

It was true he didn't know much of anything about piano music, but it was a lie that he didn't feel it. He did. As he sat there and listened, the notes almost seemed to talk to him. They lifted him up. Swirled him around. There was sadness in the music. But a good, pure sadness. Not like the Jenkins trailer sadness. Or mom-who-left-after-you-were-born sadness. More like a big, all-encompassing human sadness. A we're-in-this-together sadness. The world together, leaning in and pushing toward something greater. Something everyone deep down knows they need but can't quite reach. That elusive something that finishes people and makes them real.

It almost made Bones cry.

The lounge door creaked, and a middle-aged guy in boots and a cowboy hat stepped through, then held it open for a woman. She smiled when she saw Jimmy playing, and they made their way to a table near the stage.

Jimmy nodded to them slightly, his fingers all wrapped up in blue notes.

Juan came over and waited on the couple. They ordered steaks—his rare, hers medium well—and whiskey highballs. The cook smiled and then moved off to make the drinks. Nobody noticed Bones in the booth.

Cowboy Hat took off his hat and laid it, brim up, on the floor beside his chair. His recently cut hair was a tiny bit gray at the temples, parted hard and combed to the side. His face was freshly shaven save an impossibly thick mustache. His shirt, starched and pressed. He had a sharp crease down the front of his Wranglers. His boots caught and reflected the lights from the stage. A very put-together dude, Bones decided.

The woman was a few years younger, not more than thirty-five. She had sharp features and close-together eyes that reminded Bones of a ferret. Her hair was cut short, that style some women still insisted on and she was too young for, all business in the front but sticking straight out in the back like she'd been startled from behind. It was bottle-brownish with bright-blond streaks in it. Neither of them wore a wedding ring. Some kind of awkward first date, maybe. Something about the whole thing made Bones feel sorry for Cowboy Hat guy.

The man gestured at Jimmy to get his attention. "Hey, buddy. How about some Dwight Yoakam?"

The woman let out a two-packs-a-day sandpaper laugh. "Who the heck is Dwight Yoakam? One of your old country guys? Let the man play something classy."

The man laughed too, though his laugh felt forced. "You never heard of Dwight Yoakam?"

"Nobody has."

Bones decided he didn't like her. Plus, she was full of it. Even he'd heard of Dwight Yoakam.

"What you're in need of is some serious musical education," the man said with a put-on, good-natured grin.

The woman snorted. "Where would I get that? Juilliard? Does Mr. Yoakam teach a class on yodeling? Or banjo? Or how to marry your cousin?"

On the stage, Jimmy paused his playing. "I could probably rustle up a little 'Bakersfield' for you, pal. Dwight has some good songs."

"See, Cynthia?" the man said.

"How about Sinatra? You know any Sinatra? Would you please tell my date this is a lounge and not a honky-tonk?"

"Frank Sinatra don't have nothing on Dwight Yoakam in the class department," the man said.

"You did not just say that out loud."

Bones liked her even less.

Jimmy went back to the song he was playing before. "Tell you what.

You two discuss it between yourselves, and then whoever's still alive at the end can let me know what they want to hear."

The man leaned back in his chair, face easing into resigned lines. "Ah, I guess a little Sinatra wouldn't hurt if you've got some up your sleeve."

Cynthia smiled, revealing the whitest and smallest teeth Bones had ever seen. They looked like shiny Tic Tacs. She put a manicured-nails hand on Cowboy Hat's arm. "Honey, you're a quick study. You'll do just fine."

Jimmy started in on a song Bones had heard but couldn't remember the name of. It was cool, though. Dark and bright at the same time, like the Venus.

Juan brought the drinks. "Two of the best highballs this side of Tijuana."

Cynthia sipped.

The man did the same. "*Excellente*, amigo."

"*Bueno*. I'll get your steaks going." Juan turned and left.

Cynthia set down her drink. "I love these old standards. Let's dance."

Cowboy Hat looked around. "Here?"

"This is where the music is, isn't it? You'd rather dance outside with the wolves?"

"Mostly coyotes around here."

"Coyotes, then?"

The man stood. "Sure. All right."

Bones watched the two come together in the dim light, piano tinkling behind them. They moved slow, close. Cynthia had her eyes closed. The man gave her a slow twirl, then pulled her back. She seemed to like this.

When the song ended, Cynthia clapped. Jimmy had a big jar on the piano with the word *Tips* written on it. Cowboy Hat stepped up on stage, pulled a few bills from his wallet, and dropped them in. Jimmy nodded his thanks and played on. They danced through a couple more songs before the steaks came. Then they settled into eating and didn't talk much. Guy was serious about his steak.

Bones watched Jimmy. The biker gave the appearance of being lost in his music. Somehow Bones had the feeling he was anything but.

Jimmy rolled into "Tennessee Whiskey." Bones knew the name of that one. It was always on the radio. The lounge door swung open again, and a couple of guys walked in. Bones recognized the pair right off. Kyle and John Oaker. Rich kids. At least, rich for Paradise. They'd been a few years ahead of him in school before they graduated. With their identical blocky builds, they looked so much alike that lots of people mistook them for twins. Didn't help that they shared a school grade after John had to repeat his sophomore year. Bones hadn't seen them in a while.

They'd obviously been out riding dirt bikes. Still decked out in most of the gear, though they'd ditched motorcycle boots for the slip-on plastic sandals they had on over their socks. Their mousey-colored hair was helmet-plastered. Their riding jerseys layered with dust. They took a table directly across the room from Bones. When Juan approached they ordered burgers to go and cherry Cokes while they waited, paying with cash on the spot.

"Why'd we stop here, man?" Kyle said, watching Juan walk away. He kept his voice low, but Bones could hear him fine. "Twenty minutes into town and we could have had something good. This place is weird."

John leaned his head back and closed his eyes. "Because I'm starving, dude. If you hadn't forgotten the ice chest, you could complain. And how do you know what the food's like? Maybe they got good burgers. This place has been here a long time."

"Good burgers? Seriously? We could have gone to Shandy's. Alissa's working tonight."

"Alissa doesn't know you're alive, man. You need to get over that."

"But this place is like a bar or something. The food's gonna suck." Kyle was the type of guy who always laughed when he said stuff, even when nothing about it was funny. He laughed now and pointed at Jimmy. "Check out that dude. They got a Hells Angel playing the piano."

John glanced over. "So?"

"I'm just saying it's a weird place, that's all."

John closed his eyes again. "I'm too hungry to care."

Kyle slipped out of the booth. "What's the dude playing? I'm gonna see if he can play something good. Jerk him around a little."

"You're gonna jerk around a Hells Angel?"

"He's a piano dude. Relax."

"Leave him alone. Let's just get our food and get out of here."

"We got a few minutes." Kyle walked over to the stage, still laughing his nervous laugh. "Hey, man, you know anything good?"

Jimmy didn't answer him for a measure or two. "Sure. Do you?"

"Sit down, Kyle," John said.

Jimmy paused his song, leaned down, and pulled his metal box from his pack. He set it on the piano.

"What's that thing?" Kyle said.

Jimmy shuffled through the pack again and came out with a framed sign, the words printed on it small but clear enough for Bones to read. *Free Disappearings—One Per Customer.*

Bones straightened in his seat a little.

"What's a *disappearing*?" Kyle said.

Jimmy started a new song. "What it sounds like. Put something in the box, and off it goes. Disappears."

"Off it goes where?"

"That's the question, ain't it? Where does the sunrise go? Where does the wind go?"

Kyle looked back at John. "You hearing this? Dude's a trip, man. I told you this place was weird."

"Just sit down." John's cheeks were red as he glanced at the cowboy and his lady.

Kyle put his hand on the box. "So it's a trick box or something like that?"

Jimmy shrugged and played. "It's a box, that's all."

Cowboy Hat tapped the table and called to Juan at the bar. "Amigo, another highball. Double whiskey this time, if you would."

"So you put something in and it disappears and then comes back?" Kyle said.

"If you read the sign carefully, it says disappears, not comes back," Jimmy said.

"I don't get it, then."

"That's sad. Ain't gonna get any clearer if I say it again."

"But it's free?"

John stayed where he was. "Kyle, don't be an idiot. It's a scam."

Kyle laughed at this. "Dude, *you* don't be an idiot. How can something be a scam if it's free?"

"Put something in the box, Burt," Cynthia said. So Cowboy Hat's name was Burt. "I want to see it work."

"Nah, I don't have anything I care to lose."

Kyle ran a finger over the box. "I can put in anything I want?"

"Whatever you want," Jimmy said.

"Like a buck or something?"

"You don't want the buck?"

"It really doesn't come back?"

"That's right."

Kyle shook his head. "Dude, that's only like half a trick. You gotta make it come back. Or make it show up in my pocket or something."

Jimmy shrugged. "Is what it is. Nobody's twisting your arm."

"Kyle, c'mon. Remember the fair?" John said. "Every year those dudes suck all the money out of your pockets and you never even see it coming. Just sit down."

"What if I don't have anything on me I don't want back?" Kyle said to Jimmy.

Jimmy played a smooth run on the keys. Crazy how much straight-up cool could fit into a handful of notes. "I guess it ain't your night, then."

"You know what you should put in there, Kyle?" John said. "Your head. You never use it anyway."

Cynthia seemed to think this was funny. She poked Burt's arm. "I know you have something. Don't be such a stick in the mud. It's only for fun."

Burt focused on his recently arrived highball. "Like the kid said, it's a carnival trick."

"So? Carnival tricks aren't fun?"

"They ain't fun to me."

She took a drink of her cocktail, then leaned back, crossed her arms, and stuck out her bottom lip. "You don't have to get all irritated about it."

"I'm not irritated." Burt downed the rest of his drink and stood. "Here, kid." He tossed his empty glass to Kyle, who managed to catch it. "If a glass is empty, I ain't all that interested in it. Make that go away, if you want."

"That belongs to the restaurant," Cynthia said.

"It's not really going anywhere. It's a trick. If it don't come back, I'll pay for it. Don't worry about it." With this, he headed toward the restrooms.

"Don't fall in and drown," Cynthia called after him. For some reason both she and Kyle found this statement high comedy.

Kyle held up the tumbler to Jimmy. "This okay?"

Jimmy shrugged. "Long as Roy Rogers will pay for it, you can be Dale. Drop it in."

"Who's Dale?"

"Before your time."

"I put it in? Not you?"

"It's all you, brother. Playing this here piano takes two hands."

Kyle opened the box and set the glass in. "Now what?"

"Shut the lid."

Kyle did.

"Now open it."

Kyle opened the lid and stared. "Dude, that's crazy. John, check this out. Seriously, it's totally gone."

John still stayed where he was. "Of course it's gone, man. It's a stupid trick box. Dude probably bought it on Amazon for fifty bucks to mess with people like you."

"Nah. Box like this you don't buy," Jimmy said. "It's been around a while."

"Yeah, man. It looks old," Kyle said. "Check it out."

John finally got up and joined his brother. "There's a hidden compartment. I'm telling you, you can get these things anywhere. Beat it up a little, and you have an ancient mystery to fool fools."

"Try shaking it," Cynthia said. "If there's a compartment, you'll hear the glass in there."

"Can I pick it up?" Kyle said to Jimmy.

"Be my guest."

Kyle shook the box, then spent several long seconds studying it from every angle, inside and out. He handed it to John. "Okay, man. If there's a hidden compartment, show me."

John looked inside the thing. "It's here. You just can't see it. That's why it's called hidden."

"She's right, though. If there was a hidden compartment, we'd hear the glass."

"Not if it's padded."

"That's true." Cynthia again. "I didn't think of that."

Kyle took the box back, felt around inside again. "No way. There's no room for a compartment."

"Sleight of hand, then," John said. "He made a switch somehow. I'm telling you, it's basic stuff."

"How? He was playing the piano the whole time. With both hands. Dude never moved. I was watching."

"It's called an *illusion*, man. Like David Blaine and those guys."

Kyle shook his head. "There's no way."

"You see the stuff David Blaine does? You'd never figure it out. Like this, but this isn't as cool."

Bones watched as Burt made his way back to his table. He didn't sit, just looked down at his date. "You ready?"

"Not yet. I want to see what happens with this box. It's something interesting for a change."

Burt sighed and sat. He signaled to Juan for another drink.

John looked at Jimmy. "First one's free, right? That goes for me too?"

"What the sign says."

"Cool. I'll be right back." John walked outside and returned two minutes later with a big rock. It looked like it would barely fit in the box. He hefted it. "Check this out. Gotta be fifteen, twenty pounds."

"Probably about right," Jimmy said.

John grinned. "You think you can slip this up your sleeve?"

Jimmy jutted his chin toward the box. "There she is. Have a party."

The rock scraped the sides of the box when John shoved it in. Jimmy, focused on his music, didn't even look up.

"You're gonna let me shut it like Kyle did?"

"That's the way it works."

"You're not even going to watch, man? A rock this big?"

Jimmy stopped the song and sighed. "Sorry, brother," he deadpanned. "I'm all yours. Yeah, look at that rock. It's big. How exciting is this?"

John laughed. "Whatever." He felt the top of the rock again. Got down close. "I wanna watch it till the lid closes."

"Don't blame you," Jimmy said. "Done that a time or two myself."

"No way this rock's going anywhere."

"You wouldn't think so, would you?"

John lowered the lid slowly, leaning in to watch the rock as the crack narrowed. He paused. "You know what? I bet there's a false bottom. Whatever's in the box goes down into the piano, right?"

"Pick it up, then," Jimmy said.

"I can hold the box while I close the lid?"

"You look like a big strong guy. Why not?"

"There's no way."

"So you keep saying."

"All right, then." John cradled the box in one arm while he slowly closed the lid with his other hand. The moment the lid made contact, his eyes widened a fraction.

"What?" Kyle said.

"It got way lighter as soon as the lid closed. I actually felt it, man." He opened the box. Showed the inside to Kyle, then to Burt and Cynthia. "There's no way. It's impossible."

"Crazy, ain't it?" Jimmy said, milky eye glinting.

John set the box down, then knelt and looked under the piano. "Where did it go, man?"

"I told you," Kyle said. "Let's put something else in."

"Now you're talking," Jimmy said. "You can do all the rocks you want. Empty the desert. I'll stay here all night. Only five bucks per disappear."

"Five bucks?" John said.

"First one's free. Second one ain't. I'm working for tips, here."

"How about one more free?"

Jimmy jutted a chin at his sign. "Rules are rules."

"Yeah, but they're your rules. You wrote the sign."

"Five bucks. That's the way it goes."

"Give me a five, John." Kyle held out his hand.

"Just used all my cash on the burgers."

Bones could see the wheels slowly turning in Kyle's head. "You take a debit card, man?"

"Nope. With the box, cash is king."

"All we have is a card."

"My condolences to you in your predicament."

"You gonna be here tomorrow night?"

"If the boss don't fire me."

"We'll be back, then."

"I will count the minutes."

With a last look at the box, John and Kyle returned to their table, where their burgers waited. Ignoring his nearly full glass of cherry Coke, Kyle picked up the bag and followed John out the lounge door. A few seconds later doors slammed, a truck engine turned over, and headlights swept the window.

Jimmy rolled back into Sinatra.

CHAPTER SEVEN

Bones pushed himself back farther into the booth.

Burt's eyes were more than a little glassy as Cynthia stood and pulled him back out onto the dance floor. More money went into the tip jar—Bones even noticed a hundred-dollar bill pressed up against the glass. They were still dancing when closing time neared, and Jimmy slowed and ended the song he'd been playing.

Burt looked at him. "You play dang good."

"Not nearly as good as you tip. Thanks."

"Where'd you get the box? It's quite a trick."

"Popular story is it came from a lady deep down in a bayou."

"Popular stories ain't always real stories, though, are they?"

"Probably why they get so popular."

Cynthia walked to the piano and ran a finger over the box's side. "It looks so old."

Jimmy played something slow. A minor scale. Even Paradise schools had a music class you had to go to, so Bones recognized what it was. Chords, whether the music got soft or loud . . . all that stuff got named and demonstrated. But they'd never talked about jazz or piano in particular, let alone the blues.

"Yeah, old. Looks ain't deceiving," Jimmy said.

"It's just us now. Can you show us how you do it?" Cynthia said.

"Of course he can't show us how he does it." Burt's words came out spongy around the edges. "That'd reveal his trick."

She laughed. "Or it's really bayou voodoo. Put something in now."

Burt squinted and shook his head. "Nah. I'm tired. And I got nothing on me I don't want back. You heard the man. Once it goes in the box, it's gone forever."

"Exactly. That's what I like about it."

"What's that supposed to mean?"

"I think you know what it means."

"I don't."

"Look me in the eye and tell me you don't have that stupid ring in your pocket."

"What ring?"

"You know what ring. Your wedding ring. You carry the thing around like a security blanket."

"I do not."

"Look me in the eye."

Burt shrank a fraction then, like someone had let a little air out of a balloon. "You don't understand. It's not that easy."

Her Tic Tac teeth flashed. "I understand perfectly, and I'm drawing a line in the sand here. About time too."

"I was married for a long time, Cynthia. It's not that simple."

"You told me you cared about me."

"I know I did."

"If you really care, then forget about her. Put the ring in the box."

"No."

"You want this to end? Us? Because I'm done competing with a ghost, Burt. The past is dead. *She's* dead. I'm the future. You need to wrap your brain around that."

"I know. It's only—"

"If you know it, put the ring in the box. Now."

Burt sighed and dug into the pocket of his jeans. He pulled out a ring, gold shining in the low light. He stared at it.

Cynthia opened the box, then sat down at the table and crossed her arms, ferret eyes fixed on Burt. "Hon, it's been a good night, don't you think? Let's end it right. Make a new start. Go ahead and do it."

Burt walked over to the box, still staring at the ring in his hand.

"Mind if I take a look first?" Jimmy said.

Burt handed it to him without a word. He looked like he might throw up.

Jimmy polished the ring on his pants leg and then studied it in the light. "You sure? It won't come back."

"He's sure," Cynthia said.

"It's your call." Jimmy flipped the ring back to Burt like it was a coin. "Only yours."

The man looked at it in his palm, looked at Jimmy, then tossed it into the box with a metallic clank. He turned to Cynthia. "There. You happy?"

"Close it," she said.

Burt reached out, and the lid went down.

Cynthia walked over and opened the box. She smiled. "See? That wasn't so hard."

"Wasn't it?"

She looped an arm through his. "Let's go. You've got a lot to look forward to."

"You okay to drive?" Jimmy said.

Burt shook his head. "Nope. But I'm staying here. Already have a room."

"Don't you mean *we*?" Cynthia said.

Burt took her arm and moved toward the door.

As the couple walked out, Jimmy started playing a song so slow and sad Bones thought his heart might break. Still, he stayed where he was and listened to the whole thing.

The door opened. Burt. Alone this time. He walked straight to Jimmy. "Hey, partner. Thanks."

Jimmy lifted a shoulder. "Where's the Sinatra fan?"

"Gave her my truck keys and sent her home. *Her* home."

"Leaves you without wheels."

"I'll have a couple of the boys from my ranch pick up the truck in the morning and bring it here for me."

"Good to be king."

"Is it?" He shook his head. "She's a hard one to convince. Or maybe I'm the one who's hard to convince. She likes my money, and I get so dang sick of being lonely . . . But I think she got the picture. With any luck, I did too."

"Sometimes a direct approach is the best."

"I got blinded for a while, that's all. Get to the point it takes three or four highballs to get through an evening with someone, and I guess that's a pretty good clue it's not particularly meant to be."

Jimmy played a bar of "Amazing Grace." Everyone knew that one. "I once was blind, but now I see."

"Yeah. Let me ask you a question. You always carry brass flat washers around with you in case you need to make a ring switch for some love-sappy loser like me?"

"Let's say you're not the first. And you're not a loser. Like you said, sometimes we get a little blind. Loneliness will do that to a person." Jimmy reached into the pocket of his jeans, pulled out Burt's ring, and handed it to him. "The way I see it, sometimes the past is better put away forever and forgotten. But then again, sometimes it deserves to be treasured. Sometimes it even needs to be carried around in a man's pocket."

Burt closed his hand around the ring. "It's just that I still love my wife. Even though she's gone. I love her as much as the day I married her."

"That's a rare thing, friend. You have your memories. Don't let them go. I'll tell you this, though. When and if another love comes into your life—and I'm betting she will—she'll understand and won't step on your past. She'll even appreciate it."

"I owe you one."

"No, you don't."

"Can I at least buy you a drink?"

"Nope."

"Maybe I'll have one. You know, for the road."

"Let me suggest coffee. The highball lady has made her exit."

"You know, coffee sounds like just the ticket."

"Absolutely." Jimmy broke into some country swing. "Hey, check this out. I never had a chance to play that Dwight Yoakam for you."

CHAPTER EIGHT

BONES WAITED UNTIL THE LOUNGE was empty, Juan on his way home and no sign of Calico, before sliding out of the booth. He wished Jimmy had left the box. He'd have liked to take a closer look at it.

The ring thing with Burt the cowboy had caught him by surprise. He'd watched the exchange closely but hadn't spotted the switch. The fact Jimmy didn't keep the ring surprised him too. He could have disappeared the thing and kept it. Not for a minute did Bones believe the box was anything but a clever trick. But Jimmy had given the ring back. He was playing some game, that was sure. Bones just needed more time to figure out what it was.

He pushed open the door to the outside, then let it swing shut and lock behind him as he stepped out into the night. A million stars winked. The neon-lit Lady Venus shone by the highway. The motel porch lights fought off moths and cast soft pools of comfort. Even with all the illumination, Bones moved down the sidewalk invisible as a breeze. He wasn't tired, and the night felt good. Warm and wide. A half-moon walked a high wire over the mountains.

He cut right at the end of the sidewalk without any real reason, heading for the pool rather than back around the motel to the shop. The pool lights were off, the water smooth as glass, the reflected stars looking like floating diamonds. He picked out the Big Dipper in the shallow end, Orion's Belt over by the diving board.

"That invisible thing you do really work on people?" Jimmy's unmistakable voice came from out by the darkened highway. Bones could feel the pulse in his temples.

A cigarette glowed. "Come on over, Bones-with-the-painful-last-name. I ain't all that scary."

Thing was, he *was* all that scary with his milky eye out there in the dark by the highway, but Bones would have died before admitting it. He straightened, exited the pool gate, and walked toward the glowing orange dot.

"You always creep around in the dark?" Jimmy said.

"Do you?"

"Touché." Standing just outside the very last edge of Lady Venus's neon reach, Jimmy shook a cig from his pack, then held the rest out to Bones. "Want one?"

"I don't smoke."

"Good for you. It's a bad habit. I asked you a question. You think you're invisible or what?"

"No."

"You sure?"

"I don't know. Maybe. It kind of seems like it sometimes. It's just something I do."

"Uh-huh. You also thought nobody noticed you tucked back in that booth in the lounge last couple a nights. Am I right?"

"Nobody did."

"I did."

"Except you, I guess."

"Yup, except ole Jimmy."

Jimmy smoked for a bit, quiet. Out above the Chiricahuas, a star shot across half the sky as it died a bright and brilliant death.

"I got a gift, that's all." Bones didn't know why he said it. He never would have to anyone else. But Jimmy kind of pulled stuff out of a person with his contrasting eyes and all that quiet smoke.

"Yeah? What kind of gift is that?"

"One time somebody told me God gives people gifts, that everybody gets something. You believe that?"

"Guess what matters more is if you believe it. What's your supposed gift?"

"Nobody notices me."

"That's a gift?"

"It's just that I can sort of be background static. Like white noise. Nobody notices white noise after a while."

"No, I guess they don't. Ain't much of a gift, though. You might want to have a talk with the big complaint department in the sky about a gift like that."

"You mean pray?"

"Sure. If that's what you want to call it."

"My friend Gomez Gomez used to pray."

"Used to?"

"He died."

"Yeah? Most people do."

"Anyway, I figure if God gives somebody the gift of going unnoticed, it's most likely because he doesn't notice them that much himself. Which is fine with me."

"Is it?"

"Yeah."

"I'm not sure that logic is sound. In fact, the whole thing's a sad perspective on existence."

"I don't mind. I mean, it's not like your gift. It's not like I can make things disappear or anything, but it's cool with me."

"You think the box is a gift?"

"I wouldn't mind having something like that. Nobody would."

"Maybe, maybe not. Gifts are funny things. Way I see it, they can be a burden as much as a blessing."

"I guess so."

It got quiet again, and Bones wondered what a guy like Jimmy thought about standing there staring up at the stars. He was like a star himself. Or a comet. It was strange. He'd slid into the booth without so much as a ripple, but Jimmy had known he was there all night.

Jimmy actually noticed background static. Yeah, the guy was definitely not unidimensional.

Distant headlights loomed. A truck approached, and light washed over them. Bones caught a good view of the milky eye before the night went dark again. He shivered.

"You enjoy the show tonight?" Jimmy said. He blew a red cloud of smoke toward the truck's receding taillights.

"The music was cool."

"How about the rest of it? Those boys were pretty impressed."

"Kyle and John aren't the brightest bulbs in the string. I can't figure it out. I watched your hands and everything the whole time. How do you do the box?"

"Maybe I don't do anything. Maybe it's real."

"I'm not stupid like Kyle and John."

"The way it shapes up to me, you're far from stupid."

Bones stood a little taller hearing this. He couldn't remember the last time someone said anything like that to him. Maybe never. "You can't tell me how you do it because a magician never reveals his tricks, right?"

"I ain't no magician, Bones."

"Whatever. Illusionist, then."

"If you think about it, what's not an illusion when it comes right down to it? Who's to say what is and isn't? Maybe we're not even real. Maybe we're a figment of someone's imagination."

"I'm real."

"All right."

"The thing I don't get is why you didn't keep the ring. I keep thinking about that."

"Why does that rattle your cage?"

"You could have let him put it in the box. Then you could have kept it."

"Have you not been listening? Once it's gone, it's gone."

"There's no way stuff just vanishes. It's impossible."

"Is it?"

"Yeah, it is."

"Why?"

"Because it doesn't happen. Scientifically and all that."

"You know every rule of science?"

"No. But—"

"Do scientists know everything there is to know about science?"

"Yeah, I think so."

"Think about it. Science a hundred years ago—even *ten* years ago—was a whole different bunch of answers and facts than it is today. And those guys back then would have died on those hills. Imagine what *science* will be in another hundred years. So don't say it ain't scientific."

"So you're saying what happens in the box is science."

"Nope. What happens in the box is miraculous. That's a different thing, for the most part."

"That's even more crazy."

Jimmy smoked. "Whatever you say."

"Even if it is a miracle, I still would have kept the ring. You made the switch. He said he has money. He didn't really need it."

"That ring has nothing to do with money. It's all a matter of opinion and perspective. I imagine his would differ from yours by quite a stretch."

"You could have got some good money for that gold."

"Let me ask you a question. What do you think is the most valuable thing that man owns?"

"I don't know. Money, probably."

"What's money? Pieces of paper? Little bits of metal? A number on a screen that's gone as soon as the thing goes blank? If you think about it, money's nothing more than an abstract idea."

"Not if you don't have any, it isn't. It's real enough."

"The memories tied to that ring are that man's life. They're the most valuable thing he owns. He throws those memories away and he's a shell of what he was. Even I wouldn't do that to a guy."

"What do you care?"

Jimmy laughed a little at this. "You're a tough nut, huh?"

"You really get the box from a lady in a swamp?"

"Where it comes from isn't the important thing."

"Why?"

"Because it's just a box. You got a lot of questions for a faded chunk of white noise."

"I think it's a scam. I think you're playing the long game."

Jimmy laughed again. "Okay."

"Can I still have one of those cigarettes?"

Jimmy handed one over.

Bones balanced it on his lip like Jimmy but didn't ask to light it. "I don't mean scam in a bad way. Scams can be cool."

Jimmy looked up at Lady Venus. "Sure, kid. Scams are cool. I'm gonna get some sleep. See you around."

Bones hoped Jimmy would put his cig out on his palm again, but he dropped it to the ground and rubbed it out with his boot.

"Hey," Bones called when Jimmy was halfway to his room.

Jimmy turned.

"You ever put anything in that box?"

"Nope."

"Why not?"

"See you tomorrow." He started walking again.

"You don't have anything you want to see disappear?"

Jimmy turned again. Studied Bones for several seconds. "I got a world of stuff, Bones-with-no-last-name. A whole world. You gonna light that cigarette?"

"Maybe later."

"Uh-huh. Good night."

"Yeah, good night."

Bones watched Jimmy go, then stood for a while staring out at the desert ink. He closed his eyes and floated, became a paper-thin layer of white noise beneath the solar roar. Background static hiding behind a million blue-blink satellites and a million—no, a billion—stars. At length, he landed on his feet, turned, and walked slow steps back toward the motel, while behind him Lady Venus hummed and buzzed and offered neon solace to the empty highway.

CHAPTER NINE

Calico watched Bones cross the parking lot from the dim recess of her apartment. The lights were off inside, only the neon glow from Lady Venus giving light to the room. What had Bones and Jimmy La Roux talked about out there? A couple of loners, those two. It was strange to think of them interacting. Especially on Bones's end.

Which brought her back to her notebook and the pros-and-cons list.

She switched on a table lamp and opened the notebook to the Bones page sandwiched between her lists for bitcoins and bricks. The bitcoin list was short so far—more research needed. The brick list, there for a decision she'd been trying to make about adding a brick patio behind the motel, was substantially longer. The Bones list was long as well, and not on the pro side. In fact, she had no entries at all on the pro side.

Not that she blamed the kid. Really, as she scanned the con column, most of the issues she had with him were her own. The simple fact was she was inadequate in too many departments to deal with the kind of background and problems a young man like Bones carried. Which made her feel awful. After all, everyone deserved a shot in life. Bones had no one. But he also wanted no one. He'd made that abundantly clear. It's not like she hadn't tried, right? She'd offered to let him stay in her spare bedroom. It even had its own bathroom. But he'd insisted on staying out in the shop when Pines brought him.

Which took her mind back to Pines.

Which made her mad at him all over again.

What was he thinking bringing a kid to the Venus? And springing it on her? He'd given her an hour's notice at most. Granted, he didn't have a lot of choice in the matter at the time, but an hour? Then again, he'd trusted her enough to call when he needed help. That was big for Pines. He wasn't one to ask for assistance—ever.

Which meant he trusted her.

Which made her a little less mad.

As she sat there, each of these facts and tidbits went into either a pro or con column in her mind. But none of them helped the problem. None of them were the string she could pull to untie the knot. Because the knot was her.

She looked out through the window at Lady Venus. A dazzling, towering example of vintage neon art. Sad-eyed Venus, probably worth more than the motel and land combined. She'd been approached about selling her three times by three different collectors since she'd owned the motel. One from Vegas and two from the Middle East. But the Lady would never leave her desert post. Not as long as Calico had anything to say about it.

From a cabinet beneath her TV, Calico pulled out an old photo album. She shouldn't look through it; it would only make her sad. But she opened it to the first page, a Christmas photo of her family before her mother passed. The sickness must have been present then, moving stealthily through veins and bones.

Calico wondered if her mother had known it or at least suspected it when the shot was taken. If she had, she'd never let on. Not until it was too late and impossible to hide it. They were all smiling in the picture, a Christmas tree lit up behind them. She and Charlie, her little brother, had argued about that tree at the lot. She remembered it well. A nippy ninety degree Phoenix December day. Pine trees as natural to the desert as sunbathers in the Arctic. Charlie had won. Charlie generally won.

Charlie. She'd tried her best with him, hadn't she? With her mom gone and her dad buried in his dreams? But trying hadn't been enough. And Charlie had been Charlie. Charlie was *still* Charlie. Not that he was a bad guy. He wasn't. He just had so much of their dreamer father in him.

Charlie. And Pines wanted her to do it all over again? After her failure the first time? It wasn't fair to anyone.

She turned a page. Then another. After her mother died, Calico wasn't in many of the photos. She was almost always the one behind the camera, so how could she be? Charlie at soccer, Charlie's first motorcycle, her father and Charlie on the day their father opened his bar and motel in One Horse. A few sunset shots from her room behind the bar there. She picked up the notebook again and jotted *Can't see the sunset from behind the motel* in the con column under Bricks.

She turned back a page to the Bones list and read over the cons again. Pines was right. Her fiancé would be good for the kid. He might be able to break through his thick shell. But Pines, not her.

She was going to lose him. She could feel it.

After staring at the blank pros column for a long time, she shut the notebook.

CHAPTER TEN

In Cozy's double-wide world, Sunday and Monday nights were the two most important of the week. The rest didn't even come close. Sunday and Monday were sacred. There was no real religious element to this, though she'd be the first to admit her fanaticism would surely rival that of any zealot out there.

Sunday and Monday meant *American Idol.* A show so great, so elevated above every other show in the history of shows, that it couldn't be contained to one night of the week. And *American Idol* also couldn't be contained to the television screen.

Invariably, the minute Don left the house, Cozy would head for her bedroom, her three-way mirror on the wall, and her hairbrush microphone. The mirror was the last nice thing Don did before he fell out of love with her a thousand years ago. She knew hundreds of songs by heart. And, hey, could she help it if Simon Cowell was more than a little in love with her? She liked to mix up the judges from different seasons in her imagination, depending on what she sang.

Steven Tyler, for instance, loved her harder stuff. Katy Perry for pop, and Randy or Lionel for R and B and soul, sometimes jazz. She especially loved Katy, whom she considered a dead ringer for herself—although she had to admit Katy looked a little younger. Cozy might, too, if she hadn't given Don ten years of her life. But she hadn't *lost* her looks. She knew that.

Cozy wasn't always a singer, though. Sometimes she'd be a judge.

If she felt old school, she'd tell contestants they were *a little pitchy, dog.* She'd make fun of their moms and lambast both parents for encouraging their kids to sing in the first place. If she felt like stepping into current seasons, she'd give a rambling everybody-gets-a-trophy speech about how a contestant's shaky performance had practically saved her soul.

Because when it came to *Idol,* Cozy was a team player.

And she'd never, ever, *ever* missed an episode. It wasn't enough to stream them after the fact; she had to be watching the second they aired. Which was why it was crazy that instead of watching *Idol* last night—a precious Monday—she'd been on her laptop looking up the legalities of lottery winnings on the internet again. She'd been careful too. Not blindly believing every thread and forum but taking meticulous notes and verifying every fact. And the cold hard facts said she got half the Mega money. Period. Don couldn't do anything about it.

So she was in a good mood this morning as she picked up her brush and took her place in front of the mirror for Whitney's "The Greatest Love of All." Three slightly, but *only* slightly, older-looking Katy Perry reflections smiled back at her. Yes, last night had been worth the sacrifice. Three and a quarter big ones would buy a big, non-rolling house with a whole lot of mirrors, a real recording of herself singing, and maybe even a ticket to an *Idol* finale.

Don poked his head in. "I thought we agreed you wouldn't start killing cats until I was gone for the day."

"So hurry up and leave."

"You really need to get a life."

"Finally. Something we agree on."

"I won't be back tonight, remember?"

"So you told me a dozen times."

"El Paso's a long drive, that's all."

"Uh-huh. Just as long as you don't commit more than three and a quarter to whatever pile of metal you're going down there to see."

"I'll spend as much as I want."

"You can't, Don. Because we're married. I did more research last night, and for real, it's legally half mine. You can't spend my half."

"Cozy, we've been—"

"I'm serious. I'm getting out of this trailer."

"Anytime you want. You know where the door is." He winked. "See ya tomorrow, Porchie."

"Don't call me that."

"Break a leg. And I mean that literally."

She listened for the front door to shut, then for his truck to start. That wink bothered her. Why wasn't he concerned about her findings? It was his arrogance, that's all. He couldn't imagine her ever getting one up on him. He was like that. He thought he was invincible, the center of the world.

She smiled at the Katys in her mirror. She had Google and nineteen seasons worth of *American Idol* judges on her side.

Maybe she *should* leave. Maybe she should have done it a long time ago. Then again, it hadn't always been this way. She'd first met Don at the dirt track stock car races just outside Paradise. He'd been in the pits with a greasy crew made up of two of his cousins and a beat-up black-spray-painted 1975 Monte Carlo for a race car. She'd been at the top of her game then. The trophy queen in a red mini she'd bought at Ross Dress for Less in Tucson.

Don had taken one look at her and said, "You better be ready to kiss me up on that stage tonight. One look at you and no one's touching me out there." Except he rolled the Monte Carlo on the fourth lap. And even then he was only two cars from the back of the pack.

So she'd kissed Bill Trout instead, an out-of-towner with an actual, real car. But Bill Trout didn't roll up the sleeves of his T-shirt like Don did. He didn't have that smile. So Don got all the kisses after that. At least all of them *off* the winner's stage. He'd never once had a trophy in his hands.

Don lived his life chasing the ever-elusive checkered flag. It was fun for a while. Exciting, even. But excitement fades a lot like pink paint on the outside of a double-wide. When Don first bought the trailer, it seemed like a castle. Now it was more like a prison. A couple of years ago, a development company had cleared some land right across the street and put in one of those new tracts. The Harbors, they called it. What a joke. As far as Cozy knew, the nearest harbor was in San Diego, almost two whole states away. But she'd feel free over there compared to this dump.

The dumbest part? Since Don hit the Mega—the only thing he'd ever won in his life—Cozy could probably buy like twenty of those places. Maybe even the whole neighborhood. But stupid Don had his eyes fixed on stupid cars and only stupid cars. They could take that money and even live on a beach somewhere. High on the hog for once. The Caribbean, maybe. Or Florida. Or even Vegas. But Don wouldn't hear of leaving the double-wide.

He hadn't even cashed in the winning ticket yet. He said he had eight weeks to do it, and a buddy in Phoenix was supposed to be some kind of financial advisor working on the next move. As if she didn't know more racing was what the next move would be. Don wasn't going to El Paso to look at roller skates, that was sure.

She ran through most of Whitney's greatest hits. Nailed them all. Did a Pink song. Then a Johnny Cash—with her own spin, of course. Luke Bryant went nuts over that one. Then her throat got tired, so she took a break.

Her sudoku book was full. Nothing on TV. Dejected, she sat on her front porch steps, cigarette in one hand and a glass of sweet tea in the other. It was midmorning, stay-at-home-mom jogging hour over at The Harbors, all their kids probably stuck with some babysitter or nanny. They had a brand-new perfect sidewalk over there that ran around the perimeter of the whole development.

Fifteen minutes later, she'd seen at least six jogger-jerks. Well, they *should* jog, the way most of them tried to squeeze those size-large thighs into size-small yoga pants. Maybe they were too embarrassed to go the gym.

One of them looked over, smiled, and waved. Cozy offered a slight cigarette lift and blew smoke sideways. They all knew Don had won the Mega. Don had never been a guy to keep things to himself, especially when they had to do with him. That's why they waved. Although, when she thought about it, they'd waved before. Never mind that, though. They were judging her. She could feel it. See it in their smirky little jogger eyes.

All those nonmoving houses. All those yoga pants. All those outfit-matching water bottles. Happy joggers. So cheerful. So hydrated. So normal. Hydrated people living normal, hydrated lives.

Cozy hated drinking water. All her life people had given her a hard time about it, as if it was some kind of social deformity. It wasn't like she had a chocolate chip wart on her nose. Don didn't get it either. He actually claimed water had no taste. As if. *Here, have a tall cool glass of dirty socks.*

She inhaled on her cigarette and then blew smoke toward a pair of purple yoga pants.

On top of everything else, now the doctor said she had kidney stones. It was gross. The thought of a kidney somewhere down there under her skin was disgusting enough. Then add stones to it. He said she needed to cut out salt, which was a sneaky way of saying cut out soup. And then, of course, the old standard—drink more water.

If Don got his way, she'd never get out of here. He'd promise the world like he always did, then lose it all within weeks. They'd be lucky if they could share a plate dinner at Junior's Barbecue. She'd be sitting in front of this faded pink house on wheels watching Harbor ducks jog till they buried her dried-out, kidney-stone-riddled body in the Paradise cemetery. If she could even afford to be buried.

She sighed. It wasn't like she wanted a lot. Was a house that didn't move too much to ask? Don would blow it all if she let him. She knew him. He'd have a deal in place for a car and trailer and truck and crew . . . The whole wad would be gone the second the Mega check cleared. Then his feelings would be hurt when she wasn't over-the-moon happy for him.

No way. Not this time. She'd never get another chance to change her life. The minute Don said he was getting the money, she'd make her move.

Another jogger waved. The worst kind too. One of those rare, endangered Harbor ducks who actually fit into their tiny yoga pants perfectly. Cozy narrowed an eye but otherwise ignored the woman. She sipped her sweet tea again. She could tolerate tea as long as it had enough sugar in it. And she knew for a fact there was a ton of water in tea, so all those doctors and health gurus could get lost.

Another duck waved. Didn't these people ever get tired?

She went into the kitchen, poured herself more tea, spooned in extra sugar, toasted the doctor, then took a big gulp. She leaned back against the counter and gave the place a long once-over. She should cash the ticket herself. *If* she could find it. Don probably had it hidden out in the shop with his pile of girly magazines he didn't think she knew about. It was probably tucked in there with Miss November. But she'd wait. Her time would come. He didn't have a leg to stand on legally. For once, she held the cards.

She smiled as she walked back outside with her tea and stood on the porch. The only thing worse than living in a faded pink trailer was being bored in a faded pink trailer. A screen door slammed, and Marla, the neighbor to her right, walked out of her own faded trailer, this one baby blue.

Marla waved. "How's it going, Coz?"

Cozy lit another cigarette. "It's going." Marla had a crush on Don and made no secret of it. She was also five foot two and weighed a good two hundo. Cozy watched the little troll waddle to the mailbox, pull out a handful of mail, and start back, red-faced and huffing.

The troll feet stopped near the fence line. "So . . ."

"So, what?" Cozy said.

"Nothing."

"What?"

"Maybe it's not for me to say."

Cozy sipped her tea. "Since when is anything ever not for you to say, Marla?"

"You know, you make it sound like I'm some sort of gossip."

"No, *you* make it sound like you're some sort of gossip every time you open your mouth."

Marla wiped her troll nose and leaned on the fence. Her jean shorts were too tight and too short, practically choking her blue-veined thighs to death. But her eyes flashed victory, and Cozy suddenly had a strange feeling in the pit of her stomach. "I have things to do inside," she said.

"Sure. I was just wondering where Don was going with Tanya so early this morning."

"What's that supposed to mean? Tanya?"

"Only that I saw them gassing up at Joe's when I was picking up breakfast."

"You mean picking up donuts."

"That's what I said."

"Tanya from the Pick-a-Part?"

"That's the only Tanya I know."

"You're sure?"

The troll eyes went mock wide. "You mean you didn't know they were going somewhere together?"

Cozy took a pull on the cigarette. "Yeah, of course I knew. Don had to help her with something, that's all."

"I'll bet he had to help her."

"You better get in with that mail, Marla. You might get too hot out here. Those legs look like they might pass out, already."

"Just thought you'd want to know about Tanya. I only wanted to help."

"Sure you did. Already knew. Thanks. Bye."

Marla didn't hide the troll smirk on her troll mouth as she turned. Cozy waited until the woman was tucked back into her double-wide cave before picking up her phone and punching Don's number on speed dial.

CHAPTER ELEVEN

Two o'clock. Bones's lunch hour. Late for some, but cleaning rooms and the hundred other things Calico found for him to do around the motel made for kind of different hours. They tended to work mornings, then take a late lunch. Sometimes, like today, they'd even take the rest of the afternoon off unless something pressed.

Calico stood behind the bar. Juan, towel draped over his shoulder, sat on a barstool drinking soda water.

"So he made a glass and a rock disappear in his box. And a ring," Calico said.

"Right," Juan told her. He'd been in the kitchen when Burt came back for the real ring, so the cook didn't know about Jimmy's switch. Bones considered mentioning it but decided instead to stick that particular card back in his deck and the deck in his pocket. You never knew what tidbits of info might wind up having value down the road.

"He didn't even make money on the things that disappeared," Juan said. "He said the first one's free, and they were all firsts."

"He got the ring, though," Calico said. "That's worth something. It sounds shady."

"Why?" Bones said. "The cowboy guy put it in himself. He knew he wouldn't get it back."

Calico freshened her coffee from the pot at the end of the bar. "That's the thing. People still expect what they put in will come back. That's what always happens with these tricks. Then all he has to do is say *I told you so* and keep whatever he feels like keeping. Who's going to question a guy who looks like he'd bite your head off and spit it down your neck? But I hired him to play piano, not do a Chuck E. Cheese meets Easy Rider magic show."

"Is it called *hired* if he's only working for tips?" Juan said.

"And a room. Don't forget the room. I just think it's weird. What does he want with someone else's wedding ring?"

"You ever heard of pawn shops?"

"If that's the case, it's weird and wrong and sad rolled into one ball of tacky."

Bones changed his mind. "Nah. Jimmy's cool. Anyway, he gave the ring back to the dude. He switched it out with a washer, and that's what went into the box."

"Really?"

"Yeah, I saw it."

"Don't talk with your mouth full," Calico said.

Bones swallowed, then took an extra-large bite of his burger before talking around it. "Why? Because it's rude?"

"No, Bones. Because it makes me want to gag."

Bones picked up a fry and stuck it into his mouth with the burger. "Why don't you ever make me eat salad?"

Her coffee cup paused on the way to her mouth. "You want to eat salad?"

"Not really."

"Then what in the world are you talking about?"

"I'm just curious. Can I have some ketchup?"

"You know where it is."

Bones had kept an eye out for Jimmy, but the biker hadn't shown. They had a few customers in the place for lunch today, though—even this late. An older couple eating club sandwiches and drinking ginger ale with cherries at the bottom. Then there was Phyllis, the sporadic afternoon regular. She sat a few stools down from Bones. As far as he could tell, the woman had a closetful of identical denim pantsuits and an endless supply of mud-colored hair dye. Her sole diet seemed to be bourbon neat and pretzels, but for some reason she always smelled like clam chowder.

At the moment, thick red lipstick smudges showed on the woman's whiskey glass, which Bones found both fascinating and disgusting. He kept trying not to look, but he couldn't help himself. After a while, full, he pushed his empty plate across the bar and stood.

"Where are you going?" Calico said.

"To work on my bike, I guess. The rooms are all done."

She pointed at the plate. "Are you going to wash that? Do I look like your mom?"

He picked it up. "I don't know what my mom looked like."

"Boo-hoo," Phyllis said.

Calico turned on her. "Don't be mean, Phyllis."

Phyllis munched a pretzel and rolled her eyes.

Calico looked at Bones. "Do I look like *anybody's* mom?" She stood there, hands on her hips, looking even taller. For some reason, her full lips and wide mouth always made Bones feel slightly strange in the pit of his stomach. "No. I've never seen a mom like you."

"Good answer, kid," Phyllis said, signaling Calico for a refill by tapping a fake nail against the side of her empty glass.

Calico softened slightly. "You can take the rest of the day, Bones. But go wash your plate first."

"That's right. Everybody pulls their weight at the Venus," Phyllis said.

Calico poured the woman her shot. "Do they? What weight do you pull, exactly?"

"I tell you the news."

"I have a radio. Even a television, if you can believe it. All the way out here in the sticks."

Bones left the women to their conversation. In the kitchen, he washed his plate, then took a can of root beer from the big refrigerator and two single-serving bags of nacho cheese Doritos from the pantry. A door on the other side of the freezer led to the back side of the motel. A lot faster than walking all the way around.

The day was warm, the sun high. The little stone building Calico let Bones use hugged the rocky mountain base not a hundred feet behind the motel. It was much older than the Venus. Nobody seemed to remember whose it had been originally or what it was used for. At some point in the past, somebody had installed electricity and plumbing, and it became the caretaker's shop for the motel. They just didn't have a caretaker at the moment except for him, not that he took care of much.

He climbed the steep footpath trying not to think about Calico not looking like anyone's mom. On the shop's tiny concrete porch, he paused and looked back. The Venus itself sat on a rise a few hundred feet above a dry ocean of desert. The shop sat even higher. From here Bones could see straight over the motel all the way to where the Chiricahua range sawed into the distant sky with black-red volcanic teeth. Above it, a daylight moon hung pale and weightless, the only thing breaking up the deep-blue blanket of sky. Opposite the valley, behind the shop, pine-topped mountains rose, the forgotten debris of ancient fault lines stirring—or if you preferred local legend, the result of the devil rolling over in his sleep.

Inside, the shop smelled like grease and ghosts and stale tobacco. He'd liked it as soon as he'd stepped inside. It was private and had a bathroom, and he could be close to his bike. Being close to the bike was important. The 1972 Honda CB 360 was the only thing in the world he was proud of. He'd found it in the back lot behind the Jesus Is Coming Soon Thrift Store and talked them into selling it to him for eighty-five bucks. A repair manual along with a slew of parts cost him another hundred and fifty.

The purchase had cleaned out what little savings he'd had, money he'd saved from washing cars at his dad's lot before the whole thing went upside down. It was worth every penny, though, because when he got the thing running, he'd be free. Free of this town, free of the past, free of all those shadows and spooks and memories that sunk hooks into a guy and wouldn't let go.

In the back of the shop, he stashed one of the Doritos bags in a good-sized, hollowed-out hole beneath a loose floorboard under a counter.

He'd started collecting food that would last a while. Well, chips so far, plus a few cans of root beer. It was a perfect hiding hole, totally invisible unless you knew it was there. A guy had to be prepared. If life had taught him anything, it was that any situation, no matter how solid it seemed, could change in a second.

Floorboard replaced, he sank onto his cot, opened the root beer and the second bag of chips, and stared at the Honda and the box of parts beside it. Jimmy would probably laugh at a Honda 360, a guy like that with a Harley. Where had he been before the Venus? Where was he going after? What would that be like? To just be? To get on a bike and go? Bones was close to finding out.

He finished the root beer and chips and laid back, hand behind his head, still looking at the Honda. Less than a year before he'd be old enough for a motorcycle license, not that he cared. He'd do what he wanted and go where he pleased. He wasn't old enough to legally be on his own even though he felt like he was a million. That was the problem with time. A guy could live a hundred lifetimes in fifteen years, and some social worker would still be looking over his shoulder till he turned eighteen.

What was so great about eighteen anyway? It was a number. Like three, or fifty, or four hundred and sixty-seven. It had nothing to do with how tired and sore your spirit was. But again, who cared? Pretty soon there'd be no shoulder for any social worker to look over. Just Honda dust.

He had a bunch of books on a shelf above the cot. They were his only real family. He knew every title, and they all meant something to him. He pulled down a Roddy Doyle novel. He'd read it before. No matter. He'd spend an hour or two on Dublin's north side any day. He loved the way the characters talked. He hadn't understood it at first, but after a while he got used to it, and these days he was fluent in Doyle Irish brogue.

That was the thing about books. They took you past the desert, past the Chiricahuas. They let you see and experience other places. They could put you right there, thousands of miles away in an instant. He had a complete history of the Canary Islands in the stack and had read it cover to cover. New York, Los Angeles, the Australian outback—you could go anywhere you wanted. A whole other galaxy, even. Down at the Jesus Is Coming Soon you could buy paperbacks for a quarter, hardbacks for seventy-five cents. Ten bucks worth of books could last practically forever. The thrift store shelves had become his ticket to the world.

At least until the Honda ran and he could go for real. No one would be able to track him. He didn't even own a cell phone, and he didn't want one. Why would he? Why would anybody? They called him a freak at school because of it. Maybe they were right, but he didn't care. What was more bizarre? Walking through the world unplugged and untethered and unowned? Or willingly staring into a few square inches of glass every minute of the day while it slowly sucked all the recognizable parts out of you? High school was like living in some zombie movie.

And the dumbest part was the kids there literally had all knowledge known to man at their fingertips, but all they seemed to care about was texting each other and posting photos of themselves as if anything they did was actually unique.

And they said *he* was the freak.

He read for a while. Outside, wind began to moan. It got louder. A hot wind up from the desert. The kind that carried ancient secrets and shoved them through the cracks in the walls. After a while his eyes got heavy. The wind sound lulled him, and soon he was slipping into sleep, Roddy on his chest, Harley Davidson pipes booming along dark and damp Dublin streets.

He must have been out a few hours. It was dark when he woke, the sun having worn itself out shining throughout the day, a couple of stars appearing through the only window. He'd read about northern states where the light lasted longer. Alaska where it sometimes never set. What would that be like? He didn't think he'd care for it. Here in the desert the sun knew its place. And Arizona didn't challenge the order of things with something as useless as daylight saving time.

The wind had stopped insisting, down to a gentle breeze now, carrying with it Jimmy La Roux's moonlight blues up from the lounge. Bones lay on his cot listening to the snatches of melody floating in the air for a while. Falling asleep in the daytime for a chunk of time wasn't unusual for him. He didn't need much sleep. A few hours usually worked. He'd most likely be up most of the night working on his Honda. That'd be later, though. After he hung around the lounge waiting for whatever happened with Jimmy tonight. And something would happen. Bones felt it. Jimmy was that kind of dude.

He took a can of coffee down from the shelf along with a bag of sugar and his old percolator. He got water from the tiny bathroom and started it heating on his hot plate, another thrift store find. Cozy Jenkins had given him a hard time about drinking coffee. Said he was too young. Whatever. He'd been hooked on the stuff since he was ten. Although the six spoons of sugar he'd dumped in back then had whittled down to a more manly three.

Coffee cup in hand, he knelt next to the bike. New tires, new shocks, wiring exactly how the manual said. He'd had the motor completely apart and back together three times now. The rotor was the hardest part. He had to borrow a puller from John Little Feather over at the Exxon for that. He'd worked on the thing until his fingers bled, but it still wouldn't turn over. He opened his toolbox, selected a ratchet and socket, and started in on the crankcase.

Ten minutes later he was down to the rotor again and wondering if John Little Feather was sick of him yet. Another stinking mechanical dead end. Disappointing, even though he knew it was coming. He left the crankcase on the floor, screws inside it so he could find them later, and poured another cup of coffee. Only two spoons of sugar this time. He was almost out. He'd have to ask Juan for more. Maybe he should put away a store of it under the floorboard.

The clock said eight as he stepped out into the night. Even though he couldn't see it, he felt the mountain's pressing bulk behind him. Out past the highway, stars hung over the valley, wild and primal like a painting he'd once seen. Or maybe a photograph in one of his books.

He tried to remember, but the image hung just past the edge of his consciousness and wouldn't come any closer.

A few lights on in the motel rooms below, someone moving around in a bathroom behind frosted glass. Across the parking lot Lady Venus lent her neon splendor to the stars like the queen she was. More cars down there than usual. Blues floated on the breeze, lifting, hanging, questioning, then spinning back down again in tight swirls. Bones tossed the last bit of his coffee into the brush, left the cup next to the door, and headed down the hill. Light spilled out through the kitchen's screen door, making an irregular, weedy rectangle on the ground in front of it.

Bones went in and let the door slam shut behind him.

At the counter, Juan pointed toward the stove with the knife he was using to cut peppers. "Chili verde. Get a plate and a couple tortillas."

Bones did. Juan ladled a generous helping of the chili, then served a couple spoonfuls of beans and rice before tossing on some diced peppers and squeezing lime juice over the whole plate.

"Peppers are hot tonight," Juan said. "Definitely cure what ails you."

"Nothing ails me. I'm not sick."

"It's a saying, *guey*. Walk among the living for a change. Poke your head out of your cave once in a while and you might learn something, eh?"

"I learn a lot. Like never to eat cow's stomach." Bones picked up half a pepper from the cutting board, popped it into his mouth, and chewed. He felt like he'd been punched in the mouth.

"I told you," Juan said.

Bones coughed. Blinked away tears. "It's not that hot."

"Yeah? Then why is smoke coming out of your ears?"

Bones headed for the lounge. A lot more people than usual, like the cars outside. Twenty at least. Jimmy played smooth and low. The box on the piano reflected the blue stage light, and his tip jar was already half full. Burt sat at one of the tables, an empty plate and what was no doubt yet another whiskey highball in front of him.

Bones took a stool at the bar across from Calico.

She glanced at him. "Looks like your buddy up there brought in a few people."

"He's not my buddy."

"That's right. Bones the lone wolf. Well, he's my buddy tonight, weird box or not. I actually had to stay to help Juan serve."

"Has he made anything disappear yet?"

"Nope. But not for lack of people asking."

"People are asking? Those guys from last night must have spread the word around town."

"I really don't get it. One half-mediocre trick and all these people show up?"

Bones looked toward the stage. "If I heard about it around town, I'd want to check it out. What else is there to do around here?"

"A lot. But I can't figure the guy."

"Because he's not unidimensional."

"Is that a thing?"

"I don't know. But it is with him for sure."

"What about his room?"

Bones took a healthy bite of rice. "What about it?"

"You're talking with your mouth full again. You cleaned his room today, right?"

"Yeah."

"Don't try to tell me you didn't snoop around in there."

"That would be wrong, wouldn't it?"

"I'm serious, Bones."

"There was nothing to snoop. He travels light. That pack is all he has."

"Yet I feel like there's more to the guy than meets the eye, and that alone is enough to make me uneasy. I don't want him conning customers or anything like that. You're always around, Bones. I know you see and hear things. I want you to tell me if there's anything I should know. Even if you think it's not important. I hate surprises. And I especially hate not knowing things I should."

"You're saying you want me to spy on him?"

"Did I say I wanted you to spy on him?"

"Yeah, a little bit you did."

Calico glanced at the stage. "I just want to know what's going on at my motel. Everything that's going on."

Juan poked his head through the kitchen door. "Hey. Plates up. I got my hands full in here."

Calico nodded. "On it." She looked at Bones. "Hurry up and eat. I might need your help tonight."

"In here?"

"No, on the moon. Eat." She went into the kitchen, then returned, pushing through the kitchen door with a tray of plates. *Eat,* she mouthed as she passed. No more than two minutes later, she was back. "Help me remember this. One rum and Coke, two martinis extra dirty, a Captain Morgan Spiced on the rocks, and three Coors Lights. What did I just say?"

"One rum and Coke, two martinis extra dirty, a Captain Morgan Spiced on the rocks, and three Coors Lights."

"Good." She grabbed his plate, put it under the bar, and shoved a cutting board toward him. "Now slice some limes."

"I wasn't done eating."

"Didn't ask if you were. I need help." She handed him a knife.

"Can I at least have a cup of coffee?"

"Slice!"

Bones took it and cut into a lime. "I don't think a kid is supposed to be working at a bar."

"So now all of a sudden you're a kid? It's not a bar. It's a restaurant. And you're not handling alcohol. You're slicing limes."

"Yeah, to free you up to handle alcohol. Seems kind of like the same thing."

"Just slice. A lot."

Five minutes later, the music stopped, pulling Bones's eyes to the stage. Jimmy stood, stretched, and then tucked the box into the crook of his arm before weaving his way through the tables and out the lounge door.

Calico grabbed a lime slice off the cutting board and stuck it on the rim of the rum and Coke. "Where's he think he's going?"

"Smoke break, probably."

Calico arranged the drinks on her tray. "A lot of people in here listening to just wander off on a smoke break."

"He doesn't really operate like that."

"He should."

"I'm gonna go check it out." Bones slid off the barstool, about to be invisible.

"No you don't," Calico said. "I still need your help."

"You're the one who told me to keep an eye on him."

She hoisted the tray. "Oh, fine. See what he's up to, but come right back."

Outside, Bones spotted Jimmy's cig glowing beyond the motel lights at the edge of the parking lot. The glow swelled and dimmed as Bones approached.

Jimmy's face was hard-shadow, milky-eye ink. "I won't ask if you want one. You probably haven't even smoked the one I gave you."

"You shouldn't contribute to the delinquency of a minor," Bones said.

"You're absolutely right. I get the feeling you already contribute plenty to your delinquency yourself. You out here checking up on me for the boss?"

"Maybe."

"She doesn't trust easy, does she?"

"She's letting you play, isn't she?"

"True story. Crazy wind today, wasn't it?"

"Yeah."

"Guess it didn't like the neighborhood and moved on."

"Nothing holding it here."

Jimmy leaned back. Looked up at the sky. "Nice night, though."

"I heard people are asking about the box."

"People always wanna pet the cat once it crawls out of the bag."

"You gonna do it tonight?"

"If the music's right, maybe."

"What's that mean?"

"Means what it sounds like. Things gotta align."

"When's that?"

"Just something I feel."

"Feel how?"

"You ever run out of questions?"

"Sometimes. If I ever get answers. Which you don't give many of."

"What happened to white noise?"

"It doesn't work on you. Plus you told the cowboy dude the direct approach is the best."

"I said sometimes it's the best." The cigarette glowed, dimmed.

Bones pointed at the box still tucked under Jimmy's arm. "You should go into town and try it by the square under the big oak sometime. People play guitars and stuff for tips there. You'd get a crowd. Bigger than here if you go on a Saturday when the tourists are up."

Jimmy smoked, Lady Venus reflected in his milky eye. "Nah. I'm cool here with the Lady."

"The Venus?"

"Who else?"

"I'm just saying a lot of people are up in town this time of year. Artsy crap and all that. You'd make a lot of cash."

"I think I'll just kick it here and see if the wind left any extra tumbleweeds rolling around."

"You say a lot of stuff that isn't stuff."

"Who doesn't?" Jimmy smoked.

After a bit, Bones pointed at the box again. "How old is that thing really?"

"Old enough."

"Where did you get it?"

"You don't think it came from a lady in a bayou?"

"Sounds like something you made up."

Jimmy smoked.

"You don't want to say?" Bones said.

"I got it from my pop."

"For reals?"

"For reals."

"Where'd he get it?"

Jimmy grunted a laugh. "More questions."

Headlights swept the desert sage as a car pulled into the lot. They watched it park in front of the lounge. A big old boat of a car. Like a Cadillac but not. One of those cars that could be cool if it was a convertible but looks like it belongs to some seventies polyester grandpa and has a roof. This one had a roof—peeling Naugahyde. The headlights went off, but nobody got out.

Jimmy watched it. He didn't look at Bones when he said, "What's with the grease on your fingers? You been working on a car or something?"

"Yeah, something."

"What kind of something?"

Bones pushed his hands into the pockets of his jeans. "A Honda I got from the thrift store."

"Bike or car?"

"Bike."

"What model?"

Bones felt blood rising in his cheeks and was glad of the dark. "A 1972 CB 360. Not a Harley or nothin'."

A guy didn't have to see that milky eye to feel it. "You know what makes a bike a bike, kid?"

"Two wheels?"

"The spirit of the rider."

"I'm not a rider. I can't even get the thing to run."

"What's wrong with it?"

"If I knew that, we wouldn't be talking."

"Why?"

"Because the day I get that thing running is the day I'm outta here."

Jimmy looked out at the desert dark. "Yeah, I get that."

This surprised Bones. "You do?"

"Sure." Jimmy smoked. "Your mom and dad dead or something? Why do you live here?"

He said it just like that. Like he was talking about the weather or baseball.

Bones kicked at the dirt a little. "I never knew my mom. She left, but I don't remember it. My dad was in prison for a while until recently."

"In prison for what?"

"He shot a guy."

"Yeah?"

"Yeah."

"Kill him?"

"No."

"What'd your dad do before the joint?"

Bones liked the way Jimmy called prison *the joint.* Wished he'd thought of it first. "He owned a big car dealership."

"Rich?"

"I guess."

"Goes to show you can't go around shooting guys, even if you have dough. Sucks for you, though. You said he was in until recently. Why aren't you with him?"

"Because he's buried six feet under in the Paradise cemetery."

"He got killed in prison?"

"In the joint, yeah."

"Sorry."

"I'm not."

Cig glow. "Some dads are like that, sure enough. I'm still sorry, though."

"Yeah."

"And now you've landed at the Venus to clean rooms and pester me."

"I guess so."

"Until the bike runs."

"Yeah."

"Don't you have any friends around here?"

"I had one once, but he died."

"How?"

"He got bit by a snake."

"A snake. That's tough." Two cig breaths before he pointed toward the not-Cadillac and said, "You know that car, don't you? I can see it on your face."

"Yeah, I know it."

"You're not happy it's here."

"Makes no difference to me."

The car's driver's side door opened, and a woman got out, high heels awkward on the gravel.

"Who is she?" Jimmy said.

"Cozy Jenkins. I stayed with her and her husband for a while. Fosters."

"The guy who won the Mega?"

"How'd you know about that?"

"Like the song says, it's a small world after all." Jimmy's cig threw a spark as it arched into the night. "I think the music might be feeling right, kid."

CHAPTER TWELVE

"WHAT'S SHE DOING HERE?"

Calico followed Juan's gaze as a woman made her way through the tables and took a booth against the wall. Thirty-fiveish. Pretty in a slightly disheveled way. Something about her reminded Calico of a little girl playing dress-up. Hot rollers had been involved at some point. That was obvious. And at least a full can of hairspray. Blonde-red hair exploding out of some sort of barrette. Tight white jeans and a white blouse with one too many buttons undone. Her gold belt sparkled in the light and matched the heels she didn't seem especially good at walking in.

"Who is she?"

Juan looked over, eyebrows raised. "You don't know? That's Cozy Jenkins. The lottery lady. That's why everybody's looking at her. I'm surprised she'd come here after she and Don kicked out Bones."

"Maybe she doesn't know Bones is here."

"And maybe my name is Elon Musk and my car drives itself and I own my own rocket ship."

"Funny."

"Do you have any idea how a small town works? Everybody knows Bones is at the Venus."

"I come from a town smaller than this, remember?"

The door opened, and Jimmy La Roux strode in with his box. He threaded through the tables to the stage with purpose, then took a seat and started playing. A few bars in, Calico recognized the song as Merle Haggard's "Silver Wings." One of her dad's favorites.

"You better go take her order," Calico said.

"Do I have to?"

"Hey, she won the lottery. Maybe she'll tip big."

Juan headed off with a shake of his head.

Jimmy had just started in on "Kansas City" when several men entered the lounge. Older guys with the exception of two late-teen-looking kids. She'd seen the men together before. They were in Shorty's Cafe up in town for breakfast so often she'd wondered if they had cots in the back. Afternoons usually found them in the town square playing dominos. They moved through the room toward the stage in a loose knot.

Juan came back from Cozy's table. "She wants a sweet tea."

"That's it?"

"Put it in a dirty glass."

"You're a real comedian tonight."

Juan poured the tea, then nodded his head toward the group that just arrived. "Would you look at that? They've left their natural habitat and ventured out into the wild."

Calico smiled. "I've seen them in town."

"Very common animals. Every place has 'em. They tend to do a lot of scratching and telling of tall tales, and they always run in herds."

"You've put a lot of thought into this."

"What can I say? I'm an observer of human nature."

"And I never knew your river ran so deep."

"Now you do."

A stubby, round man with a pink face nearly matching his pink golf shirt broke from the group and made his way to the bar. "Heya."

"Heya," Calico said.

"Your piano man gonna do the box thing?"

"I don't think he's anybody's man, and I have no idea. Can I get you something?"

"Hope he does. I want to see how he works it. My grandsons over there were in here last night and told me about it. Knuckleheads have convinced themselves the thing's real. It's got people talking up in town."

Calico swept a hand, indicating the expanse of the room. "So it seems. I'm not complaining."

Pink had one of those infectious favorite-uncle-type grins. "I haven't been out here in a while."

"Welcome."

Pink nodded at Juan as the cook walked up with an empty tray. "How you doing there, Juan?"

"Can't complain, Mike. Surprised to see you boys out after dark. Isn't *Matlock* on or something?"

Mike's eyes crinkled, and he laughed a high-pitched wheeze. "Hey, brother, the world is my oyster."

"Now all you need is a few pearls."

"I thought pearls came in clams."

Juan shrugged. "Maybe you're right. I can't remember."

"Missy, you have any Woodford Reserve back there?" Mike said to Calico.

"Sure. I'll even pour you some if you promise never to call me Missy again."

"Deal. How about one for each of my compadres? Long dry drive out here."

"All twenty minutes?"

"Ain't the length of the journey, honey. It's the trials you meet along the way."

"It must have been rough. Rocks or neat?"

"Neat."

"Woodfords coming up. I'll bring them over myself."

Mike gave a thumbs-up followed by an okay sign followed by another thumbs-up and then rejoined his herd. They'd gathered on the dance floor in front of the stage with an air of expectation. Jimmy, deep in his song, seemed not to have noticed them.

Calico poured the whiskies, loaded them on a tray, and then carried them over and passed them out. A jovial group. The kind of old men who wore perpetual mischievous grins and told the same jokes every Thanksgiving.

Jimmy's song ended.

"Hey, you make things disappear, right?" Mike said before the biker could start another.

Calico stayed put, curious to know what the guy was up to.

Jimmy fingered a note or two. "That's the rumor, though I mostly just sit here and watch."

Mike grinned. "Oh, yeah, right. It's the box."

"Hard to tell. It's only an old box, but you know how it is. Sometimes the most ordinary things are also the most mysterious." Jimmy played a few more notes.

"My grandsons here told me about the rock you got rid of."

Jimmy gave a slight nod. Looked at the boys. "'Lo, children are an heritage of the Lord, and the fruit of the womb is his reward.' Arrows in your quiver and all that jazz. Good stuff whatever way you shake it."

"Thing is they think the box is for real," Mike said.

"Smart boys."

Mike laughed. "Not so's you'd notice, believe me. I told 'em I'd come and check it out. Tell 'em how you do it."

"Hey, good deal. You work it out, let me know too."

"That's a good schtick, brother."

Jimmy played a full chord.

"You worried I'll crack your cover?" Mike said.

"Scared to death."

Mike rocked on his heels a little, eyes sparkling. "You ever heard of the Great Nowak?"

"Can't say I have, but don't let that hurt his feelings. I don't get out much."

"That's me. On account of my last name's Nowak."

"Very clever marketing."

"Played all over the Midwest back in the day. Have to tell you, I made a few things disappear myself."

"He's serious. He was almost on with Carson one time." This came from one of the herd.

"Sounds like you know your stuff," Jimmy said.

"You could say I've crossed a few creeks and climbed a few mountains. C'mon, let's do it."

Jimmy stopped playing. "Mr. Great Nowak, you do seem to be a man who won't be deterred."

Mike lifted his Woodford in salute. "I will not, sir."

Jimmy smiled. "Then, as you say, let's do it."

CHAPTER THIRTEEN

BONES DIDN'T FEEL ANYTHING ABOUT Cozy. Like he wouldn't feel anything about a cactus or a book that didn't catch his attention. Cozy *was*, that's all. Maybe on some level he should be mad at her—or even hurt that she didn't seem to mind too much when he was booted out. But he knew that was all Don. He was mostly just glad to be out of the whole Jenkins-vortex-of-tension carnival fun house.

The woman hadn't even looked his way when he'd come in behind Jimmy. Then again, he'd gone invisible right away. It was weird she was here alone, though. Very un-Don-like to let her out of the trailer without him. She sat down at a table, not far from his booth near the stage, and he tried to read her. Cozy had sort of a resigned sadness about her. Like an overripe fruit. He almost felt sorry for her. At least as sorry as you could feel for a cactus or a book about German dancing.

Out on the dance floor, Kyle and John didn't have the cocky thing going tonight. They stood there looking at Jimmy like he was a movie star or something. Bones had to laugh inside. It had only been a rock. Bones knew Mike and the others even if they didn't know him. They were always around town. The whole Great Nowak thing was a surprise, though. He couldn't picture Mike on stage with a cape and top hat. Or anything besides golf clothes, when he thought about it.

"So what do I do?" Mike was saying.

"Ain't complicated," Jimmy said. "Put something in the box you don't care if you ever see again. Then"—he made a whistling sound—"off it goes. Buh-bye, adios, sayonara."

Mike nodded, then winked at Kyle and John. "Mind if I look at the box first?"

"Figured you might want to."

They had the attention of the whole room now. This was exactly what people had come to see. Except Cozy, maybe. She was staring into her glass looking lost.

Mike picked up the box, turned it over slowly, studied all sides. He opened the lid and felt the inside walls. "Not real big, is it?"

"Can't get your wife or mother-in-law in there if that's where you're going," Jimmy said.

Mike laughed. "You must be a mind reader too."

"Nope. Just heard about every joke that goes with this thing over the last billion miles."

Mike gave a fake wince. "I guess the Great Nowak isn't all that original, is he?"

"I wouldn't take it too hard. It was real funny the first dozen times or so."

"Buddy, I'm old. I don't take anything too hard. Let's do this. Make something disappear."

"Whatcha got?"

"To be clear, I really don't get it back?"

"To be clear, you really don't."

"Guess a hundred-dollar bill would be a bad choice?"

"That's all relative. I've met a few who wouldn't miss a Benjamin any more than a George."

"I bet you'd love that. A hundred-dollar bill. Make for a decent night's work."

Jimmy shrugged. "Like I said, once it's gone, it's gone. Doesn't affect me one way or another."

"Sure it doesn't." Mike fished a quarter out of his pocket. "Tell you what. Let's start with something not quite so rich."

Jimmy tapped the box. "Your call. Five bucks a pop."

"My grandson said the first one was free last night."

"First one *was* free last night. But this ain't last night, and you ain't your grandson."

Mike wheezed-laughed and reached back for his wallet. "The old bait-and-switch. I love it. How about I make you a deal?"

"Talk to me."

Mike pulled out a hundred-dollar bill. "I'll give you this—in your hand, not in the box—and you give all my compadres here a turn. But by the end of it, if I can tell you how you do it, I get my hundred dollars back. You can keep the quarter."

"The Great Nowak is a confident man. Admirable."

"Call me a student of the craft."

Jimmy held out his hand. "Sure. Why not?"

Mike gave Jimmy the bill. "I get to put the quarter in myself, right?"

Jimmy leaned back. Started playing. "She's all yours."

Several people had left their seats and were now pressed behind and around Mike's group. The room was quiet except for the piano. Bones—in ultra-invisible mode—shifted out of the booth and up by the stage curtain for a better view.

Mike lifted the lid and dropped the coin in with a metallic clunk. He looked at Jimmy. "Now what?"

"Now shut the lid and open it again."

"You're not even going to touch it?"

"Nope."

Mike shut and opened. He picked up the box, shook it, felt around inside.

"Gone?" one of his friends said.

"Like it was never there. Knew it would be, though." He handed the box to the asker, who studied it before passing it on.

"How'd he do it, then?" somebody said.

Mike took the box back and surveyed the bottom again. "Not sure yet, but I'm getting there. Who's next? Make it something bigger. Harder to work with."

A man in a John Deere hat and a long-sleeved cowboy shirt held up his empty whiskey glass. "How about this?"

"Perfect," Mike said.

"Long as you pay for it when it doesn't come back," Calico said.

Mike turned to look at her. "It'll come back. If not, I'll buy you a whole new set. How's that?"

John Deere stepped up and set the glass in the box. Mike shut and opened the lid.

"I'll be danged," John Deere said. "You just might be saying adios to that hundred dollars, Mike."

"Nope. I'll figure it. Who's next?"

A man at the edge of the dance floor held up a water glass. "How about this? It's almost full."

Mike looked at Jimmy with an I-got-you smile. "How about liquids, chief? You all right with liquids?"

Jimmy winked the milky eye. "Whatever floats your boat. Which I guess would be liquids if you want to get technical."

Mike shook his head. "No way you can hide liquid. Can't be done."

"Great Nowak oughta know," Jimmy said.

Fifteen seconds later, Mike stared into the again-empty box where the full glass of water had just been. He turned the box upside down. "It's impossible."

"Yet, there it is," Jimmy said.

"I don't believe it." Mike leaned down and looked under the piano.

One by one, the men placed items in the box. Every time, the object vanished. When the last man had had his turn, a large cup of sand he'd retrieved from outside, Mike shook his head. "There has to be an answer. How about another round?"

"For another hundred?" Jimmy replied.

Mike licked his lips, contemplating.

"Thought you could figure it, Mike." John Deere's lips twitched. "Looks like maybe you got a little ahead of yourself."

"Maybe that's why you only *almost* made it on Carson," another said, laughing.

Mike's face broke into a good-natured grin. "Maybe it is. But another hundred is getting a little steep."

"You saying you can't afford it?" John Deere again. "Give us a break."

Kyle took a step forward. "I told you it was real. I knew it."

Mike shook his head and pulled out another hundred, then passed it to Jimmy. "Fine. One more round, then. At least it's entertaining. Ah, heck, how about another two hundred and I buy you for the night? Anybody here who wants to have a go at the box can."

Jimmy took the money. "Sounds fair enough."

People pressed in, several of them slapping Mike on the back, others shaking his hand. Mike, all smiles and benevolent generosity, moved off to the side to give them room. Even Cozy was watching now. Juan had come out of the kitchen. All eyes on the box. So only Bones saw the lounge door open and the man come in.

CHAPTER FOURTEEN

Bones gave the guy the once-over. He definitely wasn't your typical Paradise, Arizona, type. City head to toe. Average height. Maybe late thirties or forty. Dyed jet-black hair cut and brushed to try to hide the fact it was thinning on top. Black T-shirt, black jeans, black boots, black everything. He took in his surroundings, looked at the knot of people around Jimmy, and smiled. Then he walked around to the back of the bar like he owned the place, poured himself a drink out of a bottle that looked expensive, sipped, and made his way to the back edge of the crowd.

Good thing Calico and Juan missed all that.

Mike was next to the box again. The guy definitely loved the limelight. He pulled a small photo from one of several plastic sleeves in his wallet and waved it at his friends. "Tell you what. Jackie's been a little extra naggy lately. Can't fit a wife in there, but a wife pic couldn't hurt."

Laughs all around.

"I'm playing cards with her tomorrow, Mike," a woman from the crowd said. "I'm sure she'd like to hear all about that little crack."

Mike held up his hands. "I'm kidding!"

More laughs. These people sure were easy to amuse.

"No pictures," Jimmy said.

Mike laugh-wheezed again. "C'mon. I was kidding about the nagging. She's a solid old gal. It's only a photo. I have loads of 'em. It'll make for a good story down the road."

Jimmy fixed his good eye on the man. "I'm sure it would, but no pictures. Choose something else."

"I'd listen to him." The man in black had made his way close to the stage now. "What goes in the box is gone forever. You don't want to lose a wife. Even if she is a . . . How did you put it? Solid old gal?" He turned toward the piano. "Buy you a drink, Jimmy?"

"Ah, Nelson. Figured you'd be along eventually."

"You'd get to see more of me if you'd hold still for more than a few days at a time, at least a little more often. Lucky you."

"Uh-huh. Wouldn't that be a kick?"

Mike's eyes bulged with sudden recognition. "Wait a minute. You're Nelson Black."

The man ignored Mike. "How's tricks, Jimmy?"

"Oh, you know, 'bout the same."

"You gotta be kidding me," Mike said. "I can't believe I'm standing here looking at Nelson Black."

"No?" Black said. "I look at him in the mirror every day. It takes a while, but eventually the novelty wears off."

"You know the Great Nowak, don't you, Nelson?" Jimmy said. "Man who almost made Carson?"

"I can't say I've had the pleasure."

"I watched your special on Netflix," Mike said. "I can't believe you're standing here. Nelson Black! Right here in the Venus!"

Black turned back to Jimmy. "Where'd we leave off, Jimmy? What were we up to?"

"You know, it's completely escaped my mind."

"Mr. Black, could I get an autograph?" Mike said. "It's—"

"Seven hundred and fifty," Black said to Jimmy. "That's where we left off."

Jimmy played a slow blues run. "Ain't no we about it, Nelson, if memory serves. That's where *you* left off."

"Are you ever going to be reasonable? It's a trick."

"I feel plenty reasonable."

"That was seven hundred and fifty *thousand* dollars, by the way."

"Was it?"

"It was."

Jimmy shrugged. "Answer's still no."

"All right. I'll give you a million. A *million* dollars, Jimmy. For one trick."

"Can't do it."

"I'm not sure you heard me. I said a million dollars."

"I do got me some pretty good ears."

"Are you crazy? A million dollars for one trick! That's unheard of. Historical, even."

"I very well may be crazy. It is a lot of dough."

Black stared at the box for a few seconds, then sighed. "Think about it, Jimmy. Tell me you'll at least think about it."

Jimmy started playing again. "Night and day, buddy. You and your million bucks will be ever on my mind."

"I'll stick around while you consider."

"Of course you will." Jimmy pointed toward Calico behind the bar. "That's the lady to see about a room."

At the bar, everyone watching, Black booked his room. Then, with a salute and a bow to the crowd, he turned for the door, setting his empty drink glass on an occupied table on the way out. As soon the door closed behind him, conversation broke out all around. The name Black on repeat. The word *million* a close second.

Jimmy, a half-smile on his face, started in on "New York, New York."

"That . . . that was Nelson Black," Mike said to him.

"I'm fairly sure you've established that fact, Great Nowak," Jimmy said.

"Did he just offer you a million dollars for that box?"

"Thing about ole Nelson is that he gets a thing in his craw."

"He's the greatest illusionist alive. Maybe the greatest of all time."

"So they say."

Mike looked back at the lounge door. "Nelson Black. I'll be danged."

"You just might, brother," Jimmy said. "Guess we'll have to wait and see."

CHAPTER FIFTEEN

THE CROWD HADN'T THINNED.

"Hi."

Calico looked up from the beer she was pouring, surprised to see Cozy Jenkins standing across the bar from her. "Hi."

"I'm Cozy."

"Calico. Can I get you something?"

Cozy wrinkled her nose. "You know who I am, right?"

"I think everyone around here knows who you are."

"Yeah, because Don won the Mega. But you know who I am because of Bones."

"I won't deny that connection was pointed out to me."

"So you probably hate me."

Calico delivered the beer, then came back.

"Why would I hate you? I don't even know you."

"Yeah, but it was an awful thing to do. I'd blame it totally on Don, but to be honest, I wasn't sorry to see Bones go."

"At least you're up front about it."

"The thing is he wasn't much fun to have around. Still, I wouldn't have made him leave. At least, I hope I wouldn't have."

"He can be challenging, that's true."

"Don said we took in those kids because we needed the support checks. Maybe we did, but I always felt sorry for them. At least most of them."

"And now he doesn't need the checks anymore."

"Not yet."

"Not yet?"

"He'll lose it all. He can't help himself." Her face set. "But it's somebody else's problem now, isn't it?"

What did that mean? The woman obviously had loads on her mind. Calico weighed her options. It was still busy, and she didn't feel like getting caught up in someone's personal drama. She wrestled this against Cozy's shipwrecked eyes. "Can I get you more tea?"

"Yes, please."

Calico poured from a pitcher and slid the glass over.

Cozy added sugar, tearing four or five packets at once and dumping them in. She started to stir with her finger.

Calico handed her a spoon. "Here."

"Thanks. And don't worry."

"About what?"

"About me spilling my guts. I know you're a motel owner, not a priest confessor."

"Am I that obvious?"

"One hundred percent."

"Sorry. It's only that it's busy tonight, and I lost one of my help recently."

"Sure. I know Denise. She lives a few doors down from me. If she's after workman's comp, don't believe her for a second. She does Pilates in her backyard every day."

"She is, and I don't." Curiosity got the best of her. "So where's Mr. Mega tonight?"

"El Paso. And unfortunately, not alone."

"Oh?"

"That's really why I'm here. I'm done with him. I want to get a room for a few nights, and I don't want to stay in town. I don't want everyone staring at me."

"Wow, that's tough. I'm sorry."

"He's with Tanya from the Pick-a-Part. Can you believe it? Have you seen her hair? I'm sure she gets extensions. And he didn't even deny it when I called him. He acts like it's all my fault. He always does that. But I'm done this time. I told him I was leaving, and he said, 'Good, don't come back.' He's moved on."

"I don't know her."

"You're better off. The funny thing is she wouldn't give him the time of day till his ticket hit."

"Surely you're entitled to some of the money as his wife?"

"Half according to Google. The thing is"—she made jazz hands—"surprise! We're apparently not married."

"Apparently?"

"He dropped that little nugget on me today. Said his friend who married us, this chaplain guy who used to follow the races around, never filed the paperwork because he wasn't really an ordained minister or whatever. I don't even know what ordained means."

"I suppose it means you're not legally married."

"So Don says. So Google says too."

"Still, you've been together for a while. It seems like you'd have some kind of legal recourse."

"Maybe. Google didn't say, but I didn't look very deep. Honestly, when I look it in the eye, I'm kind of tired of fighting. I mean fighting everything. Fighting a race car, fighting Pick-a-Part women, fighting the stack of filthy magazines he keeps in his shop and thinks I don't know about. I'm even tired of the Harbor ducks."

"What harbor ducks?"

"Yoga pants and water bottles. It doesn't matter."

Juan approached with a notepad list of several drinks, dropped it on the bar, and scurried into the kitchen. Calico looked at it, then started taking down bottles.

"I could help you," Cozy said.

"Help me?"

"With the drinks. I used to bartend. That's why I mostly drink tea. I got an eyeful back in the day."

"Really?" Calico slid the notepad around. "You know how to make these?"

Cozy ran her eyes down the page. "Sure. You've been nice enough to listen. It's the least I can do."

Juan bumped back through the door, forehead beaded with sweat. He tapped the bar as he passed. "I got some more plates up when you get a chance."

Calico looked at Cozy. "You're sure you can do this?"

"Absolutely. I'd like it. It'll take my mind off things for a while."

"I wouldn't normally do this, but I'm kind of desperate at the moment. So fine. Have at it. And thanks."

Calico left her to the mixing and stepped away to help Juan deliver plates. Onstage, the music and disappearing continued—Jimmy, as always, looking more focused on the piano than on the box.

Plates delivered, Calico returned to the bar. She stopped short, stunned to find the whole list of drinks already made and sitting on a tray. A good-looking array garnished to perfection, much better than she herself would have managed in a rush. "Wow, you weren't kidding when you said you knew how to do this. I hope they taste as good as they look."

Cozy picked up her tea. "They do. If you like that sort of stuff."

It took Calico a few minutes to get the right drinks into the right hands.

Juan sidled up to her with a whole new tray. "Can we keep her, Mom? Please?"

"She's not a puppy."

"She has puppy eyes."

"I can't argue with that. I don't even know if she's looking for a job. She's working off heartache tonight."

"Ain't we all." He handed a Rob Roy to an extended hand. "It won't hurt to ask. We get more nights like this and I'm gonna lose my baby fat. Big is beautiful."

"We wouldn't want that."

Calico rejoined Cozy behind the bar. "So you're really wanting a room?"

"Absolutely."

"It's on the house tonight. Plus I'll pay you. Happily. The same for tomorrow if you want to help out again."

"Seriously?"

"Seriously."

"As in a job?"

"We'll see."

"I'm in."

"Good. I need a Tom Collins stat."

Cozy set her tea behind the bar and started mixing. "I'm not supposed to be drinking tea. I have *stones*. Can you believe it? It's so gross. I love sweet tea, though. I can't help it. That's my problem. I can't help a lot of things. I couldn't help falling for greasy old Don when I met him. Couldn't help letting him step all over me all these years while he chased his dumb dream."

She looked toward the stage. "Oh, brother, I love this song. I have dreams too, you know. But his dreams were all we were ever allowed to talk about. I wanted to be a singer. It sounds ridiculous when I say it out loud, but I did." She put the Tom Collins on Calico's tray.

"Not so dumb. You don't want to anymore?"

"I don't know. I wanted to go to this place in Tucson. You know, the kind that records you with tracks? But I probably won't now."

"Dreams like that don't just go away. Why don't you do it?"

"Yeah. Why don't I do a lot of things?"

Calico took Cozy's tea and dumped it into the sink. She rinsed the glass, filled it with ice and seltzer water, squeezed a lemon into it, and handed it back. "This is better for you. My dad had kidney stones, and this helped."

Cozy looked at the glass and wrinkled her nose. "No sugar?"

"No sugar."

"Okay." Cozy sipped. "It's not bad. Not good, but not bad."

"So go ahead."

"Go ahead and what?"

"Go ahead and sing."

Cozy set the glass down. "What?"

"You have a dream. I have a piano player and a stage. Go sing. No drink orders at the moment, so you have a few minutes."

"No way. I could never do that."

"Of course you could. You know the words to that song?"

"Everybody knows the words."

"So? What's the worst that could happen?"

"People could laugh at me. There's that."

"So what if they do?"

"You're really serious? Will he let me? The piano guy?"

"It's my lounge. I say who does what. You want to sing, sing. Call it an audition."

"An audition for what?"

"Look. The thing is I need help. And if you don't mind me saying, it sounds like you do too. At least for the short term. I'll give you a room and pay, you help do a little cleaning and work with Juan here in the lounge. And you can sing anytime you want if you sound good."

"You're not joking?"

"Not at all."

Cozy looked at the stage again. "I might, you know that? Oh, brother, what would Don think? He'd die of embarrassment if he heard I was singing here."

Calico arched a brow. "Would that be bad?"

Cozy stepped from behind the bar. "I can't believe I'm saying this, but . . . I think I'm gonna sing."

▼

Cozy couldn't believe they were actually doing it, but there they were, her crazy legs, the same ones she'd had all her life, carrying her across to the stage like she was floating on a cloud.

The piano player looked rough but gave her a half smile when she stepped up. "Did I just inherit myself a vocalist?"

Her answer came from someplace else. Another body. "I said I love this song, and Calico said to come up. Do you mind?"

He pointed to a microphone on a stand. "That thing's on, but it ain't really doing anything but standing there. It's all yours. This a good key for you?"

"I have no idea. I only sing in the mirror."

"Guess we'll see, then." He rolled back to the intro chords, starting the song over. "Sing when you're ready. Don't worry. I'll follow."

No Simon, Randy, or Paula. No Keith or Lionel, Luke or Katy. Just a room full of people. Most weren't even paying attention because they were too busy playing with the metal box. Still, her ears roared. She felt dizzy. Then she started in, singing about music and tunes and heaven and the moon. Ella Fitzgerald, one of her favorites.

Even as she sang, she prayed the crowd would all stay focused on the box. Don always told her how horrible her voice was. Like a cat screaming. He always said that right before he smacked her rear end and tried to make out. What if he was right? After all, she only had her mirror. What if it was all in her head? What was she thinking?

Then someone actually looked up. A woman in a lemon-yellow top. She smiled. Smiled! Then another before the noise around the box died down and Cozy was singing. For real. To people, not to her own triple reflection. And then, feeling like it had lasted only two seconds, the song was over and people were clapping. Really clapping. For her.

"I'm Jimmy," the piano guy said.

"I'm Cozy."

"How about singing another, Cozy?"

"Really?"

He pointed into the room. "Don't want to upset your fans."

She looked toward the bar, where Calico nodded. "Okay, sure. But then I have to help make drinks."

He started to play. "You know this one?"

Her own smile felt like it would break her face.

CHAPTER SIXTEEN

The pine trees whispered and waved, stirring a wind on the mountainside as she walked. Calico breathed deep. She loved the smell of pines. Loved the thin feel of the air up here. It was like breathing silk. And as much as she loved the place, every once in a while it was good to get away from the Venus. Last night the crowd had been good for the first time in a while. Money had come in. She even had new help in the form of Cozy Jenkins. Things at the Venus were looking up, at least at the moment, and she should be thrilled.

But she missed Pines. Their last conversation had been hard. Her anger had faded, but frustration remained. And honestly, it wasn't all directed at him. A healthy portion of that frustration came back on her.

Which was why she needed to get up here on the mountain this morning and think. She needed clarity, and the clear mountain air was just the ticket. Pines called this route the Path of Ghosts. Maybe it was a Native thing. Or maybe it was just Pines. Whatever it was, Calico lingered, walking slowly, a deep carpet of pine needles deadening her steps.

She began mentally picking apart the Pines-Bones knot. Making a pros-and-cons list in her head. Was she being unreasonable? She didn't think so, but nothing was ever black or white. Pines had a big heart and too often felt responsible for the world. And he and Bones did have some history.

After a while, as often happened on this trail, she started thinking about her mother. Or maybe it was the other way around and her mother was thinking about her. After all, it was the Path of Ghosts. Her mother had died on the Saturday after Thanksgiving, not long after Calico's twelfth birthday. Calico had been at the bedside and watched her slip away into the next life, leaving barely a ripple as she left this one. A pale, fragile thing, pulling in a breath one second, then simply not attempting another, her soul floating away as rare-as-gold hail pecked at the Phoenix hospital room window. Twelve is a tender age to watch a parent depart. Twelve is a balancing beam on top of which a child wobbles, arms outstretched for balance. A fence separating the relative safety of childhood from all the mystery that lies beyond.

In a normal world a kid climbs down when the time is right and explores that mystery a little at a time, uncovering its joys and challenges slowly and wonderingly as they present themselves. But desert hail and flat-lined heart monitors and clear plastic bags of morphine no longer dripping all tend to roll themselves into one massive fist. And that fist hits the tender fence walker hard enough to knock her several years into the future. There'd been no choice in this, only landing. Working to get her feet under her and learning to walk again. To survive in a world as sudden and confusing as a tornado on a clear day.

Up until a few weeks before her death, Mom had been the rock of the family. And if her mother had been a rock, her father had been a stream. A little trickling stream dreaming of the next bigger stream and then the river and finally of the eventual glorious ocean. So many dreams packed into one man. The world needs dreamers, true. Without them the planet would be a dull and stagnant place. But as is often the case with true romantics, Bob Foster's dreams had left very little in the way of solidity in her post-mother life.

And so she'd planted herself, tried to grow roots and spread branches out far enough to shield both her and her little brother. She'd tried to replace the missing rock. In the end, she'd done the best she could, but she'd still been only twelve years old when the world changed.

Funny how her father's ghost never came to her here. It wasn't that she hadn't loved him. She had. It was simply that she didn't *need* him. Not like she needed her mother. Even after all these years, she listened for her mother's quiet, solid voice. Hoping for answers. Hoping for insight. Hoping for hope. Hoping for anything.

The trees thinned as she reached the cliff. She stood on the edge, the desert floor spreading into the clear distance far below. A spectacular view. Wind gusted up from the valley, warm against her skin. It tugged at her clothes, lifted her hair, swirled, laughed, and sang. She especially missed Pines here. This was a special place for the two of them. His history deeper—he'd scattered his friend's ashes from the cliff up ahead—but she felt a connection to this spot as well. She'd watched him come to the end of himself here . . . and the beginning of them. They'd shared their first kiss here. It sounded so high school, but she loved the thought anyway.

Above the trees, the sky stretched to infinity. Slight whisps of high-altitude clouds. A big rock near the cliff edge had become *their place* over the last months, and she sat there now, taking in the distance.

She pulled out her phone and punched Early's number.

"Hey," he said.

She tried to read his mood, but he just sounded like Pines. "Guess where I am."

"Up on the cliff."

"How do you do that?"

"I have a tracking device planted in your ear."

"You can hear the wind, can't you?"

"No place else in the world sounds like that."

"You're right. Are you okay, Pines?"

"I'm working on it. Are you?"

"I won't lie to you. I don't know if I'm okay. I'm frustrated at the situation."

"Me too."

The wind picked up, quelled, picked up again.

"Salad," she said after a bit. "That's the problem."

"Salad is the problem?"

"Bones asked me why I didn't make him eat salad."

"Why did he ask that?"

"I don't know. But that's the thing. I probably should be making him eat salad. I didn't even think about it."

"So make him eat salad."

"It's not about the salad. I miss you, Pines. And I love you. But you can be so thick, you know that?"

"Sure I do."

"I should have thought of it first. What kind of kid has to ask someone to make him eat salad?"

"Calico, he doesn't really want you to make him eat salad."

"Doesn't he? Who knows what he wants? You don't. I definitely don't. He's an enigma."

"He's not an enigma. He's a kid."

"Is there a difference?"

"Yes, there is."

"What are you going to do, Pines? I need to know. I've thought about all kinds of things. Do we wait to get married? Do I jump into something I'm not ready for? Dive into a situation where I might hurt someone? You or Bones?"

"You won't hurt anyone."

"You don't know that." She closed her eyes and imagined his profile. The crooked nose. The hard angles. The scar. He had a single gray hair in his eyebrow. She loved that gray hair. Crazy how fast it had happened between them. It wasn't like her at all, yet here they were.

But this . . .

"I don't think I'm ready for a package deal, Pines. That's all."

The wind stilled.

A hawk circled a thousand miles above the valley.

The phone might as well have been dead.

"Pines?"

"I'm here."

Her heart beat against her ribs. "It's not that I don't want to marry you. I do."

"I know."

"I'm working on it, okay? I am. This is hard for me."

"I understand."

"Do you?"

"Yeah, I do." The distance in his voice killed a little bit of her.

"You're angry with me."

"What am I supposed to do, Calico? Let them throw him into some other foster family that wants him only for the money? Ship him off to someplace he doesn't know? What about Gomez Gomez? What would he think?"

Calico bit her lip. "I didn't know him. You know that."

"I'm just frustrated."

"And I know that too. But please don't second-guess us."

"Last time we talked it sounded like you were the one doing the second-guessing."

"I wasn't, Pines. I was just upset you were making decisions without me."

"I understand that, but I'm still frustrated."

"Ugh. What gets me is that you're right and I'm wrong. But I can't help how I feel."

"I'm not asking you to help how you feel. Or to change how you feel. I just wish you felt differently."

"Like I said, I can't help it."

"I know."

"What are we going to do?"

More quiet. "I don't know, Calico. I really don't right now. Listen, I just got to the station for a meeting. I have to go."

"Pines?"

"Yeah?"

"I'm sorry."

"Me too. I'll call you later, all right?"

"Sure."

And then he was gone.

And the wind felt cool against the tears on her cheeks.

CHAPTER SEVENTEEN

MAYBE IT WAS THE NEWNESS of it, maybe the fact that she was out of the trailer, or maybe simply the freedom of being somewhere she wasn't berated at every turn, but Cozy found she didn't mind cleaning motel rooms.

Jimmy La Roux's room went quickly. So did Nelson Black's—the guy was a neat freak. Then room ten, occupied by the Pecks—not neat freaks. The couple owned Pecks Furniture out on Third. They'd come out for the music and the box and opted to stay the night. They'd left early this morning. Only one room to go. The whole thing was almost therapeutic, and Cozy was a little disappointed more rooms weren't occupied.

"I can do the last one by myself," she said as she closed room ten's door.

Bones eyed her. "Yeah?"

"Sure."

"Cool."

"Hey, I should have said this earlier, but I'm sorry Don kicked you out. Maybe if I'd—"

"It's cool."

"You sure?"

"Is that why you want to do the room by yourself? Because you think you owe me something?"

She shook her head. "I don't think cleaning a motel room makes it even steven for making a foster kid leave, do you? I can just do it, that's all."

"You don't have to feel guilty."

"Really?" Bones looked like he meant it, but she'd like to be sure. Anyway, with Bones it was hard to tell.

"Yeah, I'm cool."

"Okay, thanks."

"You're welcome. But you'll owe me one down the road."

"I will? Like what?"

"Nah. I'm kidding."

"Wait. That was a joke? Did Bones the Sullen really just make a joke?"

He walked off toward the pool. "Don't get used to it."

"You just made a joke," she called after him.

"Whatever."

"You must like me a little bit."

"Whatever."

A big, brand-new Dodge Longhorn pickup was parked in front of room eleven. Cozy knocked on the door but received no response. Another knock. Nothing. She used the master key and pushed the door open slowly. "Hello?"

"Oh, hey." A man sat on the couch by the wall, one booted foot crossed over a knee. Cozy recognized him from the lounge last night. The sharply dressed cowboy. He was staring at a gold ring in his hand, working it through his fingers, then back again. Looked like a wedding band.

"I knocked, but you didn't answer," she said.

"Sorry. Guess I was lost in my thoughts. I get like that from time to time."

"I'm here to clean the room, but I can come back later."

He had a comfortable Sam Elliott mustache Cozy liked right away. He shook his head. "Nah. That's all right. You got a job to do, and you might as well do it. You want me to leave while you clean? I can take a walk. Or a drive."

"Oh no. It's your room. Please stay. You're sure you don't mind?"

"I don't mind at all."

Cozy lifted a bucket full of cleaning solutions, brushes, and rags from the cart outside the door. "That's a nice Longhorn out there."

He was staring at the ring again. "I suppose it is. Cost enough. Prices they get for trucks these days is a special kind of robbery."

"That a Cummins Turbo Diesel?"

The ring stopped moving and went into his pocket. "You know trucks?"

Cozy started dusting. "Mister, I know everything about everything with a motor. But not because I want to."

"It's just a truck. Gets me from one place to another."

"Just a truck? The guy I thought I was married to for ten years would kill his own mother for a truck like that. If she weren't already dead."

"How does a person only think they're married?"

"He won the Mega, and suddenly I find out the whole thing was a sham."

"Don Jenkins."

"That's the joker."

"Once had him do some work on a couple of rigs out at my ranch. Tell you the truth, I didn't care for him."

"Tell you the truth, he cares for himself enough for everybody."

"Ten years doesn't sound like a sham to me."

"He's taken up with a girl from the Pick-a-Part. Told me she believes in his dreams. What she believes in is his six and a half million Mega bucks."

"That'll do it. You still love him?"

It was a personal question, but the man's quiet demeanor disarmed any concern. Cozy found she didn't mind answering at all. "I think I loved him once. But that was a long time ago. It's hard to love somebody who only loves himself."

"I wouldn't know about that. My experience was quite a bit different. Opposite in fact. Ivy was one of those rare people who always gave more than they got, no matter how much they got."

"Was?"

"My wife passed away five years ago."

"I'm sorry."

"Me too. They say time is supposed to heal all wounds, but I'm still waiting on that. I think about her every minute of every day. I'm not even sure what I'm doing anymore." He waved a hand. "This, for instance. Sitting here in a motel room. No plans to even check out because I plain old don't have anywhere I need to be. Feels like no real point to life."

"You said you have a ranch?"

"I own the Bar-O over in Heaven's Canyon. But I got a good crew. These days I think I mostly tend to get in their way."

"I'm sure that's not true."

He laughed a little. "I'm sure it is. Ask my foreman. Do you like cleaning rooms?"

"It's my first day, but so far, so good. I definitely like not being cooped up in Don's trailer watching Harbor ducks all day."

"Harbor ducks?"

"That's what I call all the ladies who live across the street."

"Why?"

"It all has to do with yoga pants and nonmoving houses. It's a long story."

"Sounds like it. I'm glad you like it here, then. Away from the ducks."

"It's interesting for sure. I cleaned Nelson Black's room today. He's on television. Do you know him?"

"Can't say I watch much television, but he did make quite a stir in the lounge last night."

"You don't even watch *American Idol*?"

"What's that?"

"You're kidding, right?"

"I'm afraid I'm not."

"Oh boy. You should at least watch *American Idol*. It's the best show in the world."

His mustache lifted on the edges when he chuckled. "I'll be sure to give it a whirl."

"And then late last night a man named David August checked in." She sucked in a breath. "Ooh. I don't think I was supposed to say his real last name. But Calico says he's famous too. Have you heard of him?"

"David August the author?"

"That's what Calico said. He made reservations a week ago but used a different name. He says he's staying indefinitely."

"What in the world is David August doing way out here at the Venus?"

"All I know is Calico told me he just disappeared into his room and hasn't come out yet, not even for something to eat. The Do Not Disturb sign is on his door handle too."

"Have you read any of his books?"

"No. I've mostly played sudoku and watched *Idol* and the Harbor ducks. Have you?"

"Sure. The man's brilliant. Or was. Haven't seen anything from him in a long while. Didn't even know he was still around. I'd like to meet him."

"Really? Calico said he looked like a homeless guy."

"David August at the Venus. I'll be darned."

"And don't forget Nelson Black."

"I'll try not to."

"Anyway, it's an interesting place to be. And I'm meeting interesting people for a change. Interesting like you."

"Oh, I'm not all that interesting."

"I think you're very interesting. A whole lot more interesting than the Harbor ducks."

Now his eyes crinkled with a full smile. "You're a nice person. And you have a real nice voice."

Her cheeks heated. "It was my first time in front of people."

"I dang sure hope it's not your last."

"Really?"

"You were very good. Took me out of my uneasy mind for a while."

"Really?"

"Really. You have a very peaceful voice."

"I've never heard of a peaceful voice."

"I imagine that's because it's a rare thing."

Cozy pulled the sheets up on the bed. "Well, I think a love like you have for your Ivy is a rare thing. It's beautiful."

"You remembered her name."

"Of course I did."

"It's sad is what it is. All my moping."

"Sometimes the saddest things are the most beautiful."

"Are you going to sing tonight, Cozy?"

"I think so. If there's time."

"Make time. I could sure do with more peaceful."

CHAPTER EIGHTEEN

"The thing about offing a guy," Sal was saying, "is that you can't get all caught up in it. You gotta think about the job like you're stepping on a cockroach. You do it, and that's it. The guy's a bug. Then he's gone. End of story."

The Pontiac's windows were rolled down, and Rufus Miller—in the passenger seat because Sal always insisted on driving—let his hand move up and down in the wind. Sal had been talking since Nogales. He could be like that once he got on a subject that interested him. Killing people seemed to be one of them. Rufus shook his head and laughed a little.

"You think it's funny? Offing a guy?" Sal said.

"I think it's funny that you talk about it. You say *offing a guy* like you've done it before, man."

"How do you know I haven't done it before? Back in Brooklyn—"

"I know. Brooklyn, Brooklyn, Brooklyn."

"New York is the real deal, man. Guys get offed in the city."

"Sure they do, but it wasn't you doing the offing. That's all I'm saying."

"You think I'm too soft to off a guy?"

"Yes, Sal, I do think you're too soft to murder someone. Which is a good thing, man. You should take it as a compliment, not an insult to your manhood."

"How did I end up with a sap like you, anyway?"

"Easy. A guy hired both of us to do stuff he didn't want to do."

"Yeah, but that guy's been in prison for a year, and you're still here."

"Because over time you realized you needed a calming influence in your life. It's like a yin-and-yang thing, man. Roll with it."

"Yin-and-yang . . . What's that? A Chinese cartoon? Man, what am I doing out here? I'll tell you what I'm doing. I'm driving through the middle of nowhere with a hippie surfer. I don't know why I ever left Brooklyn."

"You didn't have a choice about leaving Brooklyn."

"I could off a guy, Miller. Any day of the week I could off a guy."

"Look. If I hurt your feelings by suggesting you may not be a sadistic killer, I'm sorry. And I'm not a hippie, man. The hippies all turned on, tuned in, and dropped out like fifty years ago. I'm just relaxed. And while we're on the subject of me, stop calling me Miller. I've told you a thousand times it's Rufus. Miller reminds me too much of things better forgotten."

"Things better forgotten. See, if that ain't a stinking hippie thing to say, I don't know what is."

"I'm relaxed, man."

"So you said. Twice now."

"Yeah, so I said."

"They'd eat you for lunch in Brooklyn. You know that?"

"Cool. They could put me on toast."

"Cool, he says."

Rufus pushed a sun-bleached strand of hair out of his face. "Man. Todos Santos. That was some beach. I've been this side of the border only a day and I already miss Mexico."

"I don't miss nothing about it. It's desert-y and sandy and nobody speaks English and all they got is Mexican food down there."

"You should have learned to surf, man. I told you I'd teach you."

"Do I look like a surfer to you? You know what I look like? I look like a sausage. A big fat Italian sausage any shark with half a brain would swim a hundred miles to take a bite out of. I ain't even sticking my stinking sausage feet in the ocean. Not ever."

"You don't know what you're missing, man. I'm telling you."

"It's easy for you. You're all skinny and sun-dried. You're like a sun-dried tomato. No self-respecting shark would look twice at you. He'd have to practically be a vegetarian to eat you."

"You're gonna hurt my feelings."

"I never knew you were so sensitive. Anyway, we ain't going back to Mexico."

"Says who?"

"Says me. With the kind of money we're about to score, we can go anywhere we want. And it's my turn to pick. I'm gonna pick somewhere civilized."

"And where, pray tell, would that be? I seriously can't wait to hear. And don't say Brooklyn."

"Like I said. Somewhere civilized."

"Civilized like Brooklyn? Where everyone goes around offing or getting offed?"

"Canada maybe. Or Europe. How about Italy? I have relatives there."

"Sure. You're probably related to half the country. But I'm not going to Italy."

"What's wrong with Italy?"

"For one thing, they don't surf in Italy."

"What are you talking about? Of course they surf in Italy. They got an ocean there, don't they?"

"Do they? Do you even know, Sal? Sal De Nunzio, for five thousand dollars and a brand-new pontoon boat, is there an ocean in Italy? Don't forget to answer in the form of a question."

"Yeah, they do. They got an ocean."

"Incorrect. They have seas. Three of them. The Adriatic, the Ionian, and the Tyrrhenian."

"Yeah, well, you didn't say that in the form of a question, genius. So it don't count."

"Three seas, but I still don't think they surf."

"They surf. If you can surf, the Italians can surf."

"I doubt it."

"They can surf."

They rode in silence for a while. All that sand and sky. Rufus was a beach guy, not a desert guy, but he went with the flow. "Offing a guy is like stepping on a cockroach, huh?"

"Yeah. Like a cockroach."

"What if the guy's not a cockroach? What if he's cool?"

"What are you talking about? Most everybody's a cockroach."

"That's a very cynical view of life. You know that?"

"No, but Italians surf. I know that."

"Let me ask you, Sal. Do you know what the word *cynical* means?"

"Yeah, it means you need to shut up."

"It means you're distrustful of human integrity. It means you don't think people operate from sincere motives."

"That's exactly right. They don't. So I'm . . . whatever."

"Cynical."

"Exactly. I'm that."

Rufus laughed, pushed his sunglasses farther up the bridge of his nose, and went back to weaving his hand through the wind.

"Whoa!" Sal slowed so fast he almost put Rufus's face into the dash. "Look at that, man! What are those? Horses?"

Rufus surveyed the raggedy little herd as the Pontiac crept past. "Yeah, man. They've got 'em wild out here. It's no big deal."

"Are you kidding me? Just like that? They got 'em wild? Horses? Walking around?"

"Yeah. A lot of 'em. Descendants of the horses brought over by the conquistadors."

"Man, how do you know all this stuff?"

"I read, Sal. And I watch documentaries instead of cartoons. You should try it."

"Another stupid thing a stupid hippie would say." The Pontiac's tires barked as Sal hit the gas. He stared out at the horses. "Where'd they come from again?"

"The conquistadors."

"Right. Those guys."

"You have no idea what a conquistador is, do you?"

"You really like saying I don't know stuff. It makes you feel superior."

"Do you know what they are?"

"If you tell me to answer that in the form of a question, I swear I'm gonna put your face through this windshield."

"I'm only asking if you know. To pass time. Humor me."

"Of course I know what a conquistador is."

"What, Sal? What exactly is a conquistador? In the form—"

"Don't you dare."

"Conquistador. Come on."

"I don't feel the need to say it. You know what one is. You started this whole thing."

"Yeah, I know. But you don't know."

"Shut up."

"Yeah, shut up. That's your answer to everything."

"Yeah, that's my answer. But I said it wrong. What is shut up? That better?"

"You don't know what a conquistador is."

"All right, I don't know. Happy? Why don't you bless me with some of your great wisdom as we all know you can't help doing, oh enlightened one?"

"Conquistadors were Spanish soldier-explorers. A long time ago. It means conqueror."

"Yeah? Doesn't look like they did too good a job conquering this godforsaken patch of dirt. Looks to me like they got their butts kicked so bad they left their rides behind."

"I suppose that's one way to put it."

"No wonder I ain't ever heard of 'em. Anyway, I don't like them Spanish. There's this one guy, Silva. Runs a little bodega on Sixth. He's got a gold tooth and smells like he takes baths in Aqua Velva. No class at all. I can't stand Spanish."

"Silva's a cockroach?"

"Of the lowest order. I'd off him in a hot second if there was a buck in it."

"No you wouldn't."

"Bet your life on it."

"Because deep down you're a decent human being. You're a lover not a fighter."

"Stinking hippie, man."

Rufus sighed and leaned his head back.

"We should take one," Sal said after a minute or two.

"We should take what? A bodega?"

"One of them horses. They don't belong to nobody, right?"

Rufus shook his head and laughed. "Where you gonna put a horse, man? In the trunk? Or maybe he can sit in the back seat. We'll buy him a bag of chips and a Mr. Pibb."

"Horses don't drink Mr. Pibb."

"No? What do horses drink?"

"They don't eat no chips neither."

"I bet you a hundred bucks he'd eat chips."

"I bet you a hundred bucks he wouldn't."

"Would."

"Shut up."

"I'm saying a horse would eat chips. I don't know why you get so offended."

"He might eat trail mix, but he ain't eating no chips."

"Trail mix? No."

"Why do you want to argue all the time?"

"All right, he'd eat trail mix. Are you happy this time?"

"Not until you admit Italians surf."

"I'll never admit that."

More desert. More minutes.

"I know they eat hay or oats or somethin'," Sal said. "Way I figure it, we get a trailer, put it on the back of the car, catch a horse, and take him with us."

"To Italy?"

"No, to Mexico. I ain't taking him on a plane. That can't be good for him."

"Now you're worried about your imaginary horse? After you were just feeding him trail mix?"

"I'm serious."

"Just like that. You're gonna catch a horse."

"Yeah."

"Just like that."

"Yeah. I'm gonna catch a horse. Are you deaf?"

Rufus sat up a little, shifted his sunglasses down to the tip of his nose, and eyed the man. "What, Sal? You're gonna lassoo it? Like John Wayne or something?"

"It's lasso, man. Not lass*oo*. And why not? How hard can it be? If these cowboy yahoos out here can do it, we can do it."

Rufus laughed even louder at this. "There's no *we* when it comes to this, man. There's you, and then there's me. You wanna lass*oo* a wild animal and get dragged through a hundred miles of cactus, be my guest. But leave me out of it."

"I'm gonna do it."

"Go right ahead."

"I'm gonna. And I'll also off this guy if he gives us problems."

Rufus let Sal have the last word. It wasn't like he had a choice. Dude would never back down once he dug his heels in. Plus what did he think he was going to use to kill someone? A gun he didn't have? Then again, he could always sit on them. He watched the desert roll by for a while. It was like a movie out here. Like *The Good, the Bad, and the Ugly*. "Sal, I have to tell you, life is not a constant test of your manhood."

"If he gives us problems I'll off him."

"He won't."

"I don't care if he's James Dean or the Fonz or Gandhi, you understand? No problems." Sal pointed through the windshield. "Hey, is that it?"

Rufus took off his sunglasses and squinted. "That's something, all right. Big, tall neon woman rising out of the desert waving to the empty highway. Would you look at that? She's like a dream, man."

CHAPTER NINETEEN

CALICO LEANED FORWARD ON HER hands and watched the two men approach the bar. They were so different from each other it was comical. The one in front might as well have stepped off a used car lot. Black hair slicked straight back, cheap suit and cheaper shoes. Not more than five foot five and round as a ball. The other, almost a foot taller, looked like he'd been sleeping under a bench at the beach for the last year. Sun-bleached hair past his shoulders, scraggly beard, sandals, frayed chinos, and a Cubavera shirt that looked like it was stolen from a down-on-his-luck mariachi.

"Can I help you, gentlemen?" Calico said.

"Only one gentleman present, and that's me." The suit jerked a thumb toward his companion. "He's a hippie."

The beach bum slid onto a barstool. "Ignore him. Everyone else does. He's jealous because I'm relaxed."

"Whatever you say," Calico said.

Suit took the stool next to Beach. "Can you make a decent martini?"

"You insult the lady, Sal. Of course she can make a decent martini. Look at her."

"She's lovely, but what do looks have to do with a decent martini?"

"It's the way you present yourself, man. Instead of simply asking the lady to make you a martini, you asked her if she can. You gave the impression you doubt she can do it."

"I'm asking, that's all. Making a decent martini is an art."

"I'm sorry," Beach said, turning to Calico. "Sal fancies himself sophisticated because he's from Brooklyn."

"One decent martini coming up. How about you?"

"Soda water with a slice of lime, please."

"You got it."

"See how I just asked for soda water and lime, Sal? I didn't ask if she had it or if she could make it."

"I'm not gonna ask if I can put my fist through your face either. By the way, you know who drinks soda water? Hippies."

"Everyone in the world drinks water, man. Eighty percent of our bodies are water."

"Eighty percent of my body is martinis."

"Eighty percent of your body is mouth. The other twenty is hair gel."

"You know, Rufus, just because I came here with you doesn't mean I have to leave with you."

Rufus winked at Calico. "He's a very tough guy, so he feels everyone should take him very, very seriously. Don't worry. He's not in the Mafia no matter what he says. I'm Rufus, and this is Sal."

"Calico. I own the Venus. And I'm not worried."

"I do know people in the Mafia," Sal said. "I might know a lot of people."

"Good for you, man, but there's no need to intimidate the locals."

"You intimidated?" Sal said to Calico. "You don't look intimidated."

"Because you might know people in the Mafia in Brooklyn? Why would that intimidate me?" Calico finished mixing the martini and slid it across the bar to Sal. Then she poured soda water from the dispenser over ice, squeezed a lime wedge into it, and handed it to Rufus.

Sal sipped and raised an appreciative eyebrow. "Not bad. Ain't no Clover Club but not bad."

"Thanks, I think," Calico said.

Sal sipped again. Gave a satisfied sigh. "So what room is David August in?"

"Excuse me?"

"I said what room is David August in. As in the author. It's a very simple question. Now you say a number and we'll all be happy."

"David August? I don't think—"

"I'm sure there's a whole incognito thing going on," Sal said. "But it's cool. We're friends of his."

"You're friends of David August?" She managed not to point at the man's photo on the wall.

"Sure. Met him on the beach a couple of weeks ago down in Todos Santos. He suggested we stop by."

"Stop by the Venus? This isn't really a place you stop by."

"And yet, here we are."

"It's only that he talked so highly of the motel," Rufus said. "We decided we had to come see for ourselves."

"And what do you think so far?"

"So far, so good."

"The thing is," Calico said, "we take our guests' privacy very seriously."

Sal popped an olive into his mouth as he pushed his empty martini glass across the bar to Calico. "We came all this way, and we only want to say hello."

"I'll check with him, all right? It's Rufus and Sal?"

"That's us." Rufus slid his empty glass forward too. "Refill while we wait?"

"Ditto to that," Sal said.

Calico made the drinks, then stepped through the swinging kitchen door and dialed room nine from the kitchen extension. It rang a dozen times before she hung up and walked back into the lounge. "I'm sorry, but he's not picking up. He may be sleeping."

"These authors. Strange hours, am I right?" Rufus said. "How about if we enjoy our beverages and then maybe you can try again?"

"I suppose so."

The lounge door swung open, and Burt strode in. He took a stool at the far end of the bar. "*Hola*, Calico."

"Hi, Burt. Highball time?"

"I'll take coffee if you have any on."

"You got it."

Calico put cream and sugar on the bar and poured Burt a cup.

Rufus looked Burt up and down. "Hey, man. That's a cool mustache. Are you a real cowboy?"

Burt lifted a shoulder. "I've been known to work cows here and there. Made a living at it a long time. Guess that makes me bona fide."

Rufus seemed to appreciate this. "Bona fide. Man, that's cool. Let me ask you a question. Have you ever lassoed horses when you've been out there riding the range?"

Burt sipped his coffee. His eyes were very blue. "Nope. Can't say I have."

"Hold on a second," Sal said. "You're telling me you're a real cowboy, but you never lassoed a horse? That's what you're telling me?"

"That's what I'm telling you."

"Why not?" Rufus said.

"Because I'm not five years old watching old Tom Mix movies. I've *roped* a horse plenty of times, but I never lassoed nothin' in my life."

"Roped. I like that," Rufus said. "Correct terms are important. I'm Rufus, and this is Sal. What's your name?"

"Burt Calloway."

"Burt Calloway." Rufus turned the name over in his mouth a couple of times. "That's actually not a bad cowboy name."

"I'd be heartbroken if you didn't approve," Burt said.

Rufus laughed. "So it's *roped* a horse?"

"It is."

"Not lassoed?"

"Nope."

"But it's the same thing."

"I suppose so."

"So what we're really discussing here is semantics."

"I suppose we are if we're discussing anything at all. I'm mostly drinking a cup of coffee."

"Let me ask you another thing. Do you mind?"

"Fire away."

"When you *rope* one of those horses out there on the range, would you describe said action as a hard thing to do or an easy thing to do?"

"Guess that would depend on the particular disposition of said animal."

Rufus laughed. "Said animal. That's good, man. Okay, how about if you wanted to lass—rope one of those wild horses out in the desert between here and Tucson? I suppose you'd just walk up and shake its hoof and it'd follow you home?"

"I don't suppose it would, no. You want to rope a wild horse?"

"Not me. Sal here. He wants to take one home like a kitten. In fact, his exact words were"—Rufus looked at Sal—"correct me if I'm wrong, Sal. His exact words were *if these cowboy yahoos can do it, so can we*. I told him there wasn't any *we* about it. He's flying solo when it comes to catching horses."

"I could do it," Sal said. "I don't care what you say. Or the yahoo with the mustache. Talk all you want."

Burt seemed to consider this while he took another sip of coffee. Then he set his cup down, pulled a paperback from his back pocket, opened it to a dog-eared page, and started reading.

"What are you reading, man?" Sal said.

"Elmore Leonard."

"What's that? Like a book about the guy's life or something?"

Burt sighed and looked up. "It's a western."

"Like a travel book?"

"Sal, please," Rufus said. "It's a novel. Fiction. A story made up. Like David August writes."

"You know David August's work?" Burt said.

"Sure. I'm what you might call surprisingly well read. Sal here is lucky to keep the colors inside the lines in his books."

"I'm gonna be lucky to keep my fist away from your mouth is what I'm gonna be lucky to do," Sal said.

"Although I suppose Sal and I have that in common. We both enjoy colorful characters. Much like Mr. Leonard did, come to think of it.

Also come to think of it, we might be colorful characters ourselves. You too, Burt. With that mustache and roping wild horses and all."

"Whatever you say," Burt said, looking back at the page.

"Are we boring you?" Sal said.

Burt looked up again. "I wouldn't say that. But if you don't mind, I came in to have some coffee and read a while."

"What if I do mind?"

"Sal, leave the man to his book. He asked politely," Rufus said.

"I don't care if he sent it with a bow. I don't like being ignored."

"You don't have anything to prove, man. Relax."

"It ain't about proving. I don't like being brushed off. I can also tell by his face he don't think I could catch a horse. Like I'm a joke. You think I'm a joke, man?"

Burt's jaw went tight. He put down his cup. "I'm not sure what your problem is, friend."

"My problem is someone thinking I couldn't go catch a horse. I asked you, you think this is funny?"

Burt pushed his cup away from him. "Let me put it this way. I don't think a fat man in a bad suit wanting to rope a horse to take home is without humor. Does that answer your question? I also don't like your attitude, so why don't you take it someplace else before you find yourself outside on your ear?"

Sal got off his stool.

So did Burt.

"Guys," Calico said.

CHAPTER TWENTY

STARING INTO THE BATHROOM MIRROR, David August decided it was time to leave room nine even though he was beyond hungover. Not that he actually knew what time it was. He couldn't find his Rolex, and the motel's bedside clock wasn't working.

The clock was no surprise. He'd yanked its plug out of the wall sometime in the wee hours of mid-morning because he couldn't handle the light spilling from the display. That loud, loud light—so loud it made his ears ring. Boom, boom, booms of bright, like mountain-sized drops of water falling from some massive, invisible faucet. It always happened when he drank. And he always drank, so it always happened.

And so the world turns.

He'd awakened with a freight train roaring through his head and the strong suspicion that a dead cat had been camped out in his mouth at some point during the last several hours of slumber. Then sitting up slowly, stomach churning, he'd cracked an eye to see his own face smiling up at him from the nightstand. Trimmed beard. Teeth so white you could practically see through them. Longish hair lifting in the gentle trade winds in manly-gray, outdoorsy perfection. *TIME* magazine's World edition. They'd had him on the cover so many times he'd lost count.

All right, seven. They'd had him on the cover seven times. This last time because the world had learned he'd finally be writing a new novel.

He just couldn't remember why he'd taken the magazine out of his bag and put it there. But he did vaguely remember the room's phone waking him with its ringing. At least it was silent now.

Right away he'd noticed a very sad and very empty bottle of Bacardí rum next to the magazine. Another bottle lay visible on the floor. If he remembered correctly, a third had rolled under the bed, but he couldn't be sure. Still, he always made a point to travel well stocked. At least until he ran out. And he was out now. Thus the decision to leave the room.

For a good five minutes he'd debated the wisdom of standing. About his average. He figured the odds were fifty-fifty he'd stay upright if he tried it. In the end, the fact that he had to use the restroom in the worst way settled the debate. He simply had to chance it. So he'd hoisted sail and cast off.

He'd been investing in a fair bit of nautical lingo lately. Not so much because of the pirate novel he was supposed to be working on as much as the way it aligned with this latest round of copious rum intake.

Listing a little to port on the way to the head, he'd managed to relieve himself without major incident or injury. A few long minutes later, he was leaning on the sink, staring into the mirror. If his head hadn't hurt so bad, he would have laughed. *TIME* would love this. So would the *Inquirer*. Sunset-red eyes—*Ugh, terribly trite description. Remember never to use that in a book.* A road map of veins across his nose—*Not much better and possibly worse.*

His hair. He remembered it had irritated him at some point during this last, monthlong binge's Bacardí-fueled semiconsciousness. So he'd shaved it off with some electric clippers he suspected were made for either dogs or a horse's mane. The shaving effort had eased his mind in the heat of the moment but left several barely-scabbed-over gashes in its wake. His beard looked like someone had stuck it in a blender and tried to make a margarita. In retrospect, he wasn't sure that hadn't actually happened. He had, after all, just been in Mexico.

He'd been in a mood. Over a month now, he'd been in this mood of his. Which explained his being at the Venus. He always wound up here eventually when he got in a mood. Sometimes he wound up here when he wasn't in a mood. It was his retreat. His oasis. His Alamo. Sometimes he came alone, sometimes with whatever woman was in his life at the moment, always with Bacardí and a healthy contingency of limes.

Ah, Lady Venus. It had been far too long since he'd seen her face. What? Five years, maybe? He'd discovered the place a lifetime ago when they'd been filming the stagecoach scenes for *Bloody Dawn*, based on one of his first novels, back in the early seventies. His first western. Both the book and the film had been a smash. In those days people loved westerns, and in those days people also loved David August. So how could they miss?

No one had needed him on set, but not being needed had never stopped him from showing up. He'd walked around with a script in his hand, pestered the director for his own entertainment, and spent the evenings drinking and carousing with the cast. He'd always considered carousing great fun, and outside of writing, the one thing he was actually good at.

He'd spotted the towering highway Venus from the back of a horse, of all things. Or it might have been a mule or a zebra—the seventies tended to be a bit fuzzy. Rode over after the shoot, tied the animal to the door handle of someone's car, and stepped into the lounge for a drink. He'd spent the afternoon, evening, night, and early morning hours shooting the breeze with Ray Garza, the motel's original owner. Problem was they shot so much breeze he completely forgot about the horse/zebra. He eventually emerged into the desert dawn to find not only his mount gone but the entire car door as well. They never found either.

Donna, wife number something, was supposed to be with him now, but she'd opted for Monte Carlo and the up-and-coming actor playing opposite her in the heist picture she was working on. David had pretended to be disappointed and hurt when she'd called to break the news.

Truth was, he was relieved. To say she'd been getting tedious would be like asking the sun if it had a match. Let her bore someone else with her runway looks and empty head. The sad fact was they didn't make models like they used to. He studied his reflection a few more seconds before saying, "Then again, Mr. August, maybe you're the one getting tedious." Or maybe he just needed a drink. *Get it together, my friend. You're tragically out of Bacardí.* But as he recalled, the Venus kept a good supply. And Calico, the new owner, was a looker, so tracking her down would be a pleasure.

After hurriedly brushing the cardigans from his teeth and rinsing his mouth with peroxide, he rubbed a cold-water washcloth over his face and head. The scabs stung. A swim, after a drink, of course, might be just the ticket. Cold water and warm desert air to get the old brain functioning.

A minute of looking turned up his Rolex amid his bedding. The watch said 5:58 p.m. He'd been here for about twenty-four hours, then. Moving to pull his open suitcase on the floor, he pulled on swimming trunks and a silk robe he didn't bother to tie and slipped his feet into sandals.

The crack in the blinds shone bright gold. He knew that color. Here at the Venus, it was the time of day when the whole world turned to fire. He put on his sunglasses and opened the door, then squinted at the smoldering sun before leaning down to lift a gun belt from a low table. An old Wild West–style thing holding a period-correct Colt revolver. After slinging it around his waist, he buckled it. A Wild West *pistola* for the Wild West. The frontier. It felt substantial on his hip. He sniffled and said to no one, "Weigh anchor, you scallywags. The horizon awaits."

He laughed at himself, then winced at what that did to his head. *August, you're a hack, and someday somebody will figure that out. Weigh anchor, you scallywags? Don't you ever use that one on the printed page either. You'll never be taken seriously again.*

Then, with a freshening wind on a beam reach, he set sail for the lounge.

CHAPTER TWENTY-ONE

DAVID HAD WRITTEN TENSION INTO plenty of scenes. After all, tension is stock-in-trade in the book publishing racket. He'd also been around the world several times. He'd run with the bulls in Pamplona. He'd once had lunch with a dozen armed Taliban in a Cairo café. He'd been held up at knifepoint in Bangkok. Not to mention the fact he'd been married to a fairly healthy string of strong and volatile women over the years. All this to say he had a good eye for the real thing when he encountered it, and you could cut the tension in Venus's nearly empty lounge with a knife.

Two men stood squared off in front of the bar. No pistols drawn—like that time in a Nigerian beach bar—but from the set of their faces it might as well have been Normandy. A fat short man with greasy hair and a wrinkled suit had his finger pointed at a cowboy. A long-haired beach bum with sunglasses propped on top of his head sipped from a glass and looked on fairly unfazed.

David had the sense he should intervene somehow. At least say something firm and manly. But he was hungover and acutely aware he was standing in a motel lounge in parrot-print swim trunks and an open robe through which protruded his unfortunate gut. Instead of firm and manly, he opted for the simple and less headachy route. "Beautiful Calico, I need a bottle of Bacardí as quick as you can give me one."

The motel owner looked him up and down. "I'm not sure you do, Mr. August."

That's when the bum with the glass shifted on his barstool and squinted at him. He grinned. "Dave? What happened to your head?"

The fat guy in the suit stepped back and looked as well. "Yeah, man. What did you do?"

"I got a trim."

"With what?" the fat one said. "A machete?"

"Sorry. Do I know you?"

"Dave, it's us. Rufus and Sal. Todos Santos. The El Faro Beach Club."

"I was in Todos Santos a few days ago. At least I think it was Todos Santos."

"Of course it was. Rufus and Sal. From the El Faro."

David looked at Calico. "What do you mean you're not sure I do?"

"You're looking a little rough this evening. How about a cup of coffee and something to eat?"

"Eat? Why in the world would I want to eat? I'm a big boy. Bacardí and lime, please."

Calico shook her head but poured two shots of clear rum over ice into a glass, squeezed lime juice into it, and set it on the bar.

David walked around Sal, picked up the glass, and downed half. "Hallelujah. I have to tell you boys, that particular season of existence is somewhat foggy. Especially the El Faro. I'll have to take your word for our meeting."

"No kidding?" Rufus said. "And here I thought we had a real connection."

"Oh, I'm not saying we didn't. I tend to make a lot of connections in my foggy periods."

"This is why I generally make it a rule to stick to sparkling water." Rufus held out a hand. "Let's start over. I'm Rufus. That's Sal. And I have to tell you again, Dave, I'm quite a fan."

"I see. Do you mind if I ask why your friend looked like he was about to go to fisticuffs with this cowboy when I came in?"

"The name's Burt Calloway," the cowboy said.

"I told him that was a fine cowboy name," Rufus said.

"Indeed it is. A pleasure, Mr. Calloway."

Burt slid back onto his stool and picked up his coffee. "Call me Burt."

"Burt, then. A pleasure."

Burt lifted his cup and nodded. "Pleasure's mine. I've read a few of your books."

"Thank you."

"In answer to your question, Dave . . . May I still call you Dave?" Rufus said.

David drank deep from his glass. Let the alcohol burn his throat and press into his veins. "Rupert, seeing as we have such a deep Mexican connection, I suppose you might as well."

"Thanks. It's Rufus. In answer to your question, Dave, Sal was about to go to fisticuffs—I love how you call it fisticuffs, by the way. So authorish. Anyway, it was because Sal is, in a word, insecure."

"I am not insecure," Sal said.

"He is," Rufus said. "He's insecure in his own masculinity. It's a shame, really."

Sal adopted a menacing look. "How about I show you exactly how insecure I am, Miller?"

"Sal's calling me Miller is another outlet for his insecurity. He knows I prefer to be called by my Christian name, yet he insists. Miller was my father, Dave, and my father is a very sore subject. Sal and I have gone over this ad nauseam. But let me continue. The reason for Sal's unfaith in his own masculinity is his height and weight. The former being below average and the latter being quite a bit above."

"Another martini," Sal said to Calico. Then after a pause, "Please."

"Thanks for clearing that up," David said to Rufus. "Now, if you gentlemen will excuse me, I have a date with the pool." He paused and studied the two. "By the way, what are you doing at the Venus? Did you mention that yet?"

Rufus shook his head. "No, Dave, we did not. The fact is we were due for a little road-trip R and R, and you spoke so fondly of this establishment back at the El Faro we thought we'd wander up and check it out for ourselves. And lo and behold, who do we run into? You. Although you're the one who told us about it, so I suppose we can't be all that surprised."

"I didn't mention I might be headed this way?"

"If you did, I don't recall."

"Then why did you have me ring Mr. August's room?" Calico said. "You seemed to know he was here."

Rufus eyed her and smiled. "That's right. We did, didn't we? I guess you did mention it after all, Dave."

"I do tend to speak fondly of the Venus. I've been coming here for years. It's a place to get my head straight. Or get it crooked, depending on the season and mood of life."

"It certainly seems like that kind of place." Rufus indicated the signed photos behind the bar. "That's a pretty impressive gaggle of patrons, including you. Strange place for famous people to hang out, though. Kind of out of the way."

"Which is exactly the charm. I remember seeing Nelson Black in the office when I checked in. He was asking about . . . I forget."

"No kidding?" Sal said. "The dude who makes buildings disappear?"

"The same."

"That's crazy. Dude's amazing. And a little creepy."

"I imagine he'd be flattered to hear both."

Sal shrugged.

Rufus pointed at the Colt revolver. "I have to ask. What's with the Doc Holliday hog iron?"

"Just a little protection. After all, this is the desert, where snakes are often about, not all of them of the animal variety. I also sometimes have valuables about my person, and a pistol goes a long way in helping me maintain peace of mind."

"No kidding? You have to forgive my curious nature, but what might these valuables be? I don't see many pockets in that outfit."

"My valuables, friend, are none of your business no matter how deep a connection we may have established at the El Faro or anyplace else. No offense."

"None taken, Dave."

Calico cleared her throat. "I have to say I'm not sure I'm comfortable with you carrying a gun around, Mr. August."

"I assure you I'm a dead shot, and my safety practices are absolutely top-notch. And please call me Dave. I get too many misters and sirs and Your Royal Highnesses in this world as it is."

"Okay, Dave." Calico's voice firmed a bit. "But rum and pistols have the potential to be a bad combination. I don't like it."

"If those scabs on your head are any indication of your idea of safety, I'm with her," Sal said.

"Sal, please." Rufus.

"Rum and pistols. I like that," David said. "It might fit nicely in a novel I'm working on. Maybe I'll have to add you to the thanks page."

"What novel would that be?" Burt said. "I haven't seen anything new out from you for a long time."

David straightened a bit. Pulled in his gut. *Guess not everyone reads magazines.* "Good writing takes time. I don't rush it." He realized his glass was empty and set it on the bar. "Calico, looks like I'm dry. I'll need a refresher for my foray into the deep."

Calico refilled the glass.

"I imagine it does take a good bit of time," Burt said. "I meant no disrespect, Mr. August."

"You're a cognoscente of literature, I take it?"

"That's someone who appreciates good writing," Rufus said to Sal.

"Thanks, genius. I got that."

David pointed. "What's that you're reading? And call me Dave."

Burt held up the book. "Elmore Leonard."

Rufus snapped his fingers. "It just came to me. *The Base of the Mountain*. Hector had a Colt revolver like that, didn't he?"

The room swayed a bit as David gave an affirmative nod. "Based on this very gun, as a matter of fact, as well as my own marksmanship. I spent a month down in Laredo doing nothing but shooting so I could write Hector with accuracy. I killed many a pop bottle, let me tell you."

"Man, you did a good job with Hector. The guy really comes alive."

David killed half the rum in the glass. The room felt close and hot. "Thank you, kind Rupert from Todos Santos. Now, if you'll excuse me, I have an appointment with the pool."

"Rufus."

"Exactly. And you"—he pointed at Burt—"please find some acceptable reading material. Elmore will rot your mind."

"It's my opinion that Leonard is an American treasure," Burt said. "A whole lot of folks hold the same."

David squinted at the cowboy. "Well, Buck. May I call you Buck?"

"No, but you can call me Burt."

"Right. You have to excuse me. I'm a little foggy this morning."

"Afternoon," Sal said.

"Evening, actually," Rufus said.

"I'm a little foggy this evening," David said. "The sad and brutal truth is dear Elmore wrote seventh grade dialogue. He wrote shallow and trite novels for people going camping, Buck."

"Most of the world would disagree with that, including me. Elmore Leonard was a great writer."

"I'm beginning to see why Sal here wanted to punch you. News flash—every hack with a pen is a great writer to their mother. Even worse, on top of his dismal dialogue, Elmore had a very hard time holding his whiskey. I claim that as firsthand experience. A very gray and very snowy afternoon in Detroit. Then again, I might have been the one who had a hard time holding the whiskey. Detroit was slightly foggy as well."

"I believe Mr. Leonard was every bit as good as you," Burt said.

"Are you really comparing Elmore Leonard to David August?" Rufus said. "That's a stretch, man."

Burt lifted a shoulder. "Tell you the truth, I've been appreciative of Mr. August's work a long time. So much so that I'm having a hard time reconciling the brilliance of, say, *The Officer's Woman* with the man standing here in a bathrobe and pink swim trunks and a scabby head."

"I'll admit the head shave might not have been one of my finer moments."

"Scabby head or not, he's David August, man." Rufus said.

"Even the finest artists can find themselves stuck in a box canyon," Burt said. "Look at old Ernie Hemingway."

"David August is having a little vacation, that's all. He's not running off to be a hermit in Idaho."

David's stomach threatened rebellion. "Do any of you mind if I sit while you work out this little impasse?"

"Not at all." Rufus turned back to the cowboy. "To be clear, David August is the greatest writer of our generation."

"Look, partner. I'm an admirer of the man's work. But whether he's the greatest of a generation is a matter of opinion."

"No, it's not a matter of opinion. It's cold fact, man. This is David August we're talking about."

"I appreciate the support, Russell," David said. "Speaking of Russell . . . Calico, what do you say you rustle up a bottle or three of Bacardí? I want to buy whatever you have. If you refuse, I'll drive to town, and believe me, no one wants me driving to town. I am, after all, a paying guest, and unfortunately, through every fault of mine, an anvil is currently residing between my ears."

Calico sighed, shook her head, but then refilled his glass. Maybe he'd get the bottles after his swim—if he even got into the water.

David tried, unsuccessfully, to keep his hand from shaking as he raised the glass in toast. "Beautiful Calico, may your joys be as bright as the morning and your sorrows merely be shadows that fade in the sunlight of love. May your pretty eyes never cry and your pretty rum never run dry."

"That's from *A Cabin in the Hills*, right?" Rufus said.

David drank deep, the rum burning his throat. "Not that I recall, Russell."

"I'll admit, *A Cabin in the Hills* was a mite better than Leonard," Burt said.

"Absolute classic," Rufus said.

"Definitely." Sal said this with unexpected emphasis.

Rufus eyed his friend. "You never read *A Cabin in the Hills*."

"I saw the movie. Dennis Hopper, man."

Hopper? "Dennis was another person who couldn't hold his whiskey. I remember one night up in the Hollywood Hills . . . Ah, forget it. Buck, what you said about that box canyon? You might not be far off on that. In fact, I think without realizing how true it is, you have a very pointed point."

"It's still Burt, not Buck. And, yes, a man can sure get to a place in life where he's mainly killing time. It doesn't happen only to writers. Believe me, ranch owners are not immune."

David nodded. "Neither are butchers, bakers, and candlestick makers. We are a human species merely killing time. Poor time."

Burt chuckled. "And some of us choose to do it in pink swim trunks and a bathrobe."

David blinked. "In my defense, this robe is mulberry silk."

"That ain't much of a defense."

"No, I suppose it's not." David got off his stool, then walked along the bar and took another one kitty-corner to Burt. "Buck, I appreciate your honesty. It's refreshing. Let's be great friends."

"You're welcome."

"I was being honest too, man," Rufus said.

Burt cheersed him. "You as well, friend Russell. Buck, I have to admit you're on the money on at least two counts, my box canyon predicament being the first."

"And the second?"

"The second is much harder to admit. But Elmore was a tremendous writer. I've been jealous of the twerp for years." David rubbed his eyes with thumb and forefinger. "Look at me. What have I become? I'm drinking myself into oblivion and working on a pirate novel. A *pirate* novel! I'm talking eye patches and parrots and the whole enchilada. It doesn't get any worse than that, Buck. I'm telling you, the book will be awful."

"I might actually read something like that," Sal said.

Rufus rolled his eyes. "You would."

"Then why are you writing it?" Burt said.

"I don't know. Boredom? The money certainly doesn't hurt. Both the publishing advance as well as a nice little chunk of cash coming my way from Fred Katz at Global to secure the film rights. Fred didn't like the idea of cash, but I insisted."

"Cash?"

David's eyes were having a hard time focusing on the cowboy. "That's the stipulation, Buck. Cashola on the barrelhead. Two million in hundred-dollar bills or no movie. To be delivered right here to the Venus or no deal. This is where I plan to finish the book. And if not the book, at least several cases of Bacardí."

Burt leaned forward. "As your new friend, I have to say you might not want to talk about that kind of money in public."

"No banks, no governments, nor other such pestering and intrusive entities. Nobody even knows about it except me and Katz." David heard the name Katz come out of his mouth as Katzsh and gave his head a few quick shakes. "In other words, two million tax-free bills can buy a lot of rum and limes."

"What say you head back to your room and get a little shut-eye, Dave?" Burt said.

"I'm not worried about snakes." David pulled his pistol and laid it on the bar. "I'm well-heeled, as they say."

"Mr. August," Calico said.

"You know, I got this baby on the set of *Three Strangers* back in seventy-something. A gift from Glenn Ford." He toasted Glenn's picture on the wall. "Heya, buddy. Now, Glenn could hold his liquor, unlike Dennis. Anybody gets too close, I'll put one between their eyes. Snakes. I'm telling you the desert's full of them. Now, beautiful Calico, you and I really need to discuss this rum situation."

CHAPTER TWENTY-TWO

Cozy sipped her soda water and lime—the stuff was actually growing on her—and looked herself over in the bar mirror. The mirror made her think of *Idol*, which reminded her she'd hardly even thought about the show since she'd been at the Venus. That was strange. Only a few days out of the trailer, a few days away from Don, and she was already changing. She wore her hair down tonight. Still a curl here and there, but she'd nixed ninety percent of the hair spray. And she'd given up cigarettes cold turkey. It wasn't too hard. She'd really only smoked when she was bored.

She'd also driven up to Paradise yesterday looking for a couple of new evening outfits. At the Jesus Is Coming Soon, she'd lucked out and found a whole slew of women's clothes in her size, recently donated from an estate. Tasteful vintage. Quality too. In the end, and thanks to her first paycheck, she'd bought several dresses, slacks, and blouses for next to nothing.

The dress she'd selected for tonight was black, simple, and off-the-shoulder with what Google called a Sabrina neckline. Cozy had never heard of a Sabrina neckline, but she liked the way it sounded. Classy, like the Venus. She also liked feeling attractive in something that left a little more to the imagination than the clothes Don had always suggested for her. She'd picked up a string of fake pearls at the thrift store as well, and they looked good in the mirror. She wore her sparkly pumps, though. No need to get crazy.

She watched as Calico took orders from a group of at least a dozen women. They'd pushed a few tables together, smiling and laughing and having a good time. She recognized at least half of them as Harbor ducks. Out of their yoga pants and into their Nordstrom for a night on the town. She knew the drink orders before hearing them. Vodka spritzers all around. Maybe a glass or two of chardonnay if they were feeling adventurous in the calorie department.

What would Harbor ducks think of thrift store estate clothes? They'd pretend they didn't notice. Why couldn't Harbor ducks stick to the harbor? This was her retreat, not theirs.

Calico approached the bar. "Busy again tonight."

"Uh-huh. They really come out for Jimmy's box."

"True, but the box isn't up there now, and no one seems like they've even noticed. They're enjoying the food and music and generally having a good time."

"Except for him." Cozy gestured toward Burt, who was sitting alone at a table with coffee.

"He's here, isn't he?"

"Yes, but he's sad."

"I think it's just his mustache that makes him look like that. It's like a permanent frown."

"You're terrible, Calico. He misses his wife. It's sweet."

"It is sweet. But I'll tell you what, he sure pays attention when you sing."

"He told me I have a peaceful voice."

"That sounds like quite a compliment coming from a man who doesn't seem to care about going home or have a whole lot of peace in his life."

"It was nice. Don hates my singing. He calls it killing cats."

"Don's not here, so who cares what he thinks? Besides, based on what you told me about that Tanya, he's got terrible taste. And anybody who'd cheat on you is an idiot anyway. Why don't you hit the stage? I've got the bar."

Cozy glanced at the Harbor ducks. "I can wait a while."

"Why? You practiced all afternoon. Show them what you've got."

"It's still early."

"You don't mind disappointing people? I thought you wanted to be a singer."

"Burt will still be here later."

"I'm not talking about Burt. I'm talking about your fans."

"Yeah, right."

"I'm serious. See that group of women? First thing they asked was when you were going to sing. They came to hear you."

"That's funny."

"I'm not joking."

"That can't be true. People are coming down to see Jimmy's box."

"They came to hear you sing, Cozy. It didn't have anything to do with Jimmy's box or they would have asked about it too. Get up there."

"You're serious? Really? A lot of them are Harbor ducks."

"Harbor ducks must like peaceful singing."

"They've never even heard me."

"The one in the blue blouse and moon earrings has. She was here a couple of nights ago. She's crazy about your singing."

Cozy wiped her eyes, realizing they were wet. "Do I look all right?"

Calico smiled. "No. You look like a raccoon. Go into the kitchen and fix your makeup, and then get the heck up on stage."

Makeup fixed a few minutes later, Cozy took a deep breath, then stepped back into the lounge. A few of the ducks actually clapped as she made her way to the stage, and Cozy prayed the dim light would hide her flaming cheeks.

"Well, well," Jimmy said as she took her place behind the mic. "I like the look. You're doing the Lady proud tonight."

Cozy covered the mic with one hand and kept her voice low. "It's from a thrift store."

"It's from an elegant era, that's what it's from. An elegant dress to match an elegant singer with an elegant voice."

"I can't get used to people calling me a singer."

Jimmy played a chord, then rolled into an intro. "You better get used to it quick, 'cause you're about to sing."

The nerves fell away with Jimmy's chords, and once again Cozy was transported by song. It was like someone else was singing. She floated, lifting and falling with the melody and lyrics. Standards. They were beautiful songs with beautiful sentiment, and before long she was totally lost in them. An hour went by in what seemed like minutes, and everyone at the duck table, along with the rest of the room, was applauding like crazy when Jimmy called for a break. "Girl, you've got yourself some magic," he said.

"I can't believe they really like it."

"That clapping and whistling ain't no lie."

"I love it, Jimmy. I love singing."

"You've got a gift. Use it."

Her clutch vibrated, and she pulled her phone out and looked at it.

"What?" Jimmy said. "I don't think I've ever seen a face crash so fast."

"It's Don. He keeps texting. He's got Tanya and the Mega money and everything he wants, but he won't stop telling me how worthless I am. I don't know why he can't just leave me alone. Maybe he's afraid I want something from him, but I don't want anything. Ever. I'd even like to dump the name Jenkins, which might not even be my legal name anyway."

"This isn't the first time he's done this?"

"He's been sending these texts ever since I left."

"Let me see."

Cozy handed him the phone. He read, a deep frown on his face. "Who's Porchie?"

"Me."

"Why?"

"It's a long story I'd rather not tell."

"Why do you keep reading these?"

Cozy stared at her hands. "I don't know."

Jimmy started to play softly. "I think you do."

"I've never known anything but a trailer. And I'm not talking a happy trailer. Part of me keeps thinking maybe he's right. Who do I think I am? Who am I fooling? You don't know all the things I've done. I'm talking about stuff even back before I met Don."

"Everybody's got a bag or two."

"I've got a train car full."

Jimmy leaned down, lifted the box from his pack, and set it on the piano. "What do you say we start unpacking."

"What do you mean?"

He opened the lid. "You don't need to hear that junk. Put it in the past."

"You mean my phone?"

"Yes, but really the lies he tells you. It's your call, but you deserve a whole lot more than that."

"The thing is I don't."

"Don't believe the lies, Cozy. You were made for beautiful things."

Cozy looked at the box. "Really? You think I should?"

"One bag at a time, sister."

Cozy put the phone in. "I'm doing it."

"You sure are."

She closed the lid and found herself glancing out toward Burt. "Hey, Jimmy?"

"Yeah?"

"Do we have to take a break? I still feel like singing."

Jimmy's answer came in the form of the intro to Sarah Vaughn's "Lullaby to Birdland."

And Cozy sang.

CHAPTER TWENTY-THREE

Even with a late night, Bones woke up early. He'd read into the wee hours, a novel about a submarine stranded on the bottom of the South Pacific, its occupants with only hours to escape before the air ran out. Nuclear bombs were involved. A couple of foreign dictators, one with an eye patch. And for some reason, trained dolphins. He could handle the dictators and dolphins, but when the author brought aliens into the story, he gave up. He didn't mind a little action, even if it was the obvious stuff. And dolphins were cool. But he drew the line with underwater aliens. Like the dude just didn't know where to go with the story so he decided to throw in some *Star Trek*, the only thing he could think of.

At least it wasn't vampires. Bones had had it up to his ears with vampires in books.

A soft beam of summer came in through the window. He made coffee and had just poured a cup when someone knocked on the door. Probably Calico with something for him to do even though this was supposed to be his day off.

Not Calico, though. Jimmy. As usual, a cigarette hung from the biker's bottom lip. He squinted into the dim interior of the shop. "You live in this popsicle stand?"

"Yeah. So?"

"So nothin'. Looks like a decent place. I've seen worse. Heck, I've lived in worse."

"It's okay. It's quiet, and no one bugs me."

"Am I bugging you?"

"Would you care if I said yeah?"

"Not much."

"You're not bugging me."

Jimmy tossed the cig and pushed past Bones. "Cool."

"Come in, I guess."

"Don't mind if I do." Jimmy took the room in, and his eyes settled on the Honda. "This is the bike that has you all in a twist?"

"Yeah, that's it. I can't figure out what's wrong with it."

Jimmy knelt by the Honda. "Lotta new parts. You do all this work yourself?"

"I do everything myself."

"I guess you do. What tools do you have here?"

Bones handed him the box. Jimmy messed with the bike a while, taking one thing apart, then another. Grunting a "Huh" every once in a while, to which Bones replied "What?"

"I can tell you one thing for sure," Jimmy finally said, straightening.

"What?" Bones was getting sick of the word.

"I'd take a cup of that coffee if you got any extra."

"Oh. Yeah."

Bones poured. "I got sugar but no milk or nothing."

Jimmy took the cup. "This'll be fine." He stood there a while, looking down at the bike. "You got a leaky float bowl, for one thing. Might have a wire or two wrong. Battery looks old. You didn't replace it?"

"No. It still has a little juice, I think."

"These old Hondas, they hate weak batteries. A little juice might not be enough."

"I'll get one next time Calico goes into town."

"She your ride?"

"Yeah. At least until I get the bike running."

Jimmy walked outside, then just stood on the little concrete slab in front of the shop door looking out over the motel, toward the desert. Bones stood in the doorway, leaning on the jamb.

"You're lucky, man. I could get used to this place."

Bones liked the way Jimmy called him man instead of kid. "You can have it."

"That's right. Soon as the bike runs, you're out of here."

"Yeah. As far as I can go."

"You'll hit ocean eventually."

"Fine with me."

"You really want out of here."

"Yeah."

"To each his own, I guess. Personally, I seen a lot worse places."

A dove cooed in the pines behind the shop. Jimmy lit another cig.

Bones shifted a little against the doorjamb, not sure why the guy was hanging out but at the same time not wanting him to leave. "So why was Nowak so excited to see this Nelson Black guy?"

Jimmy arched a brow. "You never heard of him before?"

"No."

"Don't you watch television?"

"Not really. Sometimes if it's on in the lounge. I mostly read books and work on the Honda when I'm not cleaning something."

"You're kind of a strange kid, you know that?"

"Yeah, I know. Everybody says that. Why do you think I want to get out of here?"

"Strange ain't bad."

"I know."

"Black's probably the most famous illusionist in the world. Made a whole skyscraper vanish on his latest Netflix special. You don't even watch Netflix?"

"No."

"Everybody else does, as far as I can see. Old Great Nowak does. That's what's got the dude's tighty-whities all in a bunch over him."

Bones laughed at this.

Jimmy puffed. "You know, they say Nelson can levitate right off the ground anytime he wants."

"You think that's true?"

"Don't matter what I think. Don't even matter what's true. They say it, so there you go. Nelson's world, perception becomes reality."

"I don't get it. If he can make a building disappear, why does he want your box so bad?"

"Because Nelson wants to be the best. And he thinks he never will be if he doesn't have the box." Jimmy gazed out toward the distant mountains. "Look at all that space, man. All that empty. Some people don't like the desert. Seems crazy to me. One time I heard a man say the desert was dead. Couldn't be more wrong. There's always life. You just have to keep your eyes open. Dig for it a little."

"Yeah, I guess."

"You ever see it out here in the spring? After the rains?"

"Yeah. So?"

"Green as Ireland for a week or two. One of the prettiest things on planet Earth."

"I guess. Then again, Ireland is always green as Ireland."

"Desert's a land of extremes. Of blacks and whites. Man knows where he stands out here. It tests his mettle. You know what a cactus wren is?"

"A bird?"

"Yeah." Jimmy pointed to a shoulder-height cholla cactus a few yards up the hill. "See that nest? About the size of a football?"

"Yeah."

"You ever notice it before?"

"Yeah, I've seen it."

"Ever see the bird that lives there?"

"Yeah. It comes and goes."

"That's a cactus wren. Out here everything and its brother wants to eat either her or her eggs. Snakes, owls, cats, everything. So she builds her nest in that cholla. Surrounds herself with spines. Nobody gets close to her, you know what I mean?"

"Yeah. She does what she has to do."

"I suppose she does. But it ain't a way to live."

"Sounds to me like she doesn't have a choice."

Jimmy smoked, milky eye on Bones. "Maybe she doesn't. Things can sure get to seem that way sometimes."

"Where'd you really get the box?"

"From a swami named Shamali on top of a mountain in Nepal."

"That's not true either, is it?"

"Who knows? Every maybe has its arm around the shoulders of a maybe not."

Bones considered pressing the subject, but the ghosts behind Jimmy's milky eye waved him off. "What happened to your eye?"

"That's an ugly story not worth repeating."

"Was it a fight?"

"The world can be a rough place."

"How long have you had that Harley?"

"Long time."

"Where'd you get it? From a swami named Shamali?"

"Nope. A guy in a tavern outside Natchez, Mississippi. True story."

"How much did it cost?"

"Everything, I imagine."

"How much is that in dollars?"

"Not everything can be counted in dollars. Are dollars that important to you?"

"Dollars are important to everybody."

"Nah, not everybody."

"They are if you don't have any. I would have sold that box to Nelson Black in a heartbeat. If I had a million dollars, I'd have a Harley even better than yours and be five hundred miles from here."

"And whatever problems you got right now would be strapped on your back when you pulled out and still be there wherever you stopped."

"Maybe, but I'd still have the Harley. What happened in Natchez that didn't cost dollars?"

"Bike used to belong to this skinny biker dude. He needed something else more than a bike."

"More than a Harley? What did he need?"

"You got any more coffee?"

"No. I have to get some more."

"Too bad. Let me ask you a question. What would you put in the box? Something you'd never see again."

"I don't know."

"Think. Anything at all. You put it in, and it's gone forever. Like it never happened."

"I can't think of anything."

Jimmy snuffed the cig under a boot and then started down the path to the motel. "When you do, you'll understand what a guy might need more than a Harley. You got enough dough for a battery?"

"Yeah. I just got paid."

"Grab it. After lunch, I'll take you into town."

CHAPTER TWENTY-FOUR

Bones was wind. Sky. A shooting star. He put his arms out, convinced he would fly if Jimmy went any faster. A NASA rocket straight up to the sun. Go out in a blaze.

And Jimmy did go faster. The boom of the Harley Davidson's pipes rattled the air, shook Bones's spine. Tears streaked back along his cheeks. It was the greatest sensation of his life. They pulled in miles and highway lines. Blew past a pickup with a bunch of Native kids in the back. Dodged a big rattlesnake stretched out in the road. Raced a jackrabbit and left it in the dust.

Yeah, man. Bones was born for this. He was alive.

When Jimmy offered him a ride into town, he'd figured they'd take a direct route to the auto parts store, but they'd been riding a couple of hours now. They'd hit Paradise, looped around the town square—where they'd made an old lady cover her ears—then ridden around the mission and north out through the ranches and farms to open desert. That's when Jimmy really opened her up.

Yeah, man. Rocket ships and shooting stars.

The wind was hot, the engine hotter against the inside of Bones's legs. Jimmy didn't mess around with lanes but rode the center line like he owned all the highways in the world. Up ahead, a gas station rose up out of the desert. Couple of pumps and a roll-up garage door with a little store next to it. Jimmy let off the gas with a great *braaaap* of the pipes and let the bike coast into the shade of an adobe lean-to overflowing with used tires. Bones climbed off and pulled the helmet from his sweat-dampened head.

"Man, that was awesome."

"I could use something cold to drink. How about you?" Jimmy said.

"Cool. I thought we were just going into town."

Jimmy strode toward the little store inside the station. "Did you? You wanna go back?"

"No way. I wanna ride."

"I figured."

The gas station building itself had been baked at 450 degrees for about eighty years. Peeling white paint with a faded *Rex's Garage* painted above the roll-up door. Beneath that somebody had added *Rexaco* with a spray can. No asphalt or concrete on the ground, but decades of oil stains on the dirt around the pumps most likely kept the dust down. Jimmy went inside and came out a minute or two later with a couple of Dr Peppers. He handed one to Bones and stuck his own in the crook of his arm while he lit a cig. "Nice place."

Bones stared at the man. "You serious?"

"Yeah, I'm serious. Why?"

"Beauty's in the eye of the beholder, I guess."

"To this beholder, it's a nice place."

Bones looked out at the million miles of empty desert spreading in all directions. "Whatever you say, man."

Jimmy took a seat on a bench against the wall, stretched his legs out in front of him, and crossed his ankles. "So what's with you and the boss?"

Bones stayed standing. "What do you mean?"

"You two don't get along?"

"I don't know. We mostly sort of stay out of each other's way."

"I noticed. Who's fault is that? Yours or hers?"

"Why does it have to be somebody's fault? Maybe it just is what it is."

"Doesn't have to be anyone's fault, I suppose. Just an observation."

"We both have our own things going on, that's all. I'm working on getting my bike going, and she has a motel to run."

"You don't like her?"

"She's okay. I think she thinks I'm strange, like everyone else. But maybe everybody else is strange and I'm normal."

"I told you before. Strange ain't bad. You are who you are."

"Not like I have a choice."

"Thing is, sometimes it's better to be who you are with people on your side. People who have your back."

"Calico doesn't have my back, so it doesn't matter anyway."

"What about the detective? Her fiancé? From what I hear it sounds like he's all right."

"Early's cool. But he mostly feels bad for me because he was Gomez Gomez's friend."

"The snake dude?"

"Yeah, the snake dude."

"You took that pretty hard, huh?"

"It wasn't fair. He was just getting his life together."

Jimmy lifted a shoulder and smoked.

"I mean, I know he wanted to be with his wife and everything," Bones said. "She got killed before."

"Sounds like he got what he needed."

"Maybe. I got a dead friend. And a dead dad."

Two streams of smoke came out of Jimmy's nostrils. "Well, I wouldn't write the boss off. I have a feeling she's a deeper river than she lets on."

"I just want to get my bike running."

Jimmy took a long swallow of his Dr Pepper, then snuffed the cig on the bench. "Sure. Be good to have some wheels under you." The man didn't seem to care whether Bones had a license, which was fine by him. Jimmy crushed his empty can and stood. "Ready to get that battery?"

"Yeah."

Bones had hoped they'd keep riding north a while, but Jimmy gunned it back toward Paradise. Once there, he took another loop around the town center. Early evening now, sun slanting sideways through the branches and leaves of the big oak. A guy sat on a picnic table next to a portable barbecue while his wife and kids played in the grass. The smell of grilling meat made Bones's stomach growl. They rolled past the mission, Shorty's Café, Finnegan's Bookstore, and then took a sharp right and exited the square. Five minutes later they cruised to a stop in front of Porter Auto.

"You know which one you need? Know the number? You write it down?" Jimmy said as Bones climbed off.

"I got it in my head."

"Good enough. I'll wait out here."

Inside the auto parts store, the air was cool and saturated with fluorescent light and low-volume country music. The kid behind the counter had a name tag that said Sean. Bones had seen him around school, but the only interaction they'd had was when Bones came into the store for parts.

"Hey," Sean said. "That thing running yet?"

"I need a battery. Maybe after that."

"Cool. What size?"

Bones gave him the battery number, and the kid headed back into the recesses of the parts shelves. In the aisle opposite, a guy and his wife discussed floor mats. The country song ended and "Sweet Home Alabama" came on.

Halfway through the song Sean came back carrying a battery. "This the one?" Bones had never really noticed how bad the guy's acne was. Poor kid's face looked like it was on fire.

He looked the battery over. "Yeah, that's it."

"It's an old CB 360, right?"

"Yeah."

"Cafe bike, man. Those things are cool. You get it running, you should bring it by. I might even buy it." Sean said this every time Bones came in.

Bones took the cash for the battery from his pocket. "Probably won't sell it. If it ever runs."

The kid scratched at a zit, then wiped his fingers on his pants before pointing to the big windows at the front of the store. "You come here with that dude?"

On the other side of the glass, Jimmy leaned against his Harley, smoking, of course. Ropey arm muscles like snakes under his skin.

"Yeah. He gave me a ride."

"Man, that's sweet. I'm gonna get a Harley one of these days myself."

"Cool."

Bones stood a little taller as he counted out the bills. Then, change in his pocket and battery under his arm, he headed for the front door. An electronic bell chimed in the back of the store, and the door swung open before he reached it. He was looking down, so all he saw at first was a pair of very shiny ostrich-skin boots in his path. He looked up into Don Jenkins's face.

His old foster grinned. "Heya, Bones. What are you up to? Buying parts for your tricycle?"

Bones stepped to the side, but so did Don, blocking his way.

"C'mon, dude," Bones said.

"C'mon, dude." Don laughed.

Bones stepped the other direction, but Don mirrored him.

"Knock it off," Bones said.

Another laugh. "Get that thing running, and I bet you can get it up to thirty-five miles per hour if you got a good wind behind you. Forty if you're going downhill."

Bones sidestepped again. So did Don. And in that moment Bones no longer wanted to be the prairie dog working behind the scenes. He wanted to be the guy with the .22. His anger rose. "Get out of my way, man."

"Whoa, is Bones getting mad? You losing your cool? I thought you were made of ice, man."

Bones hadn't realized his hands were fisted.

Grinning, Don touched Bones's chest with a finger. "You want to hit me, Bonesie? Really? After how we helped you out, man? That doesn't seem very grateful."

"You didn't help anything."

Don laughed again. Then he moved, but not on his own. He moved sideways and up and back all at the same time, Jimmy La Roux with a firm hold on the back of his collar with one hand and the seat of his pants with the other.

Bones stepped outside and let the door close behind him.

Jimmy's tone sounded almost bored. "I think you were in somebody's way. The proper term in a situation like that is *excuse me*. Or *pardon me* if you're from the South."

Don spun, his face going purple. "Get your hands off me, man!"

Jimmy held up his hands and looked at them. "You're a little behind the sequence of events, bud. I already did. That can be reversed, though. You ready, Bones?"

"Yeah."

"Go ahead and put the battery in the saddlebag."

"Okay."

Don cocked a fist but dropped it when Jimmy just grinned.

"You the Mega guy?" Jimmy said.

"Leave me alone."

"You bother Cozy or Bones again, and I'll find you."

"What?"

"You heard me."

Don looked at Bones, then back at Jimmy. "What? You got a thing for kids?"

"No, but I got a thing against bullies." Jimmy pushed the glass door open and held it. "Here you go, Skippy. You got some shopping to do, don't you?"

Don turned sideways, edging inside, keeping himself as far away from Jimmy as he could. "You think that Harley makes you something? I could buy a dozen of them things right now. I could toss my wallet on you and smash you like I'd smash a grape."

Jimmy smiled and let the door swing shut. He walked to the bike and climbed on.

His helmet in place, Bones swung on behind him. "I could have handled him."

"I don't doubt you could have. But don't be selfish. That was more fun than I've had in a while." Jimmy hit the gas, and within a few minutes they were winding down the mountain. When they hit Highway 41, he pulled over and stopped. "Your turn, kid."

"What?"

"You heard me."

"To drive?"

"You don't *drive* a motorcycle, but yeah, that's the idea." They both climbed off. "Think you can do it?"

"I don't know."

"I think you can. You've ridden before, right?"

"Yeah. Dirt bikes and stuff, but never a stinking Harley Davidson."

"Not much different. Same premise. Point her the direction you want to go, put her in gear, and let out the clutch slow."

"You're really serious? You'll let me?"

"Now or never. Make up your mind."

And then, there he was, Bones on a Harley Davidson. Maybe not flying as fast or as high as Jimmy had, but he was doing it. He was riding. He was in control. He laughed out loud. He rolled the throttle back, and his heart sped with the engine. Up ahead Lady Venus waved him in. "Can we go farther?" he shouted.

"Let her loose, amigo."

Bones caught a glimpse of Calico on the pool deck right before he hit the gas and shifted gears, but she didn't turn. He laughed again as he left the ground, and the desert faded in his rocket ship exhaust. He climbed higher, then higher. He blew through the atmosphere, and his laugh became a shout as he popped another gear, wheelied the moon, and blasted through the Milky Way.

He was alive.

CHAPTER TWENTY-FIVE

"Easy, you said. It'll be easy! This is not shaping up to be easy, Sal. August doesn't even have the money. And he carries a crazy cannon everywhere he goes."

Rufus had been walking back and forth for twenty minutes. He hated being stuck inside, and room twelve was no exception. At the moment, he also hated the Venus and the desert and most of all Sal, who was reclining on one of the two queen beds watching him.

Sal yawned. "Yet. He doesn't have the money *yet.* You heard him. It's gonna get delivered here. Just like he said in Todos Santos when we practically carried him back to his room. And he said Katz was the only other person to know about it, so we're golden. Will you stand still, Miller? I'm getting a neckache."

"The guy has a gun with a barrel the size of a fire hose, Sal. One Glenn Ford gave him, of all people."

"Yeah? Well, I never heard of the guy."

"That doesn't matter. What matters is we drove all the way here from Mexico because this was supposed to be easy. Two million bucks a stumbling drunk dude told us about in a bar. Two million no one else would miss because no one else knew about it."

"Can you believe we met Nelson Black? Just like that, the dude's walking down the sidewalk. Staying in the same motel as us."

"You could have been nicer."

"Why? He started it. What kind of guy doesn't give autographs?"

"The busy kind."

"What's he busy with at the Venus? While we're here, we oughta figure out a way to rip him off too."

"Leave Black alone. Figuring out this August thing gives me enough to worry about." Rufus shook his head. "Easy."

"You're the one said this would be easy. I never said that. Two mil ain't gonna be easy on general principle."

"Man, you know how far two mil would go in Mexico? A long, long way."

"Italy."

"They don't sur—" What was he doing arguing with this guy? "Forget it, Sal. We need to get the money, that's all."

"We will."

"At this point, I'm having my doubts."

"Nothing's changed. It's just gonna take a little longer. The money's on its way, and when it gets here we'll take it and go."

"No, when it gets here we'll get shot between the eyes with a John Wayne pistol. You heard what Dave said about snakes. We're the snakes, Sal. And the stupid thing is we're broke, man. Totally broke. We can't even afford gas back to Todos Santos."

"We ain't going to Todos. We're going to Italy. And by the way, this is the problem. You're calling the guy Dave like he's our friend or something. He's not Dave to us. He's a drunk with a truckload of money. He's a cockroach. Which, lucky us, makes you and me the opposite of broke. We're gonna have two million in cash. That's a million each. So quit whining and let's see what's on TV. Maybe they got one of those fixer-upper shows on. Or sharks on Discovery or something."

"Are you hearing me, Sal? The guy has a *gun*. We're not getting that money."

"You think he has eyes in the back of his head or something?"

"It doesn't matter."

Sal sighed and lifted his shirt. He pulled a small, very wicked-looking pistol from his waistband. "Maybe we got a little something too. How about that?"

"What's that?"

"What's it look like?"

"It looks like a pistol, man."

"Give the man a cigar."

"Where did you get a pistol?"

"Tucson."

"When?"

"At the Motel 6 when you were all knocked out on Tylenol PM."

"I had a headache. It was a long drive."

"Whatever. I met a couple of guys at that watering hole down from the 6. They hooked me up with some hardware. Turns out it's leveling the playing field."

"You bought a gun?"

Sal pointed the pistol at the television set and closed one eye. "It ain't a chinchilla, pal."

"Don't point that thing, man. Why in the world would you buy a gun?"

Sal sighed and put the pistol on the bed. "I just said. You never know who else might have one, and it levels the playing field. You know, man, your lack of good old common street sense really gets to me sometimes. You spout off all these words and facts and figures, but you think we're gonna walk in here and ask a dude, drunk or not, pretty please for two million dollars, and then he's gonna hand it over, pat us on our heads, and send us on our merry way? You're living in a dream world. This ain't no beach, Miller. It's real life."

"Yeah, I thought we could. You saw the man in Todos. As much as I hate to admit it, because he *was* at one time brilliant, he's lost it. He's a walking rum sponge. So, yeah, I thought relieving him of two million dollars he'd probably never even miss, remember, or even care about would be neither a hard nor dangerous proposition. I thought we'd be back across the border by now."

"That ain't how the world works. Not when we're talking this kind of cash."

"Yeah, but a gun? It's not like we're going to kill anybody."

"You sure about that? Two mil is two mil. You wouldn't off a guy for two mil?"

"Look, man. Relieving a drunk of a little cash he doesn't need is one thing. Murder is another altogether. Murder is life in prison stuff. And now other people know about the money. He blabbed it in the lounge. These kind of people are called witnesses. Not to mention—"

"I'm curious, Miller. Why is it whenever you use the phrase *not to mention* you always go ahead and mention what isn't to be mentioned?"

"Stop it. Not to mention this is David stinking August we're talking about. The guy is a literal American treasure, man."

"He's a cockroach like every other cockroach."

"We're not killing David August, Sal. We're not killing anybody. We're the good kind of thieves, remember? We're like Robin Hood."

"Is that what you tell yourself? Do I look like I'm wearing green tights to you? Nobody wants to see that. Let me ask you something. When we *relieved* that art dealer in Costa Mesa of his retirement fund, did we give any of that dough to the poor? How about the Disney tickets scam? All those kiddies who wanted to see Mickey? They probably bawled their sorry little eyes out."

"They still got to see Mickey."

"How do you know?"

"Because they have parents who love and care for them, that's how I know. I'm sure they bought them real tickets when they couldn't use the ones we sold. They also probably teach their kids to stay away from guns, unlike whoever raised you."

"My aunt Ninetta raised me. You know that, so be very careful what you say."

"I know your aunt Ninetta raised you. What I didn't know was dear old Aunt Ninetta robbed mini-marts in her spare time."

"I'm warning you, Miller. Don't talk about Aunt Ninetta like that. The woman was a saint."

"Look. It's nothing against Aunt Ninetta, all right? I'm just worked up. I don't like guns, and I'm starting not to like this whole thing. I want to get out of this room, out of this desert, find a beach, and surf till I pass out."

"What happened to being relaxed, man? We'll scare the dude, that's all. Guy like that, he'll fold like a cheap suit. We'll relieve him of the cash and beat it for wherever we're gonna beat it to. Probably Italy."

"Mexico."

"We'll cross that bridge when we get there."

"Or Costa Rica. They have some really nice surf breaks on the Pacific side."

"Yeah? Actually, Costa Rica doesn't sound like a bad idea. What's their food like?"

"Lots of chicken and rice and beans. And probably seafood. But we're not killing David August."

"Not unless he gives us no choice. I do like seafood. They have lobster in Costa Rica?"

"Costa Rica means rich coast, Sal. I imagine they have lobster. I imagine they have lots of things. And there's always a choice. For instance, one choice would be getting in the Pontiac and driving away without murdering somebody."

"Rich coast. I like that. We'll be rich on the rich coast. We ain't driving away from two million dollars."

"Sure, we don't want to. But we will if we have to."

Sal picked up the gun and sighted it on a picture of a coyote by the door. "Rich coast. That's beautiful. We'll see. Who's up for a martini?"

CHAPTER TWENTY-SIX

His hands still tingling from the Harley, Bones felt good. Even hopeful. As soon as the Honda was fixed, he'd fly so high and fast even the satellites wouldn't see him. No more Dons or snakes or dead dads. Yeah, he felt good. And so invisible tonight he almost couldn't see himself.

Juan was blind-busy at the stove in the kitchen, so Bones grabbed a plateful of fries and a plastic squeeze bottle of salsa. Then Calico didn't look up from her computer when he fished a Mexican Coke out of the bar cooler. The Great Nowak and his pals didn't even twitch an eye in his direction as he slid into his usual booth near the stage. He could have sat on the piano bench next to Jimmy and no one would have noticed.

Nelson Black was here, sitting at a table not far from the stage, sipping a honey-colored scotch with no ice. Not-So-Great-Nowak was here too, with a couple of his tagalongs, occupying a table close to Black's. Nowak had the same drink as the magic guy, and he watched Black while the man watched Jimmy. Jimmy mostly watched his hands on the piano keys or Cozy, who was singing a Patsy Cline song.

The box sat on the piano watching no one.

Only a handful of others were in the lounge, all engaged in quiet conversation except for Burt Calloway. He sat at a table by himself, hat pulled down low, edges of his mouth turned down. He also watched Cozy.

After a minute or two, Cozy finished falling to pieces and stepped down for a break. She smiled and waved at Burt as she passed through the room. Bones was surprised to see the cheeks above the cowboy's thick mustache flush slightly as he managed an awkward nod.

Jimmy slid into some of his blue jazz.

Black turned to Nowak. "You're staring at me."

The Great Nowak looked like he wanted to crawl under the table. "Sorry, Mr. Black."

"You have to understand. You're like Jesus Christ to this man," one of the tagalongs said. He had some kind of pathetic goatee going on.

Black arched a brow, pursed his lips. "The big J. C." He leaned forward. "Really. Water to wine? Things like that? How's your water, by the way, Mr. Nowak?"

Nowak looked down at a glass on the table. The liquid in it had turned purple.

"Try it," Black said. "You'll find it much better than the Middle East swill I can only imagine they had two thousand years ago."

"How?" Nowak said, grinning.

Black chuckled. "Jesus Christ. That sounds so sacrilegious, doesn't it?"

"It was just a figure of speech," goatee guy said. "I only meant he admires you."

Black looked thoughtful. "Yes. Tell me, Mike. Do you remember the story about Christ being offered the kingdoms of the world? He could have had them all right then and there. All he had to do was bend a little." He held up thumb and forefinger demonstrating a tiny gap. "Just a little. Do you remember?"

"Yeah, sure. It's a Sunday school story."

"Why do you think he declined?"

The man shrugged. "I don't know. It's just a story."

"Of course it is. Still . . . By the way, aren't you going to taste the wine?"

Nowak lifted the glass and sipped. "Not bad."

"Not bad? That's a Lafite Rothschild. Only a 2008, mind you—let's not get carried away—but still an excellent wine." Black's hand shifted slightly, and a wine glass appeared in it. He swirled the purple liquid, lifted it to the light, then stuck his nose in the glass and sniffed. "I myself prefer the '82. Oh, I know people talk about the '89, but they're such sheep. Let's get back to *just a story*. I'll tell you why old J. C. didn't bow."

He sipped the wine, then lifted his hands. The wine glass had disappeared from one and appeared in the other. "Because too much power can be a heady thing. Frightening to some, like oxygen to others. An addiction, even. Take our friend Jimmy, here. He holds on to his metal box with white knuckles. Like a heroin addict with a needle."

"How'd he do that with the glass?" Goatee guy was chatty.

Nowak shrugged and shook his head.

"That all sounds pretty blasphemous." Tagalong two this time. "Actually, a lot blasphemous."

The wine glass disappeared again, and Black now held a refilled tumbler of scotch. "They say you shouldn't mix wine with hard liquor, but I've never found it a problem. Blasphemous—it's a made-up word, in my humble opinion. We are what we are, and we are alone. I suggest you not be so sensitive."

"Yeah, don't be so sensitive," Nowak said.

Black set the scotch on the table. A small pop sounded, and a cigarette appeared between his index and middle finger. Another pop, and the tip of his opposite index flamed like a lighter. "Calico," he called. "Do you mind if I smoke?"

"Yes I do," she called back, eyes still on the computer screen.

Black showed mock disappointment as cig and flame vanished. "So many rules these days." He picked up the scotch again.

Nowak grinned and shook his head, looking like he was about to applaud.

Black leaned back. "Tell me, Nowak the Great. Being so great, what was your greatest triumph? Your greatest trick? Did it involve doves or rabbits? Women sawed in half?"

"I mostly worked with cards."

"Cards? I love card tricks. Show me."

Nowak's cheeks flamed. "Well, I don't have a—"

"Try your shirt pocket."

Nowak reached up and pulled out a deck. "I—"

"What now? Do you ask me to pick a card?"

"I could I guess, but—"

"Go ahead, then. Ask me."

Nowak stood and approached. He fanned the deck and held the cards out facedown.

Black put a finger to his lips and narrowed his eyes as he studied the deck. He pulled out a card. "Do I look at it?"

"Sure," Nowak said.

Black did.

"Now put it back in the deck."

Black did.

Nowak shuffled, shuffled again, then pulled out a card and held it out for Black to see. "This your card?"

Black grinned and clapped his hands together. "Excellent."

"Queen of hearts," Nowak said. He flipped it over, and his face fell.

"What?" The two tagalongs spoke at the same time, as if synchronized somehow.

Nowak studied the face of the card for a long few seconds. He looked at Black. "How do you know about this?"

"About what?" By now Bones didn't care which one of the tagalongs spoke. His eyes stayed on Black and Nowak.

"Mr. Nowak's little tax issue," Black said. "It's a true conundrum. It's all printed there on the card if you want to see."

"This is private information." Nowak looked stunned more than angry.

Black smiled. "Which is what makes illusion so fun, don't you think? Hey, why don't you pick another card?"

"What?"

"Any card. Just pull one from the deck. Let's see if the news is happy this time."

Nowak pulled a card from the deck and flipped it over. He read, then pulled out his wallet and laid a few bills on the table. "I'm done. Let's go."

The tagalongs both opened their mouths, but Black jumped in before any words came out. "I'm sure you compadres wonder why Nowak here wants to leave so soon. It's all there on the card. It simply points out that when one's wife . . . in this case, Jackie, I believe. You know, the solid old gal? Anyway, she's so under the weather, it might be better form to be home where one might be needed. Even if I am considered to be on the same level as God's Son. Nasty flu, I'm afraid. At least we hope that's all it is." Black looked at Nowak. "Tsk-tsk. Shame, shame, shame."

Nowak's face reddened. "I don't see how it's any of your business."

Black winked. "Chicken soup. That's the ticket."

Nowak shook his head as he headed for the door. His friends followed, throwing a couple of confused backward glances at Black.

The wine was back. Black sipped.

Jimmy's blue jazz was a slow shuffle. "That was a mean thing to do, Nelson."

"I really can't help it. It's so easy."

"It's petty. TV preacher stuff."

"I know. It would never fly in New York or Vegas."

"Sure it would."

"Yes, I suppose it would." He sipped, then sighed. "I'm bored, Jimmy. That's the thing. Sell me the box. Rescue me from this season of mediocrity and too-easy shills. Have you considered my offer?"

"You said I'm an addict. Do you even need to ask?"

"Two million dollars."

A line formed in Jimmy's cheek when he smiled. "What's next in your little Lucifer act? You offer me all the kingdoms of the world?"

"Why not? You seem to like playing Jesus. Would it work?"

"What do you think?"

Black stood, walked over to the box, lifted the lid, and dropped his empty scotch glass in with a *thunk*. "Bedtime, I think."

"Good night, Nelson."

"See you soon, Jimmy."

CHAPTER TWENTY-SEVEN

CALICO FINISHED UP WITH THE inventory spreadsheet and left the computer to ponder its screen saver. She'd changed out the CO_2 and nitrous tanks and started dusting some of the rarely used bottles on the shelf behind the bar when Cozy came out of the kitchen. She had a bowl of Juan's menudo in her hand.

"You actually eat that stuff?"

"Of course. I'm starving."

"Do you like it?"

"I love it. Don't you?"

Calico gave a slight shudder. "I'm not an intestines type of girl."

Cozy shrugged and took a bite.

"You sound great tonight, by the way."

Cozy smiled. "I found out C is a good key for me. B and B-flat too, depending on the tune. Jimmy calls them tunes, not songs."

"Good for you."

"I like it here."

"I like having you here."

Cozy took another bite, then swallowed. "Why are you frowning?"

"I got a call from Don a little while ago. He says he's been trying to get ahold of you."

"He can try all he wants. I don't have a phone anymore."

"Oh. Well, do you want to know what he said? It's not good."

"I'm used to not good. Tell me."

"I'm honestly not sure I want to. This is an awkward spot, and I want you to know how sorry I am."

"What did he say?"

"He said he's selling the double-wide, and if you want the rest of your stuff, you should come get it this week."

Cozy stared. "He's selling it? I thought he'd never leave that place, even with the Mega money."

"Tanya's moving in with him. He's buying them a place in The Harbors."

The pain in Cozy's eyes broke Calico's heart.

Cozy didn't speak for several seconds, then said, "I think he's had his eye on her for a long time. I mean, he always flirted with any woman who came across his path, but I figured that was just him. That he didn't mean it. But he did start spending a whole lot of time down at the Pick-a-Part. And now he's rich, so it's a no-brainer for her. I can't believe Tanya is going to be a Harbor duck."

"I'm so, so sorry, Cozy."

"Thank you. I'll be okay."

"What happened to your phone?"

"I put it in Jimmy's box. Don kept texting me mean stuff, and I got tired of hearing him tell me how horrible I was."

"Couldn't you have just turned it off?"

"Some things you can't turn off. I think I was really getting rid of Don's lies, anyway. That's what Jimmy said. And I do feel better. Ugh. The worst part is stupid Tanya will look great in stupid yoga pants. What was I thinking all those years?"

"You were loyal. You're a loyal person. He's an idiot, Cozy. You're a prize."

"Look where loyalty got me."

"It got you to the Venus. And up on the stage. Hey, speaking of loyal, Burt keeps looking over here."

Cozy blushed. "He's a nice man. Very lost, but a nice man. You want to talk about loyal? He still carries his dead wife's wedding ring around in his pocket. Don would never do something like that in a billion years."

"Regardless, he's interested in you. You see that, right?"

"In me?" Cozy looked over. "I doubt that. He owns a big ranch."

"So?"

"I'm a trailer girl. Don was wrong about a lot of things, but he was right about that part. I'm not in the same league as a man like Burt."

"If you ever say that again, I'll fire you on the spot."

"Really?"

"No, but don't put yourself down. You're a special person. Anyone with half a brain can see that."

"I'm not, but thank you."

"I'm serious, Cozy. You're beautiful and nice, and you have a voice like butter and warm blankets. You're what's called a package. Any man would be lucky to have you."

"I . . . I haven't always been nice. Burt likes my singing, that's all. You're reading into it. He's in love with his wife and always will be. Look at him. I bet he's thinking about her right now. It's so sad and sweet it makes me want to cry."

"Maybe he's thinking about you."

"Stop it. I'm serious."

"So am I. I haven't seen him drink anything but coffee the last couple of nights."

"So?"

"I don't know. It gives me the feeling he's stumbled into some hope somehow. Speaking of coffee, I bet his is either gone or cold. Why don't you go check?"

"Now I'm embarrassed to even go over there. I feel self-conscious."

"Sorry, but it's your job. You do work here, don't forget. See if Nelson Black needs anything while you're at it."

"Fine. Speaking of Nelson Black, it's so bizarre. He sits there salivating over Jimmy's box like a dog over a steak. He honestly creeps me out. It's so weird to see him in person after watching him on television."

“I wouldn’t know. I never even heard of him until he got here.”

“He’s huge. You know how they say people are always different in person? I think he’s equally creepy either way. I always thought they made him like that on TV, but he’s exactly the same. What do you think of the box?”

“I think it’s a nice trick. And I think Jimmy has your phone somewhere.”

“I don’t know about that, but I really do feel better without it. Like I’ve made a step away from Don’s control. A step in the right direction. And I don’t know, but . . . I mean, Nelson Black is world-famous, but he wants that box so bad he’s still here. It’s strange, don’t you think? I mean, there has to be something more to the thing than a trick.”

“You’re around Jimmy more than anyone. What does he say?”

“He says it’s an old metal box. Like it’s nothing. But things disappear, and he won’t say anything about how or where they go. What would you put in there? How about whatever’s going on between you and Early?”

“Am I that obvious?”

“More than obvious.”

“I wish I could just get rid of it. I really do. But what’s going on between Pines and me won’t go into any box. Pines might disappear, though, no box needed.”

“No way. I’ve known Early a while. He’s the type who, if he’s really in it, won’t go anywhere. Talk about loyal, when he came to get Bones, I thought he’d knock Don into the middle of next week. Don had it coming for sure. I secretly kind of hoped Early would deck him, but he kept his cool.”

“Very un-Pines like.”

“Maybe, but you’ve changed him. At least that’s what everybody says.”

“Paradise really is a small town, isn’t it?”

“Absolutely.”

“Well, I hope I haven’t changed him too much.”

Cozy gave a slight head shake. “Only in a good way. I’ll go make the table rounds.”

"Say something nice to Burt. It's wrecking me the way he keeps sneaking glances over here."

"That's your imagination."

"We'll see."

Burt nodded and smiled as Cozy refilled his coffee cup. They talked for almost a minute before Cozy moved on. When she left, he watched her go, his hand moving subconsciously to his pocket. Which made Calico think of Pines, of course.

Everything made her think of Pines. She fingered her engagement ring. It wasn't a huge diamond—Pines wasn't a huge-diamond type any more than she was a cow's-stomach type. But it was hers, and she loved it. She loved him. But was love enough? This was real life they were talking about. It was uncontrollable, even with a notebook full of pros and cons. Things happened. Life was life. Life was unsure. Life shoved you onto the wrong side of the fence. In life, people left.

And people failed. In her mind she heard hail pelting a hospital window, saw her brother the first time she'd gone to pick him up from the police department in Tucson. He'd been sixteen. She'd been only a couple of years older. She hadn't been able to find her dad that day. He'd been out in the desert somewhere looking for a rumored lost gold mine. So she'd driven the more than three hours to Tucson by herself. And now Pines wanted her to fail all over again.

She picked up a bar towel and started wiping down the counter.

On the piano, the box glinted. She'd have to remember to ask Jimmy for Cozy's phone.

CHAPTER TWENTY-EIGHT

Bones had never seen an armored truck before. So when one pulled into the parking lot, he naturally set down his broom and went invisible. A uniformed, sunglassed man stepped out of the passenger side, hand resting on the butt of the pistol on his belt, and surveyed the property. His gaze lingered longest on the Venus sign out by the highway.

Calico stepped out from the office, hand shielding her eyes against the sun. "Can I help you?"

The man was all business. "I have a delivery for a Mr. Edgar Filmore."

Calico pointed to the truck's license plate. "All the way from California?"

"We drove through the night."

"You must be tired. I hate to tell you, but we don't have an Edgar Filmore registered."

"Of course you do." David August stood across the parking lot by the pool gate, today in a pair of bright-purple trunks with sea turtles printed on them. He had a bottle of rum in one hand and his pistol in the other. "I'm sort of Edgar Filmore. You can bring the delivery over here. And why did Fred send an armored truck? Does he want to announce this to the world?"

The uniformed man shielded his eyes in August's direction. "I'll need you to put down the weapon, sir."

August only laughed. "Will you? Just bring the money over."

"Do you have identification?"

"As Filmore? I do not. But dial up Fred Katz and tell him that besides this delivery of yours, he owes me a steak from the Dodger game bet and that his wife looks like a manatee with a mustache."

"Excuse me?"

"I assure you I'm dead serious. Call him and say exactly that."

The man shrugged, climbed back into the truck, and shut the door. He consulted with the driver for a few seconds, then got out his cell phone. He spoke, nodded, spoke again, then climbed back out. He lifted the phone, took a photo of August, pressed the screen, and waited. His phone buzzed, and he answered.

Another half minute and he looked at August. "Mr. Katz wants to know what happened to your head. He says you look like you got run over by a lawn mower. He also says you're right. Mrs. Katz does look like a manatee with a mustache."

"Did he tell you to give me my delivery?"

"He did. I'll need you to sign."

"I'd rather not."

"What?"

"I only used three words. Was it really that hard to understand?"

"I understand fine, but you'll have to sign for this. That's standard procedure."

"Look around you. You're in the middle of the desert talking to a man with a scabby head, purple swim trunks, and a pistol. Does any of this seem like standard procedure?"

"Actually, we deliver to a lot of strange situations for Mr. Katz. I'll need you to sign. This is a rather large delivery."

"Not large enough. Fred caught me at a vulnerable moment. It should be twice what we agreed on."

"That's none of my business, sir."

"Untraceable and string free, that was the deal. No signature. Call him again."

The man made another call. This time he spoke for only several seconds before ending it. "Fine. But Mr. Katz says he'll ruin your life if he doesn't see a manuscript by January. And the steak dinner is a no-go."

"He'll get the manuscript. He'll have pirates and damsels in distress and chests of gold coming out his oversized and pointy ears. Please tell him I said so, and feel free to use those exact words."

Bones caught a movement out of the corner of his eye. Rufus stepping out of his room in worn board trunks and flip-flops. He stretched, slung a towel over his shoulder, and started for the pool.

"Do you mind, Russell?" August said. "We need to finish up a little business here."

"My apologies, Dave. You go right ahead and do your thing." Rufus stepped back into the room, but the door didn't close all the way.

The uniformed man walked around and unlocked the back of the truck, opened the door, and took out a standard-looking briefcase with hard sides. He walked across the lot and handed it to August. "I don't like not getting a signature."

"And I don't like spiders and adverbs. Life is a precarious channel to navigate. How about a drink before you go on your merry way?"

"No, thanks."

August saluted by putting the barrel of the pistol flat against his forehead and snapping it down. "Dismissed then, private. Thank you for your service."

The man shook his head as he walked back to the truck.

Bones ghosted along the sidewalk to the end of the Venus, then slipped over to the pool. He took up a spot next to the pool shed and pretended to be interested in the pool-cleaning tools.

August was sprawled on a deck chair now, eyes closed. A towel protected his stubbly head from the sun. He had a bottle and the pistol both balanced on his gut. The briefcase sat on the ground next to his chair. It had no special markings. It reminded Bones of the briefcase his dad took to work at the car dealership to carry titles and contracts and lunch and a dozen other boring things Bones had sifted through when no one was looking. But car titles didn't arrive on armored trucks. And it didn't require a signature to accept delivery of a peanut butter sandwich. That truck had dropped off something of value. Big value.

August snorted a small rum-soaked snore.

And Rufus ambled onto the deck.

CHAPTER TWENTY-NINE

Bones, already invisible but wanting a little insurance, slipped into the open door of the pool shed. Something about Rufus nagged at him. The guy's body language or maybe the way he'd appeared right after the armored truck pulled up gave Bones the feeling he was up to something. And it wasn't only a swim.

Rufus glanced down at August but didn't address him or even stop at the writer's chair. At the pool's edge, he tossed his towel onto a table and slipped out of his flip-flops. He was tall, at least six four or five. Long and lean with tribal-looking seascape tattoos covering both arms and part of his torso. An ugly scar, white against his tan, ran nearly from his right shoulder blade to his waist. He stretched and leaned forward, each vertebrae visible down the center of his back. When he finally dove in, he hardly made a ripple.

Rufus swam laps for several minutes. Bones watched, hoping the whole time Calico wouldn't notice he was missing and call for him. At length, Rufus came to a stop where he'd started and propped his folded arms on the pool's edge. He made a show of leaning his head back and enjoying the sun on his face, but his eyes, narrowed to slits, were obviously fixed on August, who was snoring.

Rufus continued to watch. It reminded Bones of a nature show he'd seen one time where a praying mantis killed a lizard twice its size. The insect had blended in with its surroundings, motionless, infinitely patient until the time was right. The lizard had never seen the attack coming. And that lizard hadn't been passed out with a bottle of rum on its gut.

Rufus waited. So did Bones. The pool pump whirred to life, humming quietly in the back of the shed. A bird landed on the fence opposite the pool, fluffed its feathers a few times, then flew off. Then in one effortless, smooth motion, Rufus lifted himself up onto the deck. Water streamed silently off his body. He reached for the towel and dried quickly, then picked up his flip-flops rather than sliding them on. He glanced toward the Venus and around the pool deck, then moved on silent feet toward August.

He stopped by the writer's deck chair, eyes shifting back and forth from the pistol on August's stomach to the case. Mantis and lizard—the resemblance was crazy. Another glance around, and then he moved forward ever so slightly.

A V-8 engine rumbled to life. Sal and Rufus's Pontiac. Bones could see Sal's fat form behind the wheel. It would make for a smooth and quick getaway.

A tall aluminum pool broom leaned against the shed just outside the door. A clatter from a pole like that would wake any rummy from sleep. Bones considered the options. With a little push it was in his power to save whatever was in August's case from almost certain theft. Then again, what was it to him? The world spun, and the fittest—or the most invisible—survived to rule the day. If David August was foolish enough to drink rum and pass out in the sun with something valuable on him, he almost deserved to lose it.

Then again, he was a guest of the motel, and Bones did work here. And if the thieves disappeared with the case, how did Bones benefit? But if he happened to save the day, that might be a playable card at some point.

Rufus leaned slowly down toward the case.

Bones moved a hand toward the pool broom.

"Can I help you with something, Russell?" August said, eyes still closed.

"Oh, heya, Dave. You had an ant about to crawl on you. Didn't want to wake you."

"Aw, I never sleep all that hard, buddy. An ant's not going to hurt anything. They drink very little rum."

"Good. Good to know."

August shifted the pistol a little. "Good thing it wasn't a snake, though. I'd have had to put one through his eye."

CHAPTER THIRTY

IF THERE WAS ONE PLACE Bones would miss when he left Paradise in his Honda dust, it was the Jesus Is Coming Soon Thrift Store. It occupied an old brick building that took up an entire corner of downtown.

A gigantic, faded mural on the side portrayed an angry-looking Christ figure descending from a cloud in a rain of lightning bolts and fire. In opposing hands he held a sheep and a goat by the scruffs of their necks. Whoever painted the thing back around Moses's time had been a lousy artist, and the two animals were practically indistinguishable. The problem had been overcome simply and effectively by painting the word *sheep* under one and *goat* under the other. Under it all, in huge block letters, was the cheerful slogan LOOK UP FOR YOUR JUDGMENT DRAWETH NIGH!

The whole thing had fascinated Bones from the moment he'd seen it as a kid. Last week, when he'd been cleaning rooms, on a whim he tried to find the phrase in one of the Gideon Bibles in all the nightstand drawers. But he couldn't. He was starting to think maybe the artist had it wrong. From everything he'd read, people did stuff like that in religion all the time. Usually when they were trying to control someone else.

The double glass doors were open to let in the breeze, but it was still hot inside. Bones checked out the clothes for a minute or two, found a T-shirt that said *Fat People Are Harder to Kidnap*, and slung it over his shoulder. Then he headed upstairs to the books section.

Paradise had a couple of other thrift stores, but they had a few books scattered throughout or just a shelf or two. Jesus Is Coming Soon took books so seriously they'd dedicated a whole second-floor room with rows and rows of shelves and stacks of books when the shelves ran out. Mismatched tile floors. Old wood boards in places the tile had come up. Dusty beams of light coming through high-up windows. Musty, crusty perfection.

As usual, Bones was alone in there. Calico would be busy most of the afternoon, so he had a while. No use trying to peruse certain sections, topics, or genres, anyway. Any sense of order in the place had long ago been abandoned. It was a beautiful dice roll. You never knew what you might come across. Bones liked to start in the back and work his way forward. He'd done it dozens of times, but he always seemed to stumble across something he hadn't seen before.

He wasn't even five minutes in when he found a book about Ernest Shackleton and the ship *Endurance*. Its cover—with a tall, masted ship leaning to one side and stuck in an ice floe—caught his eye right off the bat. He picked it up and thumbed it for a few seconds. Next thing he knew he was engrossed, lost in the sweeping vistas and bitter cold of the Antarctic. He was deep into chapter four when a voice pulled him back to Arizona in half a second.

"A brave man, that Shackleton."

He usually heard the floors creak when someone came into the room.

"Yeah," Bones said. "So I'm finding out."

The man held out a hand. "I'm Nelson Black."

"I know who you are."

"And yet you don't look impressed. Aren't you a fan of illusion?"

Bones looked the man up and down. "Why do you always wear black? Is that your thing or something? Like an act?"

"I guess you could call it that. Publicists, you know? Always working an angle. All about the image. You don't like black?"

"It's cool, I guess."

"Your name is Bones, correct?"

This took Bones by surprise. He had no idea Nelson Black would know he was alive. "How do you know that?"

"It's not magic, if that's what you're thinking. You work at the Venus, and I've noticed you slinking around. You like to slink."

Bones wasn't sure what to say to this, but he went with, "I don't slink."

"That's exactly what you do. You slink." Black took a book off a shelf and considered it. "Are you surprised I noticed you?"

"A little."

"Noticing things and people is important in my line of work. I noticed you seem to do the same. You listen and you notice, and unless I miss my guess, and I rarely do, you file away what you notice." Black shut the book with a *thwump*. "Faulkner, ick. What a waste of time. I never could understand what people saw in the man."

"I kind of like Faulkner."

Black arched a brow. "You know his work?"

"I read a lot."

"Do you?"

Something about Black made Bones feel like a cat getting his fur rubbed the wrong way. "Yeah, I do. And I like Faulkner. That's why I said it."

"No need to get testy."

Bones looked back at his book, hoping the guy would take a hint and leave.

"You remind me of him, you know?" Black said.

"Faulkner?"

"Shackleton. I imagine he was like you."

"I doubt it."

"Why? You're stubborn, and you're driven. You're also smart."

"Maybe I'm complacent and lazy and stupid. You don't know anything about me. You're guessing."

"No, I'm not guessing. I notice, remember? Take Shackleton. He wanted something. He wanted to survive. Odds were monumentally against him, but he managed it. He escaped what most would consider the unescapable—the Antarctic. You want to escape too, don't you?

You want to escape your Antarctic, which is the Venus. You want to escape Paradise, Arizona. You want to see the world. And don't ask me how I know this. We've already established how."

"You notice."

"Exactly right."

"So? What if I do want to get out of here? What's it to you?"

Black picked up another book. "*How to Raise Chickens*. I suppose I'd take Faulkner over chickens, but it would definitely be close." He set the book down. "You and Jimmy La Roux are friends." This last bit a statement, not a question.

"I wouldn't say that. I barely know the dude."

"Really? You're together a lot. He took you for a ride on his motorcycle. I don't believe he does that with people very often."

"So?"

"And you're an underdog. He's a sap for underdogs."

"I'm not an underdog. You make me sound like a loser."

"Losers, Bones, are people who lose. You've lost a lot in your life. In fact, have you ever won?"

"I've won."

"I'm not talking about one of your juvenile confidence tricks. I'm talking about really winning. Really getting ahead. I believe getting ahead in life has so far eluded you. So if I were to say you were a loser, it wouldn't necessarily be a slight. Simply fact. I believe you've done the best with the hand you were dealt. The thing is, cards are easily manipulated. So the hand you're dealt isn't the hand you have to play."

Black studied the spine of a period romance, a woman on the cover clinging to a shirtless man in a kilt. "Ick."

"You mean I should cheat."

"Of course I do. Cheating is a part of life. It's a requisite skill for survival. Do you have a problem with cheating?"

"Not really."

"I didn't think so. In fact, I think you're probably rather deft at the discipline." Black tossed the romance over the shelf into another aisle. "Have you put anything in Jimmy's box yet?"

"No."

"Why not?"

"I don't know. I just haven't."

"Interesting. I want it, you know."

"Yeah."

"I've tried to buy it, but you already know that as well."

"I heard."

"Jimmy won't sell the box. He's a stubborn man."

"Maybe. Or maybe the offer isn't high enough."

This stopped Black. "Did he say that? Does he want more money?"

"I don't know, man. I'm only guessing. It seems to me like anything would be for sale if the price was high enough."

Black nodded. "It does, doesn't it? My thoughts exactly. Unfortunately, that hasn't been my experience with Jimmy La Roux."

"Why are you in a thrift store, anyway? You're not the kind of guy who needs a deal."

"You're wrong. I love deals. I make them all the time. Plus thrift stores are fascinating places. Full of people's unrealized dreams and leftover lives."

"That's pretty dark."

"Yes, it is, but still interesting. I want you to get me the box."

"Me?"

"Yes."

"Why do you think I can do that?"

"Jimmy likes you. You could talk to him. Maybe he'll sell."

"Dude puts out cigarettes on his hand, man. He's not gonna listen to some kid."

"Hmm. I beg to differ."

"You can beg all you want. It's not gonna change facts."

"Okay. Steal it, then."

"What? No way."

"Why not? Haven't you ever stolen anything?"

Bones hesitated.

"Don't be ashamed of it," Black said. "Sometimes we want something we can't afford. Something that isn't ours. So we steal it."

"Like you want the box."

"Exactly. It's simply the way of the world. I'm not ashamed of it. And I'll do you the courtesy of not sugarcoating it. After all, you and I are men of the world."

"I'm not stealing Jimmy's box for you. It's out of the question."

"What if I paid you?"

"No way."

"You said it yourself, anything is for sale if the price is high enough. So the only question is what you want in return for stealing the box. Think about it. What's enough?"

"I don't need to think about it. Nothing. No deal."

"No? I guarantee Shackleton would have made a deal to get him out of his frozen Venus Motel."

"That was life or death."

"Everything is either life or death. That's the nature of existence."

"I'm not helping you." Bones stood. "I gotta go."

"No you don't. Calico won't be done for hours. What if I gave you what you want most in the world—to get away? That's it, right? And who can blame you? Look at this place."

"You don't know me."

"We've already established what a fallacy that statement is. Bones, my friend, I can read you like"—he picked up another book and looked at the cover—"this volume on the intricacies of renaissance dance. I think I'd take chickens over that."

"I gotta go."

"I'm not stopping you. Tell you what, though. Why don't you take a look at page one hundred twenty-three before you go?"

"In this book? Shackleton?"

"Yes, that book."

Bones thumbed through to the page and found a small, rectangular piece of card stock. Like a picture but blank. He turned it over. Then over again.

"How did you know this was here?"

"It's all about noticing. I notice."

"It's blank. So what?"

"Is it? My mistake. But are you sure? Turn it over again."

Bones flipped the card. He blinked, not understanding what was happening. He'd been certain the card was blank only a second ago. Now he was staring at a bright and clear picture of a Harley Davidson motorcycle. "How did you do that?"

"Like it? It's a CVO Limited, twin-cooled Milwaukee-Eight engine, 4.7 five-inch bore, estimated highway mileage—"

"I know what it is. It's the most expensive brand-new Harley on the market right now."

"That's right, it is. It could be yours."

"For the box?"

"Smart man."

"What if I'm into vintage?"

"Are you?"

"I don't know. What if?"

"Flip the card. See if something a little older is more to your liking."

Bones did. "How, man? That's impossible."

"A tiring word. Besides, ours is not to reason why, ours is but to do and die—"

"It's an EL Knucklehead."

"A 1936 model, to be exact. The most prized—and expensive—Harley Davidson motorcycle in existence. You'd look good on it. Or maybe you'd like something else?"

Bones eyed him. "Flip it?"

Black winked.

Bones flipped. Flipped again. And again. Then as fast as he could move his hand, over and over. Each flip showed a different Harley, every color and model imaginable. "This is crazy."

"No, it's very sane, actually. And simple. You get me the box—I don't care how you do it—and I'll give you a Harley Davidson motorcycle. Brand-new or restored vintage or whatever you want. Any one you choose. A whole different world from the two-wheeled toy you've been tinkering with out in your shop. This one will run perfectly, every time and always."

"You'd actually give me a Harley for a dented metal box?"

"I was willing to give Jimmy two million dollars. I'd give you two motorcycles. A baker's dozen if you want. Then again, you can ride only one out of here, can't you?"

"Yeah."

Black took a card from his pocket and handed it to Bones. "This one won't change. It's a private phone number. You can leave a message day or night, and I'll get it within an hour. Get me the box, and you live your dreams."

"I don't have a phone."

"You're a smart young man. You'll figure it out. Think about it. Pick out the bike, any bike, and let me know."

"An actual Harley. Any one I want. You're serious?"

"Dead serious. Bones, my friend, you'll see this world in style. That's a promise."

CHAPTER THIRTY-ONE

AFTER LEAVING THE JESUS Is Coming Soon, Bones wandered around the town square for a while. He bought an Americano at Finnegan's Bookstore, thumbed through an odd, off-the-beaten-path travel book about finding Jesus in Israel written by some guy in Idaho of all places, then checked out the new releases. But nothing caught his eye. It was hard to stay interested when his mind was elsewhere, in this case perched on a brand-new Harley Davidson motorcycle. Why did Black want that box so bad? What did he know? Then again, what did Bones care? The box could be his actual ticket out of this place.

Even as he thought about it, the idea of stealing from Jimmy made him feel kind of sick. That was the danger of getting attached to someone. But who was Jimmy, anyway? Just some guy who would play piano in the lounge for a couple of weeks, then blow. Sure, he'd given Bones a ride on his Harley. Even let him ride it himself. But in the end he'd leave like everyone else did. What would Bones have then? A broken Honda and a whole bunch of desert.

Then he spotted a book on the history of illusion on the special-interest shelf, and it gave him an idea. He exited the bookstore and headed for the library. Next to the Jesus Is Coming Soon, the library was the place in town where he felt most comfortable. Nobody noticed each other in libraries. At least they pretended they didn't. Eyes were purposely averted. Even moving from one aisle to another was done with soft-stepped care.

The Paradise Municipal Library was only one block off the square, so it took only a minute or two for him to walk there. Not many people this time of the afternoon. The librarian hardly looked up when he came in and made his way to the computer room. The library's five computers were the big kind with the old-school monitors that looked like robots out of a 1950s sci-fi movie, but you could still get on the internet if you wanted to. Bones almost never did want to, but today was different.

He put the cursor over the Google box and typed in Jimmy La Roux. Nothing much came up besides an English pop band Bones had no interest in and a few other random sites. He tried James La Roux and had a little more luck. A few people shared the name, but not one of them was his Jimmy. Next he tried *disappearing box*. This search rendered several sites on historical magic, magicians, and illusionists. Videos on how to build an amateur box. Several on how they worked at every level. The problem was none of them were like Jimmy's.

A couple of days ago he'd asked to see the box up close, and Jimmy had let him. He'd held it, studied it. No hidden compartments. No false walls or bottom. Just like everyone else said. Old, dented metal. That's all.

He kept scrolling down but came up with zero.

He tried *metal disappearing box* and found a few more things. Mostly vintage trick boxes for sale. One with a top hat and handkerchiefs thrown in. They were all obvious in their machinations with nothing remotely resembling Jimmy's box. After a while he gave up and switched to YouTube vids about vintage Honda motorcycles. He knew he was stalling, knew what he was about to do, and he hated himself for it. What was coming made him feel weak.

But there was no helping it.

Cursing himself, he exited YouTube and typed *Sonny Harmon prison death* into the Google search box. The article in the local newspaper was the first search result like he knew it would be. For the umpteenth time he read the story of his father's murder. A senseless prison killing, the result of an argument over a TV show. He knew the article practically by heart. He hated this, but for some reason he couldn't explain even to himself, he always felt obligated to revisit the story when he had internet access. Funny thing was his dad had a grave over in the Paradise cemetery Bones hadn't visited once and probably never would.

"Hey."

He turned to find Calico standing in the doorway. He scrambled to exit the screen. "What are you doing here?"

"It's a public library, Bones. I'm allowed."

"Are you following me?"

"Honey over at Shorty's told me she saw you walking this way. I figured you'd be here." She pointed at the computer. "Anything interesting?"

Bones closed the window. "I was looking up motorcycle stuff."

"Yeah? Figure anything out?"

"Not really. Are you ready to go?"

"I'm done in town, but if you have things you want to do here, I'll browse around a while. Take your time."

"Nah. I'm cool."

"You sure? I don't mind."

"Let's go."

"Okay. Whatever you want."

Outside, Calico's old Ford Tempo's back seat and trunk were packed with paper goods. It seemed motels went through a lot of toilet paper and tissues. They climbed in and rolled the windows down, letting the soft aroma of pines and afternoon clouds waft in. As they rolled down past the tree line and began winding down the mountain, a drop of rain smacked the windshield, followed by another. Lightning flashed on the horizon.

Calico rolled her window up halfway. "I like the summer storms up here, don't you?"

"They're cool."

"What did you do in town besides the library?"

"That's about it."

"I'm surprised you didn't go buy a book at the thrift. Don't you always?"

"I have enough."

"Okay." She watched the road for a while, quiet. A few drops hit the windshield, and she turned on the wipers. "Can I ask you a question?"

"I guess."

"Do you miss your dad?"

"You saw what I was looking at?" Of course she had.

"Yes. Sorry for mentioning it. I guess I was surprised you'd be interested. Then again, he was your dad, so I don't know why I should be."

"I don't miss him at all. I'm glad he's gone. I don't know why I look at that stupid thing."

"I'm sorry."

"I'm not."

"Okay."

"He didn't like me, and he told me that all the time. Why should I miss him?"

"That's terrible."

"Whatever."

The rain picked up. "Bones, do you want me to make you eat salad?"

"What?"

"Seriously. Do you want me to make you eat salad?"

"That's kind of random."

"No it's not, because you're the one who asked me about it first, remember? So do you?"

He watched a drop of rain work its way sideways along the windshield. "I don't want anybody to make me do anything."

"You sure?"

Bones picked at a scab on his knee. "Yeah. I can take care of myself. I like it that way."

"Don't pick at that."

"Why not?"

"It's not ready to come off. Just don't."

Bones dug his thumbnail in and scratched the scab off completely. Blood welled up. "I said I can take care of myself."

Calico reached down with one hand, dug in her purse, and came up with a tissue. She handed it to him. "Put this on it."

"I don't need it."

"Maybe I don't want blood all over my car. Take it."

Bones did, glad she didn't say *I told you so* about the scab.

They rode a while longer, faster now out on the open road. Raindrops climbing up instead of sideways. Calico turned the windshield wipers on low. "I wish you could put the whole thing with your dad in Jimmy's box."

"I'm okay."

"Yeah, I know. But it would be something if we could really get rid of past stuff sometimes."

"I guess." He could feel her eyes on him, but he didn't look over.

"Would you if you could?" she said.

"I don't know. Would you?"

"I don't know either. Maybe our past is what makes us what we are."

"Yeah."

"Then again, maybe part of what we are isn't necessarily a good thing."

"It doesn't matter. The box is a scam anyway."

"Really? Do you know how it works?"

"No, but everything's pretty much a scam. Jimmy isn't any different."

The rain stopped as *un*-suddenly as it started, tapering off to a few drops, then a single last one. Out on the desert the clouds parted, and a shaft of sunlight broke through. It looked almost solid, like God's finger reaching down to touch the sand.

"Pretty, isn't it?" Calico said as she turned off the wipers.

"I guess."

"Not everything is a scam, Bones."

"Whatever you say."

Bones wished she'd be quiet. He didn't want to talk. Reading the article about his dad always did that to him. What he wanted was to ride. He wanted speed. More speed than the Honda or even a Harley could give him. He wanted rocket-ship speed. The kind that sucked the breath from your lungs and made your tears run back and pool in your ears.

He dabbed at his bloody knee with the tissue. What he didn't say out loud was he'd drop the whole world into Jimmy's dumb box if he could.

CHAPTER THIRTY-TWO

Calico wished Early would come home. She wanted to talk to him face-to-face. Wanted to explain herself. It hadn't been right since their last conversation. And how could it?

It would be easier if he were clearly in the wrong and she in the right. But everything was so gray. His motives were altruistic, but in his selflessness he was being selfish when it came to her. And maybe she was selfish too, but it wasn't that easy. There were things—feelings—she felt she had no control over. And she hated that.

She loved Early.

She was mad at Early.

She wanted him to hold her and tell her it would all work out.

She was mad at herself.

He should understand.

How could he?

How could a person decipher black and white, right and wrong, when everything was always so gray?

So she did what she'd been doing the last couple of days and pushed the whole thing out of her mind. After all, Pines wasn't here, and she had a motel to run. And that meant at least right now she had rooms to clean. The good news was Cozy was proving to be a real help. Like the woman had exploded into action after years of waiting around for Don to come home. She was everywhere at once and still found time to sing in the lounge.

Calico studied her across the bed they were making. "What's different about you today?"

"What do you mean?"

"I don't know. You seem lighter. Something in your eyes, maybe. More confident?"

"I'm not usually light?"

"Not like this. Is it Burt?"

"You really need to get past the Burt thing."

"It's your Burt thing, not mine."

"Then why are you the only one who brings it up?"

"Because I see the bigger picture. All you see is Don baggage."

"I'm done with Don baggage. And thanks again for being so nice to me. I've been meaning to tell you that."

"You say that as if someone being nice to you is a rarity. That makes me sad."

Cozy straightened. "Don't be sad. I do feel lighter. That's a perfect way to put it. Do you know what they called me when I was a girl?"

"What?"

"Porchie."

"Porchie? Why?"

"We lived in this trailer outside of Parker down by the Colorado River. Other than the river, there wasn't anything around but desert and rattlesnakes and a couple of junkyards."

"Sounds quiet."

"That trailer was such a horrible place. One so-called stepdad after another. I don't know where my mom found them all. I mean, it wasn't that big of a town. Anyway, one time she talked me into inviting some friends home from school. I didn't have many, but a couple came over. It was winter. A nice day. My friends wanted to play outside, so we did. And then while we were out there, my mom opened a window and told me to remember the porch rule."

"What was the porch rule?"

"That us kids could play only on the side of the porch closest to the front door because the other side was rotten and might collapse. I never thought anything of it until that day. I thought everybody had a bad side of the porch. But those girls couldn't get over it. The next day the whole school knew. Overnight I became Porchie."

"That's terrible."

"Yeah. It was. I hated that trailer with everything in me. I hated stepdads, I hated my mom, I hated the river, the desert, the snakes, the heat, the never-ending sky . . . I hated everything."

"Is your mom still there?"

"She died in a motel room in Blythe, California, when I was nineteen."

"I'm sorry."

"I wasn't. Want to know the first thing I did when I heard? That night my brother and I drove out to that river trailer with a gas can and a propane torch and burned the god-awful thing to the ground. No fire trucks came. Nobody even questioned it. Not long after that I left town and took whatever work I could find. Mostly waiting tables or tending bar. I did that for about five years. Then I met this guy, and he asked me if I wanted to be a trophy queen at some of his car races. Hundred bucks a race paid in cash or gift cards. Why not? Two months after that I met Don. Three weeks after that I was back in a trailer collecting soup."

"Collecting soup?"

"I know it's bizarre, but we never had enough in that river trailer. Then I find myself married—or thought I was—and I wind up filling every inch of another trailer's cupboard space with soup cans. It was like I couldn't help it. I'm talking crazy stuff."

"That's understandable."

"I should be on one of those cable shows."

"Stop it. What did Don think about all the soup?"

"He didn't make a big deal of it. Probably didn't even notice. His mind was on cars, not what was for dinner. I could have fed him cat food and I doubt he would have noticed."

She paused. "Do you want to know the stupidest thing? Not long after we were married, I told him the story about the kids calling me

Porchie. I'm such an idiot. He missed the whole point. He thought it was funny. And cute. Even worse, he started using Porchie as a pet name for me. It made me want to scratch his eyes out. Or mine. On our first anniversary he got me a gold necklace with a fake diamond *P* on it. He said it was *our* thing. Part of our story. He couldn't understand why I wasn't over the moon about it. He'd get so mad if I didn't wear it, I swear I thought he'd hit me sometimes."

Calico frowned. "Yuck."

"Yeah, yuck. So are you going to spill what the problem is with you and the great lawman? When does he come back?"

"I don't know. He'll be gone as long as it takes, I guess."

"Do you miss him?"

"Of course."

"You have a date for the wedding set? When you do it, make sure you don't tie the knot on a racetrack between heats. Those knots don't hold."

"Advice taken. We haven't set a date yet."

"Why not?"

"I don't know. It's complicated right now. Make sure you get that corner tight."

"Okay."

Calico straightened and sighed. "I snapped at you. I'm sorry."

"Don't be sorry. Complicated does that sometimes."

"Pines and I kind of had a fight. Or we're having one. I'm still trying to figure it out."

"Doesn't sound like much of a fight. Anyway, fights pass."

"I'm not so sure about this one. *Fight* might not be the best word. More like we're at an impasse."

"About what?

"I love him, I do, but maybe it's not all about that. Maybe that's not enough. You know what it's like to try to deal with history. You just told me. My mom died when I was young. My dad was absent. I screwed up . . . Anyway, now there's Bones."

"What about Bones?"

"Bones was really close to one of Pines's friends."

"Yeah, Gomez Gomez. Everybody knows that. The kid used to hang out down at the guy's shack."

"Right. After the foster thing with Don, Pines isn't in a hurry to toss Bones into another foster situation."

"Does he have that choice? I mean, it's not up to him, right?"

"It's a small town. And he's Pines. He knows people."

"That's true. I still don't see the problem, though."

"The problem is I might be able to swing being a wife. *Might.* But no way can I do mother figure to wounded teen boy on top of it."

"How do you know if you don't try?"

Calico shook her head. "You make it sound simple."

"I don't know. Shouldn't it be? I mean, I was never like a real mother to the foster kids we had, but I did the best I could."

"I did try once. After my mom died when I was twelve, my dad basically checked out. I wound up pretty much raising my little brother. Between you and me and the lamppost, I didn't do a bang-up job of it. He was in and out of trouble for years."

"How does that count? You were a kid yourself. You're a woman now. A business owner."

"People don't change that much. Even when they grow up."

"Yes they do. At least they can if they try. You don't give yourself enough credit."

"Look. It's a whole stack of things. I just don't know if I'm cut out for it."

"You don't think you're cut out for Bones, you mean."

Calico paused. "Yes."

"What does your pros-and-cons list say?"

"You've noticed my lists?"

"It's not like I've gone through your notebook. But you write in it all the time. You make a list over whether to buy toilet paper."

"Come on. It's not that bad."

"Almost."

"Making a pros-and-cons list is a solid way to make a decision."

"Or you could listen to your heart. Or your gut. Tell me you don't have a list about Bones."

"All right, I have a Bones list. Sue me."

"What's on it?"

"A whole slew of cons."

"No pros?"

"Can you think of one?"

"Bones is Bones. There's no doubt about that. And I'm definitely the last person qualified to give you advice about him. Or maybe second to last after dear old Don."

"The thing is it's not about me. It's about what's good for Bones."

"And someone else would be better?"

"I'm sure they would. It's hard. And I *have* tried. I offered to let him stay in my spare room. He didn't want to. The kid puts up pretty thick walls."

"How hard have you tried to get through them?"

"I don't know."

"Maybe you have some walls yourself."

"You should do this for a living, you know that? Maybe one of those radio advice shows."

"Maybe you should have told, not offered, about staying in your apartment. Put your foot down."

"Maybe, but that's a classic example of something I already did wrong."

"Not that I did much better. I tortured the poor kid with soup."

Calico shook her head and smiled. "True, soup saturation gives tough love a whole new meaning."

"I think the kid's had enough tough in his life."

"And now there's Jimmy La Roux."

"What about him?"

"I can tell Bones is fascinated by the guy. And Jimmy took him out on the Harley."

"Is that a bad thing?"

"I'm still trying to decide about that. I'm not sure what Pines would say."

"You do a whole lot of thinking. Maybe you should let some of it go."

"I only worry about Bones."

"That sounds like you care."

Calico gave the room a visual once-over, then moved to the door. "It's not that I don't care. I'm not a mean person."

"I know you're not."

"You say that with more conviction than I feel. Sometimes I think I'm trying to convince myself."

Cozy hadn't moved from her spot next to the bed.

"You coming?" Calico said.

"Do you think Jimmy's box is real?"

"I don't know. It's a good trick, and people seem to like it. What's that have to do with anything?"

"Maybe everything. I think it's real. I think what goes in it goes away forever."

"That would be impossible."

"I'm not so sure."

"What are you talking about?"

"Remember I said I'm done with Don baggage? I put something else in the box last night. That's why I look lighter. That's why I feel free."

This gave Calico pause. "What did you put in?"

Cozy hesitated. "That *P* necklace. And with it a whole world of baggage and life and Don stuff I've been dragging around for years."

"Like closure? That makes sense. It still doesn't mean the box really makes things no longer exist."

"No. This is more than closure. I mean, closure would be understandable, and I'm sure there was some of that, but it was more. It was like somebody cut into me and took out a lifetime of pain. Took out doubt. I can't explain it, but it's real. It happened."

"I'm sorry for being skeptical. I'm glad you feel better. Did Jimmy know what you were putting in?"

"He saw the necklace, but he didn't ask questions. He didn't say anything at all. It was weird. He kind of acted like it was a solemn moment. And there was something in the music he played."

"Something like what?"

"I don't know. I'm probably being crazy. I'm the soup lady, right?"

"No you're not."

"It was just a melody. Familiar. I felt like I could almost remember the words but not quite. I think I might have heard it when I was a little girl, but I couldn't put my finger on what it was exactly. And . . ."

"And what?"

"You'll laugh."

"I won't."

"I could swear that, for a second, I heard a little girl laughing. Like happy laughing."

"I don't understand."

"Neither do I. It sounded like . . ."

"Sounded like what?"

"Like me."

CHAPTER THIRTY-THREE

Bones lifted a foot and pushed the Honda over with everything he had. It slammed the floor with a metallic crash.

He plopped down onto his cot and stared at the thing, then cursed himself as he got up and lifted the bike to its kickstand. Lucky he hadn't broken a clutch handle. That would be twenty bucks plus shipping, at least. Then again, what did it matter? Maybe he'd forget the whole thing. He'd been sure the new battery would do the trick. Jimmy had acted like it would.

Jimmy was wrong.

Dude deserved to have his stupid box stolen. Bones laid back on the cot and picked up a book, turning pages without seeing them. He knew very well Jimmy's box had nothing to do with the Honda, but his mind seemed to live in that box ever since the Jesus Is Coming Soon. Stinking Nelson Black was living in his head. Nelson Black and a brand-new Harley.

So in a way the box did have something to do with the Honda. Because the Honda wasn't a Harley. The stupid stubborn Honda wouldn't work. It wouldn't even turn over. Taking the box meant a Harley and an end to all these problems that wouldn't leave him alone.

Besides, Jimmy himself said the box was a burden. Bones would probably be doing the guy a favor taking it. It would be like setting him free.

But Jimmy had stuck up for Bones with Don. That had been cool.

But didn't Jimmy lead him to believe a new battery would work?

Bones went on for a while, not reading. Just turning the pages. Arguing with himself. None of this was his fault. He had to get out of here. He had to make it happen. He looked at the Honda again. It was like the thing was laughing at him.

He didn't owe anybody a thing. If anything, life owed him. All he had to do was take the box and pass it on to Black. But he had to do it in a way Jimmy wouldn't know who'd taken it.

But how could he? Jimmy was Jimmy. Jimmy was cool. Jimmy put cigs out on the palm of his hand and picked up guys like Don by the seat of the pants. Jimmy *saw*. Still, Bones was Bones. He could find a way. He knew he could.

But as much as he hated to admit it, the real problem was he liked Jimmy. He told himself he didn't. Told himself he didn't like anyone. But he did. He plain old stinking liked Jimmy, and it sucked. He put the book down. He didn't want words right now. He didn't want faraway places he couldn't experience except in his imagination. He wanted to feel the wind on his face. Smell hot engines. He wanted to ride toward distant horizons and pass them.

He wanted a stinking Harley.

He kicked himself off the cot and went outside. It was almost time to start work anyway. Calico and Cozy were on room cleaning, which meant he'd be sweeping the inevitable dust off the sidewalks and cleaning the pool. Plus Calico had asked him to reorganize the pool shed.

Oh well. Better than just sitting around here.

He hung a minute on the shop step, looking at the back of the Venus. Lots of closed blinds. What rooms were visible were dark against the bright day. Across the roof and parking lot, a hawk perched on top of Lady Venus, watching the desert. Far out on the valley floor, dust rose. Probably a jeep or motorcycle. Above it, a passenger jet dragged an exhaust trail across the blue.

An unmistakable rumble sounded, throttled up, and blasted south on the highway as Jimmy exited the parking lot below. Bones and the hawk and Lady Venus all watched him go.

Bones dropped down the path and entered the kitchen through the back door. Juan wasn't around, so he skipped food and opted for a can of root beer from the refrigerator before going into the lounge.

The place was closed and empty. He sat at the bar awhile, eyes on the stage and the piano. Jimmy always kept the box with him, so really, even if he wanted to steal it, what was he supposed to do?

"It's a conundrum, isn't it?"

Bones hadn't seen Black sitting at a table in the back of the shadowed room, but he wasn't surprised he was there. "The lounge is closed."

"I know, but I get so bored in my room, and I'm not much of a pool person. I could drive into town, I suppose. Waste some time. But that place is even worse than this one, which is saying something. You understand."

"Actually, I totally understand."

"I know you do, which brings us back to our conundrum. He keeps the box with him. From the way you were staring at the piano, that's what you were thinking about, correct?"

"No."

"I'm glad to hear you lie about it. Liars have little in the way of moral principle. Lying and stealing go hand in hand. Don't get me wrong. I'm not judging. We do what we need to do to get ahead in this life. I've done it many times, which is why I am where I am. We, all of us humans, do it on some level."

"I'm not stealing the box, man. So get it out of your head."

"Why? It's in *your* head."

Bones didn't see the point in denying it. "If you admit to being a liar, how do I know you'd even give me a Harley?"

Black laughed. "Is that what you're worried about? Do you have any idea how much money I have? How much I'm worth? I'd drop two million for that box in a heartbeat. Between you and me, I'd drop three million. Five if I had to. But now I realize Jimmy won't go for it no matter what the number is. Do you know why I know that?"

"Because he said he doesn't want to sell, and unlike you, he's not a liar or a thief?"

"You think he's not a liar and a thief? I almost feel sorry for you. No, that's not it at all. He won't sell because he knows he'll be nothing if he does. The box is the only thing that makes him something. It's sad when you think about it. I almost feel sorry for him too. But only almost."

"I don't think that's true. I think he'd still be Jimmy."

"The sentiment is touching, but what I'm saying is true. We were talking about the Harley Davidson, and the point is what do I care about a motorcycle? I'd buy you a dozen if it got me the box. I'd set you up anywhere you want. Give you a brand-new, glorious life. A *fun* life. I could do it legally even though you're underage. I have money, and when you have money, you have ways of doing almost anything."

Black leaned forward, laced his fingers together. "I like you, Bones. You have a sort of style. An odd style for sure, but that's not a bad thing. In fact, it's the kind of thing that often gets a person places. What if I said you could tag along with me for a while? You wouldn't believe the places I get to go, the things I get to do. I'm booked solid around the world practically all the time."

"Then what are you doing here?"

"Talking to you, of course. It's not easy to pin Jimmy down. He moves a lot. When he's stationary for any amount of time at all, I take advantage of it. It's funny, but for some reason I thought he would cave this time. I really thought he'd sell the box. After all, what does he do with the thing? Take it out once in a while in some bar and do inconsequential parlor tricks? Make rocks disappear? Bar glasses? Give me a break. It's an absolute waste."

Black shook his head. "I have no idea how it works, and if I have no idea . . . Not to brag, but I believe that makes it the most significant illusion in the history of illusion. It's bordering on miraculous. Something beyond what science yet understands. But I looked into his eyes when I offered the two million. I saw it then. He won't sell. He'll never let it go. Because the man is petty and jealous and small. It's all he has. It's the only reason he has to get up in the morning. I guess I actually *do* feel sorry for him."

"No you don't."

Black laughed again. "You're right. I don't. It was just a thing to say. You're good. Tell me, have you ever been to Manila?"

"No."

"Dublin?"

"You know I haven't. I've never been anywhere but here."

"I'm booked in both those places within the next month. Tag along. I'm serious. You're growing on me."

"I don't grow on people."

Black rested his elbows on the table. "Why do you say that?"

"Because it's true. I gotta go to work now."

"Look, kid." Black's tone had softened, surprising Bones. "I think I missed something, and that's rare for me. You and me? We have more in common than you think. For one thing, I lost my father early on as well. I also have no idea what happened to my mother. Everything I have I've had to work for. You want family? Somewhere you really belong? Come with me, and I'll show you what family is really like. And I won't ask you to be anything you aren't. You can be you."

He briefly closed his eyes, then looked at Bones with a new intensity. "I remember how much I hated that when I was your age. People pressing and pulling, telling me what was normal and how to act if I wanted to fit in. What did they know about me? And where are they now? Nowhere. Let me tell you, fitting in is overrated. You be you. And be you with a place to belong and a fleet of Harleys."

Bones considered this. "Why would you do all that?"

Bones waited as Black stood, walked behind the bar, then took down a bottle of scotch and poured himself a glass.

"Why would I do all that for you?" Black finally said. "Because nobody ever did it for me."

The last thing Bones wanted was some trip down memory lane. "Like I said, I have to go to work."

Black sipped the drink, then shrugged and downed it. "Well, think about my offer. Wouldn't it be something if you never had to say those words again?"

CHAPTER THIRTY-FOUR

CALICO RELAXED ON A BARSTOOL enjoying the lull between daytime chores and the evening dinner-and-drinks influx.

"Thing about Ella Fitzgerald," Jimmy was saying from his piano bench in between verses, "she was perfect. Listen to those early recordings. No pitch correction, no fancy equipment, just players and a singer sent straight from heaven in a big room with a microphone. She was smooth as silk. *Perfect.* That's what makes Ella songs so tough to sing. But you"—he pointed at Cozy with his right hand and kept the bass line going with his left—"girl, you nail it. I bet Ella's up there smiling right now."

Cozy was smiling so hard herself her ears went bright. Calico could see them glowing from the bar.

Early evening sunlight formed a bright pool on the wood floor as it flooded through the lounge window. Calico had unlocked the door a half hour ago, but so far the only person in the room besides her, Cozy, and Jimmy was Burt. He sat in a booth with a cup of coffee listening to Cozy and Jimmy run through the songs they were working on. He sat slouched a little, boots crossed out in front of him, his face a puzzle. Both sad and admiring, sometimes present, sometimes lost in the past or the future or maybe someplace in between.

Calico walked back behind the bar, took down a mug from a shelf, and poured hot water over a teabag. The door swung open, and David August entered. He'd ditched his usual silk robe and swim trunks for leather sandals, very worn khaki shorts, and a faded Miles Davis T-shirt. He still wore the pistol and carried the briefcase the armored truck delivered.

He took a barstool across from Calico, then nodded toward Burt. Kept his voice down. "I've seen that look before. I've worn it myself a time or two. Our Elmore Leonard–reading cowpoke is what I would call bewitched by the cupid."

"To tell you the truth, I kind of hope so. They're both lost souls. As different as night and day, but I have a theory. I think they'd be good for each other."

"He said he was killing time. A little music might make it die easier."

"He carries his wedding ring in his pocket. I asked around when I was in town today. His wife died five years ago. Breast cancer."

"Such is the stuff of life. When I look at Buck, I see a gentile in whom there is no guile. I do hope he finds what he needs."

"His name is Burt, but you actually know that, don't you?"

"How's the rum stock today, beautiful Calico?"

"Do you think calling me beautiful really works?"

"Of course. You're a woman, aren't you? All women enjoy being called beautiful. It's natural."

"That is so politically incorrect I don't even know where to start."

"I don't believe in politics. It tends to pander to the baser senses and roil the masses. Better to ride above."

Calico poured the writer his rum and lime. "The truth is there's only one voice I'd like to hear call me beautiful right now, and he's a long way away."

"Uh-oh."

"Yes. Uh-oh." Calico pointed to the glass. "I get the feeling, Mr. August—"

"David."

"David. Right. I get the feeling you might not always be quite as inebriated as you let on."

"Oh, believe me, I'm always quite as inebriated as I let on. Possibly more. I did ride the wagon after Bangkok for some years, but alas, I'm what you would call a weak man."

"Bangkok?"

"Bangkok, 1989. Bangkok and SangSom rum and an Italian model I met one rainy night in Brussels. Bangkok, beautiful Calico, was a train wreck of majestic proportions. You look a little like her, come to think of it."

"That was a long time ago, 1989," Calico said.

"I stayed dry for a while. Stayed home for the most part. I did some good work over that time, or at least the critics thought so. Then some friends and I decided Rome would be a good idea. Who says no to Campari in Rome? Oh boy, that was a train wreck too. The model in Rome was Swedish, if I recall."

"Have you ever thought models might be what wrecks the train?"

He smiled. "Models certainly don't make the best engineers. Elga. That was her name. On second thought, Rome wasn't so bad. It was more of an extremely painful kind of beautiful."

They both listened to Cozy sing a verse of Ella Fitzgerald's "Miss Otis Regrets." Calico's musical horizon had certainly expanded with Jimmy here.

"She's very good, you know," David said. "She could go places."

"She's much better than the Venus deserves, I have a feeling."

"No, no, don't ever say that. The Venus is an institution. She's a magical destination for those of us who've been blessed to dance in her light. I'm sure Ella herself would have been happy to play this room. You know, I met her a few times. Cocktail parties, an awards show or two. She was very nice."

"You met Ella Fitzgerald?"

"Sure. Even heard her sing one night up at Della Reese's place. Kind of an impromptu thing. She wasn't selfish that way. She gave away what she'd been given and gave it gladly."

"That's a nice way to put it."

He sipped his rum, then smacked his lips. "I wish I could say the same about myself sometimes."

"Can't you?"

"I don't know. I think—for some people anyway—life takes more than it gives with not a lot left over."

"It seems to me you've been given a lot."

"Does it? Maybe so. Still, I've got many holes. I don't hold much these days."

It was funny how she hadn't noticed the deep lines around his eyes before. More than lines, really. More like cracks. You could practically see daylight through them, as if the writer was coming apart right in front of her.

On stage, Jimmy and Cozy finished. "Feeling good?" he said to her.

"Good as can be."

"See you back here in an hour."

"See you then." Cozy waved to the rest of them as she left to get changed.

Jimmy played the blues.

The door opened, and Sal and Rufus walked in. They nodded and waved and then took a booth along the far wall. Juan had just come out of the kitchen, and he shuffled over to wait on them, saving Calico the task.

"Can I ask you a question, David?" she said.

"You can, but I can't promise I'll answer."

"What are you doing here?"

"What do you mean?"

"I mean, when you made the reservation, you gave the name David Scott. Then you show up, and now I'm looking at David August across my bar with your photo hanging behind it. They literally made me read your books in high school English class. I did a report on you my senior year. So here's my question. What are you doing at my little motel in the middle of nowhere?"

"What's Nelson Black doing here? He's famous."

"He wants Jimmy's box, but that's a different subject. Plus I'd hardly heard of Nelson Black. You're on a whole other plane."

"The box . . . It is an extraordinary thing. I've been thinking about it for a story."

"Really?"

"Really. You call this the middle of nowhere. You know, I wish we were in the middle of nowhere. I've looked for that particular location much of my life. The problem is no matter where I go, I find I'm smack in the middle of somewhere. What did you write in that school report?"

"I wrote something along the lines of how you were the most brilliant writer I'd ever read and that your books deeply moved me."

"Was that true? Did my stories move you?"

"They really did."

He stared into his drink. "I can't tell you how nice it is to hear that."

"Come on. You must hear it all the time."

"I do, yes. And there was a time I think I believed it. I believed in myself as a writer and an artist. Of course, like all artists, I also spent much of my time waiting for the other shoe to drop. For someone to pull back the curtain and discover I'd been making up the whole thing. Driving blind."

"But you weren't. You move people. You speak to them."

"Maybe once, but now I tell people I'm writing this pirate novel so they'll at least think I'm working. Adventure on the high seas. My only concern is wondering if there's enough time to go around for both Buck and me to kill."

"His name's Burt. What do you mean by *tell people*? Aren't you writing that novel?"

"Between you and me, I have a rough idea in my head for it, but I haven't put down a word."

"Isn't this briefcase full of some kind of payment for the book?"

"For the film rights."

"Don't you think you should write it, then?"

"Probably. But at the moment I'm busy exploring the fine intricacies of your rum. In my opinion, for whatever my opinion's worth these days, pirate novels are where writers go to die."

"Why do it, then?"

"Besides the fact I signed a contract, I think the better question is *why not.* Fred Katz at Global is willing to send over a couple million bucks in a briefcase for nothing more than a vague idea my publisher bought based on my past success. My agent even thinks a pirate novel from me will make money. It's been a long, dry season for her. Besides, how hard can it be? Toss in a ghost ship, a sea monster or two, a couple of sea battles, maybe a beautiful woman in distress. Easy formula, like all those romance novels."

"Romance as in the city girl comes back to her hometown and reconnects with her first-love old boyfriend stuff?"

David laughed. "Fiancé back in the city who hates Christmas. There's also the period ones. The titled man, the virgin, the conflict, the compromise . . ."

"Don't tell anybody, but I kind of love those stories."

"Of course you do. You and every other reader on this big blue marble of ours these days except for Buck and his Elmore Leonard. A sobering statistic that might very well call for another rum."

"Is there anything in David August's world that doesn't call for another rum?"

"You do have a point there, beautiful Calico who reminds me of an Italian model from another life."

Calico poured. "The desert seems like a strange place to work on a pirate book."

"But a wonderful place to kill time. Just ask Buck."

"Burt."

"Just ask Burt."

Calico nodded in the direction of Sal and Rufus. "Isn't it strange . . . them following you here from Mexico?"

David turned and surveyed the two, who seemed content with the drinks Juan brought them. He lifted a glass to them, then turned back. "Not strange at all. They want to steal my two million dollars."

"Really? How do you know?"

"Let's just say I might not have been quite as cockeyed in Todos Santos as they thought."

CHAPTER THIRTY-FIVE

Bones found a little cardboard package sitting on the concrete step of the shop. The wind was whipping up from the south, and he was glad the thing hadn't blown away. No shipping label or note, just BONES/COIL, GOOD LUCK, JIMMY handwritten in block letters across the top.

Once inside, he opened it and pulled out a brand-new-looking ignition coil and a printed sheet on how to install it. Nice of Jimmy, which made Bones feel bad. But he hadn't taken the biker's box. At least not yet. He'd thought about it, though. In fact, it was practically all he thought about. He felt like a guy in one of those old cartoons with an angel on one shoulder and a devil on the other, both of them constantly squawking at him.

He shouldn't take the box, but if he did, it would be for a Harley, man. Even Jimmy should understand that. Still, giving him the ignition coil was a pretty cool thing to do after the battery didn't help. He looked down at the bike. Months he'd worked on the thing. He felt like he knew it better than the factory worker who'd originally assembled it. Probably did. He gave the installation sheet a once-over, then got down to work. The project wasn't difficult, and twenty-five minutes in, the new coil was installed, the old one sitting on the workbench. Seeing if the thing made a difference was all there was left to do.

He started to climb onto the bike, but a knock on the door pulled his attention. "Yeah?"

"Bones, you want to open the door, please?" Calico's voice.

Bones did. Calico's hair whipped back and forth in the wind. She pushed it off her face. "A storm's coming up from the Gulf. They're saying it's a big one on the radio. I need you to cover the pool right away."

"Now?"

"Yes, now. Also stack the deck furniture and put all the cleaning tools in the pool shed. And hurry, all right? I'm serious."

"I kind of have something—"

"I need you right now, Bones."

"Yeah, okay."

"If you need help, ask me. Juan's taking off for home. He doesn't want to get stuck out here when we have flash flood warnings, and I can't blame him."

"I can do it."

"Good. As quick as you can. Judging by this wind and the look of the clouds coming, I don't think we have a whole lot of time."

"Is the lounge gonna be open tonight?"

"I don't think anyone will come down from town with flash flood warnings, but we still have guests. They'll want to eat, and Juan left something for us."

He watched as she made her way down the path back toward the Venus, then looked up at the sky. She was right. Black clouds were building over the mountains. The evening had a crazy feel to it. The Gulf storms rolled in once or twice a year, and they could be violent. A drop of rain hit the concrete step like a bullet, leaving a dark-gray spatter. He was wearing cutoff shorts and a T-shirt, and maybe he should change. But the day was still warm even with the coming storm, so he started down the path.

Then he stopped, surprised at himself for almost forgetting. Back in the shop he straddled the Honda, then checked to make sure it was in neutral. He turned the key one click. Months, man. Maybe this was it?

For some reason he thought about his dad then. Did rainwater make it down six feet? And his mom. Maybe she was dead too. Or maybe she was out there somewhere. Maybe she had a whole other family. Or maybe she was a CIA agent or a waitress or a heavy metal drummer. He wondered if she ever thought about him. Probably not. Why would she? He used to lie and tell people at school she was still there, at his house, just reclusive. That she always had chocolate chip cookies waiting for him when he got home.

They all knew he was lying, but even the bullies never gave him a hard time about it.

He didn't want to turn the key. In that moment, sitting on his broken Honda in the dark and shadowy shop where he didn't and never really would belong, he didn't want to turn the key that final click. He didn't want one more disappointment. He didn't think he could survive one.

So he climbed off.

Then he kicked himself for a fool and climbed back on. In the same motion, he reached up and turned the key.

And the bike roared to life.

He stared at the handlebars, felt the Honda vibrating beneath him like a living thing. Part of him wanted to hit the throttle right now. To fly into the storm. Never look back. But he needed time. Needed his things.

Later. But now he could plan, really plan.

Outside, the wind slammed against the walls. He killed the engine and swung off the bike, then stood out on the porch a minute. He knew more than most people about global weather—for two reasons. First, he'd stumbled across a book on the subject at the Jesus Is Coming Soon, misfiled in the western section between Louis L'Amour's *The Quick and the Dead* and an errant Stephen King, *The Green Mile.* Bones had been feeling good that day, and on a whim he'd bought all three. He'd figured the total would be a whopping dollar fifty, but it turned out to be a dollar twenty-five when the clerk made a face, said something about hating horror, and threw in *The Green Mile* for free.

Turned out the joke was on her, because the book wasn't scary at all.

The second reason he knew more about global weather than the average Joe was that the average Joe knew practically nothing at all. The average Joe, for instance, didn't know the hottest spot ever recorded on the planet was a little map-dot in Libya that had registered 136.4 degrees back in 1922. Or that the biggest hailstones ever recorded had killed ninety-two people in Bangladesh in 1986. They didn't know Yuma, Arizona, had the most sunny days out of the year and that Mawsynram, India, got the most rain.

He had all this committed to memory. He was a very-above-average Joe. And he especially dug weather because it was unpredictable, and in his linear Paradise world, he rarely encountered the unpredictable. Animals were predictable. People were predictable. Books, for the most part, were predictable. But weather was a lot like Jimmy La Roux. You just never knew. It could go on and on, bright sunny days until you thought it never would change, and then *bam*.

The evening should be clear and still warm, a star or two trying to poke through. No stars though. Only piles and piles of clouds stretching horizon to horizon.

Lightning over the western mountains momentarily turned one of the great cloud-bellies pink and purple. Other than a few scattered drops, the rain had not yet arrived, at least not down here in the valley, but wind whipped and whistled around Lady Venus. Tumbleweeds rolled beneath her, crashed into her base, momentarily illuminated by her glow before being yanked back into the darkness. Old average Joe would scratch his head and wonder where all this was coming from. After all, it was the desert, the blue-sky land. Sunshine and stillness broken only by the occasional dust devil.

But Bones knew differently. Knew all about the monsoons birthed out over the warm waters of the Gulf of Mexico. Rustling the palms in Hemingway's Cuba, pushing seabirds off their course, rising up with shaking fists and flinging themselves north, crashing over Texas and Mexico and the great Mojave Desert, waves pummeling a beach.

Time to go.

He struggled with the deck chairs and the pool cover. Probably should have taken Calico up on her offer of help, but he managed it in the end. He should have taken cover then, found a hole to hide in like every other creature in the desert was doing at this very moment. He had the shop or the lounge or the kitchen. But the Honda had started, sparking something in him. A wild freedom. He wanted sky and rain like metal pellets against his face. He wanted nature in all her fury and glory. He *felt* and wanted to feel more.

Then he was outside the shop again, his back against the outer wall, wind yanking his hair and trying its best to tear Jimmy's unlit cigarette from his lips. Below, a few motel rooms lit up. People were moving around inside. Like horses in stalls, restless, some primal instinct warning them the tempest surely coming wasn't joking around. A huge burst of lightning exploded, thunder right on top of it. Lady Venus flickered, went dark, then illuminated again.

That's when he saw the gun. Room twelve. Rufus and Sal. It was a pistol. Not a big one, but a gun was a gun. Sal had pulled it out of a suitcase, waved it while his mouth moved in silent, animated speech. Rufus had his hands out, gesturing for Sal to lower the thing. Sal did, then lifted it again. For a second, it looked like he was about to shoot Rufus, but he lowered the pistol again and kept talking.

After August had thwarted Rufus's theft by the pool, Bones had kept an eye on the situation. Rufus and Sal had seemed to settle in, content to sit by the pool or stay in their room, probably watching TV. Once they'd played cards in the lounge. They clearly weren't the most savory characters ever to stay at the Venus, but a gun was next-level stuff. Guns were for shooting people. Or for threatening to shoot them. Then again, David August had a gun, and if the two were determined to rip off the author of his two million, another pistol would be the one way to fight fire with fire.

Yeah. Two million bucks. August had said it plain as day to Calico in the lounge earlier. Bones, invisible of course, hadn't been surprised. After all, they didn't deliver peanuts in armored cars.

Below, Rufus picked up a suitcase, and for a second or two, Bones had the hopeful thought they might be checking out and leaving. Maybe the storm freaked them out. But Rufus only dug something out of the case and then set it down again. Then he seemed to notice the window, walked over, and lowered and closed the blinds.

Bones pretend-smoked and considered this. Besides all that money, there was Jimmy's box, which for all intents and purposes could be considered priceless to the right person or persons. It was to Black. So that was plenty more motive for stealing. Guns were excellent robbery tools.

But what could or should Bones do about this gun of Sal's, if anything? He could tell Calico, but she might try to do something about it and get hurt. If Early were around, Bones would tell him for sure, but he wasn't. He could tell Jimmy. He *should* tell Jimmy. After all, what if they actually stole the box before Bones had a chance? Goodbye Harley Davidson. Not that Bones had made up his mind about whether he'd steal it himself. He still wrestled with the idea. But why should Rufus and Sal get it?

Then the light behind the blinds in room twelve went out. Two long shadows appeared in the parking lot, shortening and lengthening as they passed the lights in front of the other rooms, then the office. Two people headed for the lounge.

Rufus and Sal, for sure.

Rufus and Sal and Sal's gun.

Calico would be in there at some point. Cozy and Jimmy too.

Bones snuffed his unlit cig on his palm, stuck it into his pocket, and started down the hill. The wind threatened to pull him off the path as the rain started for real.

Yeah, man. Things were getting stormy.

CHAPTER THIRTY-SIX

Calico looked out through her apartment window, more sure than ever no one would come down the mountain from town on a night like this. She wasn't sure what the five guests would do. Maybe stay in their rooms and watch TV if the cable held out. Even if every one of them came to the lounge, it would be a slow night, though. They barely outnumbered the staff with Juan gone. Just four if you counted Jimmy.

Still, five guests were five guests. Even as she thought it, Rufus and Sal walked by the window in the direction of the lounge. Well, Cozy would be there by now, and she could handle things for a few minutes.

She ran a hot shower and didn't hurry. The water felt good. She closed her eyes and tried not to think about Early, which didn't work. He hadn't called since their last talk, and that both confused and worried her. Her mind told her heart he was probably just busy with the case.

Her heart didn't buy it.

She made herself presentable, at least as presentable as jeans, Vans, and an untucked blouse allowed. She wasn't in the mood for anything more, and there was a storm outside. Wind hit her as she opened the apartment door, the rain thankfully slanted toward the highway at the moment. Only fifty feet or so to the lounge, but it still felt like running a gauntlet.

Rufus and Sal were seated at a table with drinks. Jimmy played low from the stage. Cozy manned the bar. The comforting aroma of roasting chilis emanated from the kitchen. Juan hadn't left them to starve.

"Sorry I took a while. I'll cover the bar," Calico said to Cozy. "Are you up for some singing? We could probably all use some Cozy tonight."

"Really?" Cozy glanced out across the room. "It'd be weird to sing for two people."

"Why? Jimmy's playing for two people."

"I think Jimmy mostly plays for himself."

"Why do you sing?"

Cozy smiled. "That's a good point."

The door opened again with a flurry of wind. David August, briefcase in hand, stepped in, then turned to shove the door closed. "A night not fit for man nor beast, and I'm afraid I'm both."

Calico put her hand on Cozy's shoulder and pushed her gently toward the stage. "Three's a crowd. Plus I'm here, so that's four."

"All right."

David pulled out a chair and sat at one of the center tables. "By all means, music from the lovely Cozy. If an occasion ever called for sweet song along with rum and lime, this is it. The night is more than unfit; it's biblical."

"You ever have any occasions that don't call for rum and lime, Dave?" Sal said.

"Very rarely, I'll admit. But I do love to hear Cozy sing. By the way, when are you boys heading out? I'm surprised you're still here."

"Tonight," Rufus said.

"Ah, back to Todos Santos?"

"Yet to be determined."

"I wouldn't recommend going anywhere tonight," Calico said. "Not with this storm. When the rain hits those mountains, it can get crazy down here fast."

Sal shook his head. "You people out west don't even know what real rain is. I swear, Los Angeles? A drop hits their windshields and suddenly brake lights everywhere for miles. It's nuts. Back east the rain comes down in sheets and nobody bats an eye."

"He's right about LA. I never understood that, man." Rufus looked at the stage as Cozy slid into "Blue Bayou."

"I'm talking about flash floods," Calico said.

Sal shrugged, took a sip of his martini, and set the glass back on the table with a *thunk*. "And I'm talking about getting back to civilization. Hey, Dave, what's it feel like to carry all that cash around everywhere you go?"

"It feels heavy, if you must know."

Sal glanced at Rufus, then shifted his eyes back to Dave. He laughed. "I'll bet it does. How about you let me take over for a while? Say for around fifty years or so."

"I'll manage, thanks." David pulled his pistol from the holster and set it on the table next to the briefcase.

Sal quit laughing. "Something I said?"

"Oh, I just like to have my weapon close at hand. You never know."

Calico walked over and set a tumbler of Bacardí and a small bowl of limes in front of David.

He tapped the chair next to him. "Sit with me. You can't be busy."

Calico considered. Why not? It was an unusual night. She pulled out a chair and dropped into it.

"'Blue Bayou.' What a song," David said. "You know, I saw Linda at the Troubadour in Los Angeles years ago. When she was very first starting out. Her producer put a band together for her, and he had Don Henley on drums and Glenn Frey on guitar. They later formed the Eagles. A historic night."

Jimmy nodded as the first song ended and rolled into "Lyin' Eyes" by the Eagles.

David toasted him. "The very ones."

Jimmy dropped "Lyin' Eyes" after the first chorus and rolled into Cozy's next number. Sal pushed his girth up out of his chair and wandered over to where David and Calico were sitting. "How about you let us see it?"

"Excuse me?" David said.

"Let us see the money. Why not? I'd kinda like to see what two million dollars looks like."

"Sal, please," Rufus said.

"I'm serious. We're all friends, right?"

"Are we, Sal?" David said.

"Dave, you hurt my feelings."

David smiled. "We wouldn't want that to happen, would we?" He downed half the tumbler of rum, then lifted a shoulder. "Why not?" He played with the combo lock on the case and then lifted the lid. Calico pulled in a breath at the sight of the tightly stacked hundred-dollar bills.

"That's two mil?" Sal said.

"To the penny."

"What's in the big envelope?"

"A short manuscript. Just something I wrote a while back."

Now Rufus got up and walked over. "That the pirate novel?"

David closed the lid and locked the case. "No, it isn't."

"Wait a minute. Was that *the* story?" Rufus said.

"A lot of stories in the world. I'm afraid you'd have to be much more specific than that."

"You know exactly what I'm talking about. *The* story. The lost story."

"What's the lost story?" Sal said.

The door banged open with the wind again, and Burt blew in, hand clamped down over his cowboy hat. "Sorry about that."

"That's all right." Calico stood. "Can I get you something?"

"Coffee if you've got any on. And whatever Juan's got back there that smells so dang good."

"Coffee coming up. Juan took off so he wouldn't get stuck out here, but he made us dinner before he left."

"Buck, you just cost me the company of a pretty woman," David said. "Might as well sit down here and have a little rum. It's no fun drinking alone. Well, not much fun, anyway."

"It's still and always will be Burt. Coffee's fine for me." He slid into a booth. "No offense. This is a little easier on my back."

"Roping those wild horses has to be tough on the body, man," Rufus said.

Burt eyed him. "Ranching ain't an easy life, but I wouldn't trade it."

"See, Sal?" Rufus said. "Man says it's not an easy life. Leave those horses alone."

Sal gave him a look like a dagger. "I could still do it."

Calico stepped into the kitchen, and minutes later she returned with a large tray. "We won't be full service tonight, but at least Juan left us the best green enchiladas you'll ever have, Burt. I can guarantee it."

"I'm starving," he said with a smile. "So how 'bout I take half of those? Everybody else can split the rest."

"Not to worry, sweet Calico," David said. "As long as the Bacardí holds out, I believe we can survive anything."

"I still want to know what *the* story is," Sal said.

The phone by the cash register rang. Calico answered it, then listened before saying, "I understand." More listening, then the man on the other end went silent mid-sentence.

"Hello?" She shook the receiver. "Hello?" She picked up her cell, glanced at it, then looked at Rufus and Sal. "It looks like you're not going anywhere even if you want to. That was the highway patrol. Highway 41 is already washed out in four places. Nobody can get in or out in either direction."

"For how long?" Sal said.

"I have no idea. The phone went dead before they could tell me. No cell service either. Everything's down. I'd guess a few days at least."

Lightning lit the window, thunder boomed, and the rain roared.

CHAPTER THIRTY-SEVEN

Bones was more than invisible. He was made of clear smoke. He felt like he could seep right through walls if he wanted to. Nobody in the lounge had batted an eye when he slipped in and took a seat in his usual booth by the stage. It was magic. He'd listened, liking it, as Cozy sang a sad song about a bayou. He didn't get up when David August opened his case. He definitely would have liked to see that much money in one place, but invisible was invisible.

When the phone rang, Bones had a feeling about it. He'd lived in Paradise his whole life, and he'd seen storms like this before. Flash floods rushing down from high up in the mountains could and would bring whole trees with them. Roads didn't stand a chance. And so, just like that, with a phone call, the staff and passengers on the cruise ship Venus learned they were marooned. Like Robinson Crusoe. Or Shackleton. Bones would have loved the fact except for the gun he felt sure was stashed somewhere on Sal's considerable person.

Calico, Jimmy, and Cozy. Burt the rancher. David August with a case full of millions and a couple of armed thieves. And then there was Nelson Black. Where was he? Black definitely wasn't the person you wanted to be stuck with on a desert island or an ice floe or a rudderless cruise ship.

"Heya, Bones."

Bones heart thumped loud enough to drown out Jimmy and Cozy

when he turned to find Black sitting across from him in the booth. Like the guy lived in his head.

"You look like you've seen a ghost, kid."

"Where did you come from?"

"Me? Nowhere. Look at you sitting here quiet as a church mouse. We walk through walls, you and I, don't we? Ain't life grand?"

"I don't walk through walls."

"Ah, it's easy. I could teach you." The illusionist glanced toward the box on the piano. "Look at it just sitting there. I'm patiently waiting, you know."

Bones didn't know what to say, so he didn't say anything.

"The thing about storms? They can present so many possibilities." Black winked as he slid out of the booth. He turned to Jimmy. "How about two and a half million?"

Jimmy laughed a little and shook his head, never missing a note.

"Three million?"

Nothing but blues.

Nelson shrugged, winked at Bones again, and sauntered off toward the bar.

Cozy finished a song and then stepped down off the stage to help Calico serve Juan's enchiladas.

Rufus slid into a chair at David's table. "Dave, seriously. Is that the story?"

"Russell, seriously. Was an ant about to crawl on me at the pool?"

"You think I'd lie?"

"I think everyone lies."

"The story, man. I gotta know."

"The story. Once again, the world has turned rumor into legend. The world always does that when it gets bored enough."

"What is this story?" Sal said. "Come on."

"They're referring, Salvador," Black said from the bar, "to David August's transcendent story. If rumor is to be believed, which it rarely should, this particular story is the greatest ever written. Life changing.

Unforgettable. Indescribable, even. Which is why no one ever describes it. Am I right, Dave?"

"No one ever describes it because no one has ever read it," August said. "Beautiful Calico? Another rum, please? On a blustery night like this, you might as well bring the bottle."

Calico brought the drink but left the bottle behind the bar.

August rubbed a hand over the scabs on his head and sighed. "Flattery upon flattery, and yet she arrives bottle-less. Am I being judged?"

"Not at all," Calico said. "You're being cared about."

"Ah! An arrow to my heart. Run away with me. We'll leave this cruel world behind."

"You've already run away. You landed here."

"Too true. The woman is both beautiful and wise, a somewhat dangerous combination in my experience, which isn't little."

Calico halted and turned on her way back to the tray. "Please don't tell a story about some model in Fiji."

"Are you sure? I could. It's a good story."

Calico and Cozy finished their rounds with the plates. Enchiladas, beans, and rice. Corn chips, no doubt still hot. Bowls of fresh salsa. They set a plate on a table near the stage for Jimmy. When they moved right past Bones, he almost laughed.

"So, Dave, what would a legendary, rumored, story in an envelope like that be worth?" Sal said around a mouthful of chips.

"Ah, a man who gets straight to the heart of what matters to him. Not what's it about, not if he can read it, straight to asking what it's worth. The answer to that, my conniving friend, is nothing. It's not worth the paper it's printed on. Or in this case, written in longhand."

"What do you mean conniving?" Sal said.

Rufus shook his head. "It means—"

Sal's fat cheeks flamed. "I know what the word means. I want to know why he called me that."

"Am I wrong?" August said.

"The story is priceless," Rufus said. "A thing like that, you can't put a value on."

Sal shook his head. "How can you know it's priceless if no one's ever read it? Maybe it's horrible. Or maybe it's nothing at all. Maybe he made the whole thing up."

"I didn't make it up," August said.

"It's priceless, Sal, because it's David August. And it's mysterious. A lost work."

Sal grunted a laugh. "Don't look very lost to me."

Black's food sat untouched. He stood behind the bar sipping a scotch he'd poured himself. "The word *priceless* is perfectly accurate. Isn't it interesting? Here we all sit, or in my case stand, in the middle of the desert, cut off from all civilization—and help—for who knows how long with two virtually priceless objects. Jimmy's amazing box and a lost manuscript written by arguably the most venerated and well-known author of our generation."

He smiled. "And just to ice the cake, or maybe toss a little gas on the fire, we also have a case stuffed full with two million dollars. Very tempting to the right person or persons, wouldn't you say? *Conniving* is such a fun word."

"When you put it like that, it makes me feel nervous," Cozy said.

Another flash of lightning, thunder booming.

"We probably should feel nervous," Black said. "Jimmy, you're awfully quiet tonight."

Jimmy swallowed the bite he was chewing. "Way I see it, you're talking enough for all of us. Calico, you're right. I don't believe I've ever tasted enchiladas this good."

"Three and a half million dollars," Black said.

Jimmy took another bite. "You gonna eat, Bones?"

Cozy looked startled. "Bones, you're so quiet I didn't even see you there. I'll get you a plate."

"It's okay. I'm not that hungry."

"I thought you were holed up in the shop." Calico said. "You have to eat something."

"I'm cool."

Cozy headed into the kitchen.

Lightning. The lights flickered, dimmed, then brightened again.

Black gave a pretend shiver. "Oh my. Abandon all hope, ye who enter here."

"You talk too much, you know that?" Sal said.

"Do I?"

"Yeah, you do."

"Sal, please," Rufus said.

"That's a very rude thing to say, Salvador," Black said.

"That's another thing. Who said you could call me Salvador? Nobody calls me that."

"Nobody?"

"My aunt. That's all."

"Salvador. I like it much more than Sal. Sal sounds like a truck driver. Or a cook in a greasy-spoon diner."

"Watch your mouth, Black. I don't care how famous you are."

"Oh, I'm very famous. You know that. But what are you going to do, Salvador? Shoot me?"

"What?"

"With your secret gun there. Are you going to shoot me?"

"What gun?" Calico said.

"The one under Salvador's shirt. In his waistband. I would guess it's a .38 caliber. He's planning on robbing us with it. That is your plan, isn't it, Salvador?"

"You shut your mouth," Sal said. "This ain't no Netflix show. Things might happen you can't edit out."

"You'd be surprised," Black said.

Sal stood.

"Not now, Sal." Rufus to the rescue. "Leave it alone."

But the pistol was out. Pointed at the illusionist.

"Oh dear," Black said. "It looks like I've let the kitten out of the bag."

Lightning.

Thunder.

The lights flickered again.

Then went out.

CHAPTER THIRTY-EIGHT

Bones heard only silence in the blackness for what seemed like hours. But it was probably less than fifteen seconds before lightning flashed, illuminating Sal standing, his gun still leveled. Then back to darkness.

"You know, Calico"—David's voice—"about now I sure wish you had brought me that bottle."

"When's the power coming back on?" Sal said.

"I don't know," Calico said. "It could be hours. Even days. Would you please put the gun down?"

"You don't have a whatchamacallit? One of those emergency electricity motors?"

"I think you mean a generator," Rufus said.

"You don't have a generator?" Sal said.

"It's on the growing list of things we need," Calico said.

"On the list. Great."

"Are you still holding a gun?"

"Yeah, I'm holding a gun. I'm robbing you. Like the man said."

"You're robbing me? Why?"

"I'm robbing everybody. Me and Rufus, we're taking everything."

Calico's voice had an edge. "I have about thirty dollars in the cash drawer. How far into Mexico does that get you?"

"It'll buy a couple of nice martinis when it's tagged on top of this two mil. It blows my mind. It really does. August here is stupid enough to carry two million dollars around with him like it's a few bills in a money clip. Not to mention a metal box apparently worth a whole lot more than that. Maybe I'm no genius, but I can at least add."

The unmistakable sound of a gun cocking came through the dark.

"I'm no expert on firearms," Black said, "but I don't believe a .38 auto sounds like that. No, I believe that's the sound of vintage western thunder. What did they call it? The Peacemaker? Interesting moniker for a Pistola, don't you think?"

"What are you going to do, Dave?" Sal said. "Start wailing away in the dark? With innocent people around?"

"No, I'm going to point my gun at the sound of your voice and pull the trigger."

"Will you both please put the guns down?" Calico said. "Someone will get killed in here."

"Over two million dollars," Black said. "You know, it's really not that much money in this day and age."

"I should have gotten more." August's speech was beginning to show the liquor. "That darn Katz. Wife looks exactly like a manatee."

"Since we're in the conversation now, and there's no putting the fluff back in the pillow, there's also the manuscript," Sal said.

"What about my manuscript?"

"Well, Dave, it's in my mind that that story of yours is probably worth several times a briefcase full of cash."

"You'll take this manuscript over my dead body."

"That's the general idea."

"Sal, please," Rufus said. "Dave, we don't want anyone to get hurt. You just need to understand. It's been kind of a rough year."

"The story goes with us," Sal said. "That weird metal box too."

"Never," August said.

"Can I interject with an interrogative?" Black.

"What?" Sal.

"He wants to ask a question." Rufus said.

"Why doesn't he just say that, then?"

"Dave," Black said. "If it comes right down to it, would you really shoot a snake between the eyes?"

"I'm not sure yet."

"I'll step on a cockroach, I'll tell you that," Sal said.

"If I couldn't bring myself to pull the trigger, he'd have to shoot me for this manuscript. When I say never, I mean never."

"No problem on my end." Sal.

"Sal, please." Rufus, still trying.

"Come on, Dave." Sal again. "You'd really die for a stupid story?"

"This story is all I have left. Not to mention the fact I'm halfway dead already."

"Don't talk like that, Dave," Rufus said.

"The compassionate robber. It really is priceless." Black this time.

It was quiet for a few seconds. Wind and rain against the outer walls.

"Boys," August finally said, "I do have to say I find your timing questionable."

"Why?" Sal.

"Even if you do take everything, where are you going to go? After all, we're trapped here."

"I meant it when I said I was a fan, Dave," Rufus said. "Nothing personal in all this, all right?"

"Shut up, would you, Russell?" Sal said. "Seriously, kissing up to the mark, man?"

"I only let Dave call me Russell. The name is reserved."

"Anyway, I'll figure out something. I'm sure there's a way out of here somehow.

"The man's right, Sal. Your timing never has been good."

"Man, did we not discuss this in the room? We had a plan. *This* is the plan. What's your problem?"

"My problem is plans have to adapt with changing circumstances and environments. Yes, the plan was to do this tonight, but certain events have occurred making said plan no longer viable. Which also makes you an idiot."

"I get very, very tired of your condensation, you know that?"

"I think you mean condescension."

"See? Right there. You're doing it again."

"If you didn't make it so easy . . ."

Bones felt the seat next to him dip. Black's low whisper came to his ear. "Perfect time, Bones. Think about it. All you gotta do is pick up the box and walk through walls."

Another press of the seat, and the man was gone.

And Bones found himself thinking about it. He could actually pull it off. Hide the box somewhere in the kitchen or even right here in the room. Then smuggle it out and hide it in the shop until the chaos died down. He'd be questioned, but he'd just deny everything. After all, he was in a dark room with admitted thieves. And Nelson Black, who made no secret of the fact he was willing to spend a fortune to get the box.

He shifted in his seat. His pulse quickened. A dozen thoughts flashed through his brain in a second. It was funny, but he could practically see the whole scene in his mind's eye. Knew how many steps to the piano. Where the stage began and ended. Where the tables he'd have to avoid were. And a booth near the door had a loose seat. As far as he knew, he was the only one who knew about it. He could lift the bench and put the box in there within seconds. A perfect hiding place. But what if the lights came back on while he was doing all this? What if he tripped? Or stumbled?

But it was now or never. He'd never get a better chance. He could be free and away. He'd have everything he'd ever wanted. Then again, what if Sal heard something and decided to shoot into the dark?

No. Impossible. He was invisible. He was clear smoke. Silent as pooled moonlight.

But then Jimmy's cigarette lighter flicked to life and the opportunity was gone. Crazy how such a tiny flame could chase away so much darkness.

Bones's eyes went to the box.

Jimmy's eyes were on Bones. "You all right, Bones?"

"Yeah. Why?"

Sal still held his gun pointed at Black, who was now back behind the bar. How he'd moved around the room so silently and effortlessly was a mystery. Then again, the dude was famous for that sort of stuff.

August held his gun on Sal.

"Now what, Sal?" Black said.

"That's an excellent question," August said. "Do we all die? This is exactly what they mean when they say the ending of a story is so important."

"Except this ain't no story," Sal said. "This ain't no book, man. This is real."

"They asked a question, Sal," Rufus said. "Now what?"

"Who's side are you on?"

"Right now I'm on mine."

"That's just great, Rufus. Just great."

"Seriously, what are you gonna do? Stand there until they get the roads fixed?"

"Why do you ask me, man? This is your deal too."

"I don't think it is. Not like this. Not with a bunch of people in here and no way to get out."

"Maybe we should all take a breath," Calico said. "Please?"

Burt, silent to this point, cleared his throat. "You want to steal some money, fine. But women and a kid are in here. They got nothing to do with this."

"Neither do you, so shut up," Sal said.

"You pull a pistol out in my presence, I got everything to do with it. Make no mistake about that."

"Sit down, Sal," Rufus said. "Sit down and use your head for once."

Sal turned the gun on August. "Give me the case."

"No."

"Sal, please," Rufus said.

"I want the case."

"Dude, he's got a gun too. What's the matter with you?"

"He ain't gonna shoot me."

"How do you know?"

"I know."

August dropped his gun. "He's right. I'm not going to shoot him. I don't even know if this thing is loaded. I haven't checked it in years."

"Are you serious?" Rufus said.

"Oh come on. That's beautiful," Black said.

August unlocked the case, took out the manuscript, then closed and latched the case again before pushing it toward Sal, his gun on top. "Congratulations. Two million untraceable dollars. Go wild."

"See?" Sal said to Rufus. He sat down across from August and pulled the case and gun in front of him. "I still need that manuscript."

"Not happening."

"We'll see."

Bones jumped a little when Jimmy offered up a one-handed string of notes.

"Music. Just the ticket to soothe the troubled soul," August said.

"Sing a little, Cozy?" Jimmy said.

Cozy had been pressed up against a wall next to the restrooms. Her face was pale in Jimmy's flickering flame. "What? Now?"

"Sure. Why not?"

"Maybe because up until a minute ago two men were pointing guns," Calico said. "She's scared, like the rest of us." Her hands shook as she started lighting a line of candles she'd placed on the bar.

"I can try to sing," Cozy said.

August nodded, then drank his glass dry. "Nobody's judging you, lovely Cozy. And I, for one, will much appreciate it. After all, I've recently taken a large financial downturn. Calico, in light of recent developments, what are the latest rules on the rum?"

CHAPTER THIRTY-NINE

Listening to Cozy sing about a nighttime train in a shaky voice, Bones came to the hard realization that on the fence was an uncomfortable place to exist. He wasn't an indecisive person. And one thing in life he'd learned from an early age was you had to scrap for what you got. And in a scrap, sometimes people got hurt.

But could he hurt Jimmy La Roux? That was the question, and it confused him. He wanted the Harley, and he wanted freedom. Even as he thought it, though, he knew he had a third option. He could simply ride out on the Honda and forget the box, Black, the Harley . . . Forget everything. Freedom was the thing that really counted. No strings to hold him. The Venus, Calico, Jimmy? They would all be nothing but memories once he was down the road. And memories didn't count. Memories could be stuffed into some trunk in the back of a person's head and forgotten.

But he couldn't shake the way Jimmy's Harley had felt beneath him. The roar of pipes. The speed. Jimmy would understand, right?

He glanced at the box, shining in the candlelight. He should have taken it when he had the chance. He hated the box in that moment. Wished he'd never seen it. Never heard about it. Wished it didn't exist at all.

Burt gave a low chuckle.

"What?" Sal said.

"I was just thinking this has to be the slowest robbery in the history of the West."

Sal looked at Rufus. "What are you laughing at?"

"He's right. You have to admit the situation isn't without humor, man."

"I don't find anything funny about it at all." Sal pointed his gun at August again. "What's the combo?"

August waved a hand at the pistol. "Do you have any idea how uncomfortable it is to look down a gun barrel? It's 4572."

"You better not be lying."

"Sal, that might be the dumbest thing that's come out of your pie hole yet," Rufus said. "Why would the man lie?"

Sal worked the lock and opened the case. He lifted out a stack of hundreds and sniffed it. "All this money, man. For a made-up story? That's crazy. It ain't right."

"It's called art," Rufus said. "Have you ever read a book?"

"Of course I've read books."

"Did any of them speak to you? Make you feel something?"

"Not that I recall."

"You've never read a book."

"I have. *Jaws*."

"You saw the movie."

"You don't know that."

"Name a book that isn't a movie and tell me something about it. Anything."

"You know what? Shut up. I don't have to prove anything to you, and I'm sick of you making me feel like I do."

"I'm just saying a book can be a priceless thing."

"Don't blame Sal," August said. "Not long ago I'd walk through an airport or ride a subway, or even go to a restaurant, and see a hundred people reading a book. Today it's all about the four-inch screen. I'm afraid the written word is rapidly going the way of the dinosaur. It's a fading art and a lost discipline."

"I still read," Rufus said.

Sal groaned. "You're such a kiss-up."

Thunder crashed, shaking the walls. Wind moaned outside the window. Cozy sang about someone having too many angels. Sal started pulling out stacks of bills.

"What are you doing?" Rufus said.

"Setting up the game."

"What game?"

Sal grinned and pulled a deck of cards from his jacket pocket. "When's the last time you played five-card draw with two million bucks on the table? Ante will be a Benjamin."

Rufus considered the money. "A hundred-dollar ante?"

"You got a better idea? Tiddlywinks? Thumb wars? What else we got to do during the slowest robbery in the West? Let's play."

"With only two guys?"

"I'll play," Burt said. "But Rufus holds the firearm."

"Nice try," Sal said. "Tell you what. You'll play anyway."

"I don't think so."

Sal picked up his pistol. "Get over here and sit down."

Burt did as he was told. "I've only got about two hundred bucks in my pocket, so this game might be short as far as I'm concerned."

Sal slid several stacks of hundreds in front of the rancher. "It's your lucky day. Don't get used to it, though. You ain't keeping it. August, you're in too."

"You're inviting me to play poker with money you're stealing from me?"

"No, I'm inviting you to a game with money I *already* stole from you. Money you don't deserve anyway."

"He deserves it and more," Rufus said.

"Why? What's he need money for? He's holed up in a dump motel drinking himself into oblivion. This two million is nothing but a weight he has to lug around."

"He does have a point there," August said. "I believe I might be getting carpal tunnel syndrome."

"He's a drunk," Sal said. "When's the last time he wrote anything? I bet he can't even do it anymore."

"I can," David said.

"Yeah? Go ahead. Make something up."

August scratched at a scab, then pointed at Sal's pistol. "'Put it away, Lucas,' Vernon said. 'Orville, shame on you.' Vernon, a stout character in a flannel shirt, knocked Orville's gun away with one hand and then slapped the lad's peach-fuzzed face with the other. Orville staggered back, eyes wide with shock, a red handprint practically glowing on his pale cheek.

"Vernon stepped in then, throwing a right to Orville's ear, a left to the lad's gut. A scream cut the room, causing Vernon to step back. A woman trembled in the hallway opening, her own pale face a mask of horror. She held a stained silk robe tight at the throat with one thin hand. She held the other over her mouth. Vernon stood, fight drained out of him at the sight of her. His arms hung at his sides now, his breath coming in ragged gasps. 'I love you, Claire. It had to be done.'"

David took a sip of rum. "How's that?"

Sal stared. "You just made that up? Right now on the spot?"

"There would be edits and rewrites, of course, but it's a decent rough."

"That's crazy."

"I told you," Rufus said.

August picked up a stack of bills and thumbed it. "In the inevitable film adaptation, Orville would be played by some pretentious teen-idol television brat, maybe a singer trying to parlay his rap career onto the screen. I think America—maybe not his sixteen-year-old fans but the rest of us—would thoroughly enjoy seeing the kid get roughed up."

"What was wrong with her?" Sal said.

"Wrong with who?"

"The woman in the hallway. She's sick, right? Dying? But Vernon loves her even though it's hopeless?"

"Could be."

"So you gonna finish that story or what?"

"I'll think about it. In the meantime, let me win some money back."

"You can play, but don't get any thoughts. The money's mine."

August sipped again. “What thoughts? My mind is an empty room.”

“Need a fifth at the table?” Black said from his barstool.

“Not a chance,” Sal said. “You stay where you are.”

“But I do love cards.”

“I bet you do. You probably have a dozen up your sleeve with your rabbits.”

Black chuckled. “You are fun, Salvador.”

Sal tapped the pistol. “Don’t call me Salvador. And you ain’t seen nothing yet, Merlin.”

“Oh, I’m on pins and needles.”

“Who’s dealing?” Rufus said.

Sal looked around the table, brows knit.

Black held up Sal’s deck of cards. “Are you looking for these?”

“See?” Sal said. “That’s exactly why you ain’t playing.”

Black tossed the deck to Sal. “They’re shuffled. You’re welcome.”

CHAPTER FORTY

Sometimes an inanimate object can be the loudest thing in a room. That night in the Venus lounge, rain drumming and wind moaning, candlelight throwing distorted shadows across the walls, Sal's pistol definitely fit that bill. It sat on the table never more than an inch or two from the man's hand, blued steel reflecting dull light.

Cozy sang, her voice gathering some strength as she went on. Jimmy played. Calico stood behind the bar, her back straight with nerves. Black maintained his barstool-perch eyes on the poker game.

Bones took all this in from his booth by the stage.

For an hour the men shuffled, dealt, and played. Stacks of money went back and forth, nobody's stack growing faster than the others'. They barely talked.

Even without discourse, Sal kept a superior air about him. He sat erect in his chair, barking an occasional order about who's turn it was to deal or who hadn't bet or who needed to draw. On one particular hand that had come down to August and Sal, a large stack of hundreds between them, Bones watched August fold with a straight flush.

Sal laughed when he played a pair of sevens. "You gotta learn to read the bluff, pal."

"I make it a general rule not to call bluffs when the man across the table has a pistol." August sipped his third rum. His words were getting downright soggy now.

"You saying this gun gives me an unfair advantage at this table?"

"Absolutely."

"What about you, Burt? This gun a distraction for you?"

Burt shrugged. "It don't help."

Sal grinned and patted his weapon. "Good. Your deal, Rufus."

"Yeah, all right."

"What's the matter with you?"

"I'm bored, man. That's what's the matter with me."

"How can you be bored? We're playing poker with hundred-dollar bills."

"So? Nobody has any real skin in the game. Might as well be playing with toothpicks."

"Well it ain't changing. Better than sitting here staring at the walls."

"Not much." Rufus dealt.

Betting went around. Discards, draws, more bets. The pot grew to at least fifty thousand or so. August folded again. So did Rufus. Burt wound up taking the money. Sal laughed. He was a few martinis in and doing a lot of that.

Bones considered the situation. All that money. The guy with the pistol drinking martinis. August slumped down in his chair a little now. Burt looking more and more agitated. Sal hadn't said anything about Jimmy's box yet, but he would when the time came. What would Jimmy do? Bones couldn't see the biker rolling over when it came to the box, pistol or no pistol.

Jimmy ended a song, and Cozy started to step off the stage.

"What do you think you're doing?" Sal said.

"I just want to take a break. It's been a while."

"We're still playing, so you're still singing."

"It's just that I—"

Sal picked up the pistol. "You're still singing."

"Put that down," Burt said.

Sal looked at the rancher. "You want one in the knee, man?"

"Put it down or I'll take it from you and shove it down your throat."

"I want to hear the lady sing."

"And the lady wants to take a break."

Sal got to his feet and put the pistol barrel against Burt's forehead. "How about this? You still feel like arguing?"

"Sal, stop," Calico said. "Sit down, and I'll bring you a cup of coffee, all right?"

"You'll bring me another martini."

"Burt, I can sing," Cozy said. "It's fine. Really."

"You want a break, take a break," Burt said.

"Are you crazy or something?" Sal said. "You've got a gun against your brain."

"Held by a little man who's in way over his head. I'm tired of everything about this. You want to pull the trigger, go ahead. I don't think you've got the sand."

"You'd die for a lounge singer?"

"You're a bully and a child. Either pull that trigger or put the gun down before I take you over my knee and give you the spanking you deserve."

Sal's face went red, his knuckles white.

"Sal," Rufus said. "Robbery is one thing, killing a man is another."

Sal glanced at Cozy, then back at Burt. He smiled. "You like her, don't you?"

Burt said nothing.

"Tell you what. I'll let her take a break. As long a break as she wants. But it'll cost you something."

"I don't have anything you want. You've already got my two hundred."

"You been acting all high-and-mighty like Arizona's better than Brooklyn ever since we got here. I can rope a horse anytime I want, and I didn't say I wanted anything from you. I said it would *cost* you something. I got big ears, and I hear things. For instance, I hear you got a ring you carry around in your pocket."

"So?"

"So take that ring out of your pocket and put it in Jimmy's box."

"No."

"Do it."

"I won't."

"I'll sing. I don't mind," Cozy said.

"Sal, stop." Calico's face was white.

Jimmy was still and quiet. Black was smiling, expectant.

"Sal," Rufus said.

"Shut up, Miller. This guy still don't think I could rope a horse."

"Why are you still on about the horse thing, man? This is what I'm talking about. Your insecurities—"

"Take the ring out of your pocket and give it to me," Sal said.

"Pull the trigger," Burt said.

Sal pressed the gun hard enough to push back Burt's head. "You think I won't?" He looked at Rufus. "And you. You think I can't rope a horse? You think my timing's bad? You think I'm stupid because I don't read books and know a bunch of words? You think I got nothing going except this gun? You're like the rest of them."

"Get a grip, man, please," Rufus said.

"It seems our triggerman is in a very fragile place at the moment," Black said.

Sal swung the pistol toward the illusionist. "You want to say that again?"

"Look, Sal." Rufus. "This whole thing is about two million dollars, which you now have. That's all we came for. We're going to Italy, right? To hang with the surfers."

"Don't you dare patronize me."

"I'm not. Sure they surf in Italy. I was just yanking your chain before. Just put the gun down. I know you want to."

Sal stepped back and swung the gun toward his partner. "You know what, man? You got all the answers all the time. Here's a question. How you gonna feel when I drive away with this case and leave you here with your washed-up drunk writer?" He swung the gun to August. "Speaking of you, give me the story."

"You can't have the story. I've made that clear."

"Give it to me now."

August shook his head. "I'm with Burt on this one. You might as well pull the trigger. I mean, why not?"

"Sal," Rufus said.
"Give me the story, August."
"I can't do that."
A piano note rang throughout the room.
Then another.
Then a slow blues run.

CHAPTER FORTY-ONE

BONES WATCHED FROM HIS BOOTH as Sal stared at Jimmy.

"What do you think you're doing?" Sal said.

Jimmy paused on a passing chord, felt it, and rolled into another run. "Sit down, Sal."

"You think you can tell me—"

"Sit down." Jimmy's voice wasn't loud, but Bones had never heard such authority. "I know you don't want to shoot anybody."

Sal slowly sank into the chair but kept the gun in his hand. "Who do you think you are?"

Jimmy lifted a shoulder, his milky eye pinning the guy. "Tell you what. You want to steal Dave's story? Why don't you listen to it first?"

"What's that got to do with anything? It's worth money. I don't care nothing about what it is."

Jimmy lifted both shoulders this time. "You cared what happened to the lady in his little made-up scene, didn't you? Maybe you'll want to hear this one too."

"Are you nuts? I want to leave, is what I want."

"Sure, but you can't. What can you do but go sit in your car or your dark motel room?"

"I'm taking the story. And I'm taking your box too."

"Still, it's not every day you're stuck in a storm with a famous writer with a legendary lost manuscript. I'm curious, aren't you?"

Sal shook his head. "You're too much. I'm holding a gun, and you think it's story time?"

Light reflected off the milky eye. "Put the gun away, Sal."

"I'll say when—"

"It's not loaded. Put it down. I'm telling you right now, you'll be relieved."

"You think I'd come in here with an unloaded gun?"

"Probably not on purpose."

"What's that supposed to mean?"

"Want to tell him, Nelson?"

Black sighed on his stool. "How do you do it, Jimmy? Seriously. I'm the best."

"Do what?" Sal said.

Black reached into his pants pocket and pulled out a handful of cartridges, let them drop one by one onto the bar.

Sal looked at his pistol. He ejected the magazine, then shook his head. "How did . . . I've had it with me the whole time."

Black shrugged and lifted another bottle of scotch.

"Thank God," Calico said.

"Amen and pass the gravy," August added.

Jimmy modulated from one key to another. "So what do you say, Dave?"

August took a long sip of rum. "I say no."

"It's all right. Tell you what. I'll provide the soundtrack. It'll be a night to remember."

"As if it isn't already?"

"Let it go, Dave. It's time, don't you think?"

August swiveled and stared at Jimmy. "What do you know about my manuscript?"

"Just what I've heard. Which isn't much."

"Are you sure about that?"

"You'd be surprised how in the know our Mr. La Roux is," Black said.

"You're obviously carrying a burden, Dave," Jimmy said. "Something you'd take a bullet for. I'm just thinking it's a night of letting go. How about it? Look around. You have a literal captive audience."

"My day is long past."

"Ain't nobody believes that but you." Jimmy rolled into a smokey tune. "How's this?"

"I can't."

"Of course you can."

"I don't know how to start. I'm lost, Jimmy. That's the thing."

"Nah. Maybe out in the rough and the weeds a little, but you'll find the highway again."

"How do you know?"

"I'll put it this way. What do you have to lose?"

David drained his rum glass. Then with shaking hands he lifted the envelope from the table and opened it. He pulled out a thick set of pages. Bones could see the words were handwritten.

August looked at Jimmy.

Jimmy nodded. Then keeping a slow bass line going, he reached over and opened the box.

Wind pounded the walls and rattled the window.

And David August, rum-soaked and scabby-headed, began to read.

CHAPTER FORTY-TWO

The story started with a name, and when the writer spoke it aloud, Calico felt like she'd been punched in the stomach.

It was *her* name. Calico Foster.

Calico moved to the edge of the bar, dumbfounded, listening to the first few sentences, then the next. How could David August know? How could he know about the sun slanting in through the window of the first house she could remember? About the king snake they found in the kitchen that time?

And then, several pages in, the rare-as-diamonds desert hail against a hospital window.

And it went on. Hours of it. Days. Years. Her teens and how she would lie in bed stressing about Charlie not coming home at night. The weeks she'd run her father's middle-of-nowhere bar while he was out on some wild-goose chase looking for a lost mine or Spanish gold. Then her father's death and Charlie running off to Los Angeles. The palms of her hands began to sweat when August brought Pines into the story. Then the Venus. Then Bones . . .

And David August read on.

Rufus leaned forward, his hands white on the table. His mind telling him what his ears were hearing was impossible. How could August know all this stuff?

The story had started with a name.

Rufus Miller.

CHAPTER FORTY-THREE

THE STORM DIDN'T END ABRUPTLY. It gave up the ghost in increments, its lifeblood draining slowly away into the gray, weather-stunned dawn Bones could see barely beginning to get its breath through the single window. He listened as the wind quieted from moan to whisper against the walls. A less-insistent rain pattered against the window. The thunder only a distant rumble now, high up in the eastern peaks.

Jimmy had played for hours. His music shifting from quiet blues to jazz to soaring major crescendos as the story dictated.

And the story of Bones's life was laid bare to the world—or at least to the room.

He'd never been less invisible.

Then David stopped.

So did Jimmy.

Cozy wept quietly at a corner table. The others sat open-mouthed. Tired eyes and disbelief. Like they'd lived through something tragic and brutal and wonderful. Like they'd died and resurrected. Forced into battle, emerging bloody and battered, grieving fallen comrades but glorying in the new dawn. But why them?

"How do you know all that?" Burt said. "You never even saw me until a few days ago. How do you know all that?"

"Saw you?" Rufus said. "He just told you *my* life. I don't understand what's going on here."

August stared at the men. Then down at the manuscript. "What?"

Only Black appeared unfazed. He gave a few slow claps. "Fantastic. Unbelievable. David, tell me. What did you just read?"

"I read an autobiographical sketch. A story of a man staving off demons. No longer of use to the world and walking slowly into a dying sun."

"No you didn't," Calico said. "I don't understand this at all. What's going on?"

"I think Jimmy is going on," Black said. "How, Jimmy? I've never seen anything like it. Is it the box? You opened it before he started reading. It has to be the box."

"It's just a box, Nelson," Jimmy said.

"Wait. We all heard our own story?" Calico said. "That's impossible."

Rufus stood. "It *is* impossible."

"A very overused word around here," Black said. "I've seen master hypnotists. Studied them, the best of the best. But I've never seen anything like this. What can I offer, Jimmy? Let's end this. What will you take?"

"Answer a question for me, Nelson," Jimmy said.

"If I answer it, will you give me the box?"

"We'll see."

"Shoot."

"What story did *you* hear?"

Bones hadn't seen the illusionist with anything but complete control. But he saw him slipping now. The man's eyes tightened. He looked older.

"I'd like to know," Jimmy said.

"I'll give you four million dollars."

Jimmy started to play.

"Four and a half million."

Jimmy worked an intricate run. "You a fan of Coltrane, Nelson? I love the guy's stuff."

"Five million dollars, Jimmy. Are you listening to me?"

"You know, Nelson, not really."

Then the lights came on.

CHAPTER FORTY-FOUR

CALICO STOOD AT THE WINDOW staring out at the gray creeping over the desert. "She's still down."

"Who?" Cozy said.

"Lady Venus. She didn't light up when the electricity came back on."

"I'm sure she will."

"She should have come on at the same time." Calico turned to David. "The ending. Why did you end the story like that?"

"The ending?"

"I don't end up like that. I can't. You can't know the future."

Sal stared at Rufus. "I was thinking the same thing."

"Maybe it's just a story," Rufus said.

"Is it?" Sal said.

"I read what I wrote, that's all," David said. "I don't know what you all heard, but I read what I wrote."

Rufus stood and joined her at the window.

"What was your ending, Sal?" Nelson said.

Sal put a hand on his gun. "Let's just say it ain't much of one."

Burt leaned forward, fingers laced, elbows on his knees. "Maybe it's inevitable. Maybe our paths are marked. Built brick by brick by the decisions we've already made. It'd make sense. I don't pretend to understand what went on here tonight, but I can't deny what I heard. And my ending is pretty dang much what I'd expect."

"You can't know what hasn't even happened yet," Rufus said.

"I swear to you all, I only read what I wrote," David said. "And the ending is no surprise. I know my future as well as my past."

At the piano, Jimmy played a major chord. "I'm not at all sure that's true, Dave. Them weeds are thick, but there's always a way back."

"Or maybe it's all fate." Burt closed his eyes. "Maybe we don't have a choice at all. Maybe the universe unfurls our path as we go."

"*As we go*. That doesn't explain how we all just heard our own future," Calico said.

"Somehow, tonight it unfurled a little too much and gave us a preview," Burt said. "I don't know how, but it did."

"That can't be," Rufus said. "Like Black said, it was some kind of hypnotism. Making our stories come from our own minds."

Burt shook his head. "I didn't feel hypnotized. You make enough decisions in life, and your road gets nailed down. Ain't no changing it. Our past dictates our future. We are who we are."

"No, we're not." Cozy said this loud enough that the whole room turned to look at her. "I'm not who I was. I made a million bad decisions. Things I'm ashamed to even think about. And a bunch of others were made for me. But I'm not sitting on a broken porch giving women in yoga pants dirty looks anymore. I'm not packing cupboards with soup. I'm not beaten down by Don. I don't even sing into the mirror. My path was written for sure, but I got off it. You can get rid of the past. You can be new."

"How do you know that?" David said.

"Because *I'm* new."

Nelson walked over and leaned against the wall next to Cozy. "That's a nice thought. But the truth is you've had a change of scenery, that's all. The past is the past. It *happened*. It's like the old commandments—in stone. It doesn't just follow you; it's *in* you. It *is* you."

"The man's right," Sal said, glaring at Rufus. "We might hate it, but people don't change."

"I'm telling you I did," Cozy said. "I left the past."

"Just how did you do that?" Rufus said.

"I put it in the box."

Silence in the room.

"You can't put your past in the box," Sal finally said.

Cozy nodded. "I did. And I don't only *feel* free. I *am* free."

"It's all in your head," Nelson said. "A trick."

"Then why didn't I hear the end of my story?"

Calico was confused. "You didn't?"

"The story I heard started with my name and ended the second I threw my past into the box. You all heard yours, but I'm writing mine."

David turned in his seat and eyed Jimmy. "Whatever goes into the box is gone forever. That's what you've been saying."

"It's an illusion," Nelson said.

"Says the man who offered five million dollars for it," Jimmy said from the piano.

"What past?" Rufus asked Cozy. "What did you put in the box?"

"A necklace. In my case the past was literally hanging around my neck."

"That's ridiculous," Nelson said. "It was a trick of the mind. Like David's story."

"Maybe it was like some sort of tear in time," Burt said. "Maybe we've been made privy to information we weren't supposed to know."

Rufus stood. "No. No way, man. My story can't end like that."

"Why not?" Sal said. "Maybe you get what's coming to you."

"Because I haven't had my son yet," Rufus said.

Sal stared at him. "What?"

"It's what I've really hoped for down deep, but I wouldn't let myself admit it. I want to have a son. And I want to teach him to surf at C Street in Ventura where I grew up. I want my pregnant wife to lie on the beach while my son and I surf. Then I want us all to go and have tacos." He hung his head. "But I heard the end, man. It can't be."

"You don't even have a wife," Sal said.

"I do. Or I did. Her name is Nora."

"You were married?"

"Until I screwed it up, yeah."

"With a kid?"

"No. But Nora was the best thing that ever happened to me. I was probably the worst that ever happened to her."

"Why didn't you ever tell me?" Sal said. "Seriously, we been doing this a while, man."

"It just never came up, okay? Maybe I like to keep parts of my life separate from all the garbage. Keep them clean."

"Have you tried talking to her?" Cozy said.

"Nah. It's been almost two years."

"It's worth a try."

"I just heard the whole thing in unvarnished prose. I can't even start to imagine what she thinks of me."

"What was the end of your story, Rufus?" Calico said.

He shook his head and looked down at the table again.

"Sure, tell 'em all about it," Sal said. "Starting with how you make it out of here with the money. Tell them all about the knife in your boot."

"It's a mind game, Sal," Nelson said. "It's Jimmy. That's all it is."

"That right, Rufus?" Sal said. "Is it all a mind game? Or is that knife real?"

CHAPTER FORTY-FIVE

BONES LEANED HIS HEAD BACK against the cool leather seat and closed his eyes. He was tired. Not only from lack of sleep but plain old, deep-down tired. He wanted a bike between him and the road. He wanted a long highway and no one to bother him. He wanted invisible perfection for the rest of his days. He wanted to be like Jimmy. Top of the food chain, a lone wolf, no one to touch him and no one to hurt him.

And as soon as the roads were clear, he'd have it.

Why did he feel sad?

It wasn't like he had a choice. What was he going to do? Stay here? What was there for him at the Venus? He looked over at Calico. Nothing, that's what.

"You know what, Miller?" Sal said. "I can't even be mad about it. Hearing all the things I done, all the decisions I made, that guy in the story deserves a knife to his throat. He deserves to lose it all. I don't even care." Sal looked different now, like a big, deflated balloon.

"Then change it," Cozy said.

"You can't change what's already happened."

"I thought that too. Maybe you can't, but you don't have to live with it."

Black laughed.

"What if she's right?" Calico said.

Sal turned to look at her. "She's not. It can't be that easy."

"But what if it is?" Cozy said.

Calico looked at Jimmy. "What about it, Jimmy? What happened here tonight? Did you do it? Like Nelson says you did? What do you have to say?"

Jimmy studied the room for a few seconds. "I say what I've been saying all along. What goes in the box is gone. Cozy's exactly right."

"Come on, people," Black said. "I don't have any idea how this box works, but I can tell you it's not gonna change anybody's life."

"My life is changed," Cozy said. "I don't know what else to say."

"No, Cozy, it isn't changed. The box somehow creates an illusion. That's it, end of story. If you *feel*"—he finger-quoted the word—"better, then good for you. But it's in your head. I hate to break it to you, but you're still the same screwed-up little girl you always were."

Cozy smiled. "I'm not. And I feel very sorry for you, Mr. Black."

Sal stood. "You know what? I don't care if it's real. All I know is I don't like the guy I just met in that story. I hate him, in fact. Maybe there ain't no second chances in life, but I can at least do better than this." He looked down at Rufus. "Tell me the truth. Is there a knife in your boot?"

"Yes, Sal, there is."

Sal looked at Black. "How could my mind make me hear something in that story I didn't know and now it turns out to be true? This is more than a trick, pal." He nodded and walked over to the box. "Whatever happens, happens. I just want to say I don't know a whole lot of big words, and I may not be able to rope a horse, but that guy in the story? My aunt Ninetta would slap that guy into the middle of next year, and he'd have it coming. If there's a chance I can be better than that . . ."

He took a deep breath. "I owe every one of you an apology, not that I think you'll accept it. And I don't blame you. But for what it's worth, I hope this helps." He dropped his pistol inside the box and shut the lid.

"Wonderful speech. We're all so touched. Is it gone?" Black said.

Sal lifted the lid. "Yeah. Like it was never there."

"Maybe it wasn't," Jimmy said.

"Ooh, how mysterious," Black said. "I hope you know Jimmy's going to sell your gun to a backstreet pawn shop in Omaha or St. Louis or fill in the blank."

"All I know is that it's gone as far as I'm concerned," Sal said. "Maybe I can look at myself in the mirror tomorrow."

"Hallelujah. But what does that change?"

Jimmy started playing. Not blues this time. A soft release, an after-storm peaceful resolve. "Maybe everything. I have a thought. Why don't you check the last chapters of your story, Sal?"

"You mind?" Sal said to August.

August scanned the pages. "I'm sorry to tell you, but it's exactly what I read in the first place." He slid the manuscript across the table.

Sal walked over and picked it up. He thumbed to the back, then grinned. "No it ain't. It ends right here. This morning. It ends the second I dropped that gun into the box." He handed the pages back to David, who began reading them all over again.

Black laughed. "I really don't know how you do it, Jimmy. You're the true master here. Maybe I should talk to the folks at Netflix for you. Then again, that's not your style, is it?"

Sal sank into a chair. "It's gone. That hundred-pound pistol is really gone, man."

Rufus reached down, lifted his pant leg, and pulled a long, wicked-looking knife from his boot. "I don't have any idea what's going on here, but you were right. I was gonna figure a way to get all that money and cut and run. I even have a little place down in Puerto Escondido all picked out. One of the best surf breaks I've ever seen. Still cheap down there too."

"How long you been planning this?" Sal said.

"Since we heard about August's money sitting out here where no one knew it was. No, when I think about it, that's not true. I've been planning on splitting ever since we started talking about hitting a big score. Before we knew what it would be. Maybe even since we met. I think I've only been waiting for my chance."

"That's horrible," Cozy said.

"You know what? It is horrible. I've been stupid." Rufus looked at Jimmy. "You think there's room in that box for a knife and a life that's gone with it? Even the stuff I've never told anybody? It's a lot. It would have to be pretty dang big."

Jimmy lifted a shoulder, never missing a note. "Brother, this old box will take anything you got."

Rufus stood and looked down at Sal. "I'm not relaxed, Sal. I never was. But I definitely want to be. I'm sorry for what was in my head, man."

Knife deposited, lid opened again, Rufus crossed the room and picked up the manuscript. He read with intent for several minutes. Then he sat, leaned back in his chair . . . closed his eyes . . .

And smiled.

CHAPTER FORTY-SIX

In the kitchen, Calico made coffee, then started some eggs, bacon, and sliced potatoes sizzling on the big commercial griddle. At least the electricity hadn't been off long enough for food in the freezer and fridge to spoil.

Cozy came in and stood beside her. "One less to feed. David went back to his room. I don't think he's hungry."

"Did he take his money with him?"

"Of course."

"I can see why he's not hungry after nearly a bottle of Bacardí."

"He wasn't walking all that straight, that's for sure. The rest are still in there. Nobody seems like they want to leave. What a strange night. I can't get over it."

"I'm still trying to process. Maybe we were hypnotized like Nelson Black said. That's all I can figure. Do you think that's it?"

"Like Burt said, I didn't feel hypnotized."

"Neither did I, but how would anybody know? If you're really under hypnosis, I doubt you'd realize it."

"I think I would. I got hypnotized at the state fair once. It was really weird. This wasn't anything like that."

"You did that? I always wondered what kind of people actually went up there with the hypnotist. I mean, you know he's going to get you to do embarrassing things in front of a crowd."

"Don talked me into it. It was stupid. I wound up dancing like

Mick Jagger. But hearing my story tonight wasn't like the fair at all. That was all dreamy and gross. This was real. I was wide awake. More real than anything I've ever experienced."

"That's exactly how I felt."

"I've never seen anyone point a gun at somebody before. I was so scared."

"Neither have I."

"At least Sal's gun is gone now. He seems so different, even in the last hour."

Calico looked at her. "You really believe in that box, don't you?"

"How can I not? I've seen it work. I've felt it work."

"I just don't believe it. I *can't* believe it. And yet I heard it plain as day. David August read my life's story, warts and all, right to my face. It's so embarrassing."

"Not really. You're the only one who heard it."

"Supposedly, yeah. But I'm still embarrassed. Seriously, I've been so selfish. I tell myself I'm this way because of others. Because I'm protecting them from *me*. But that's a lie. I'm scared. That's all there is to it."

"When I look at how strong and determined you are, I can't imagine you being scared of anything, Calico. What are you scared of?"

"I don't know. Of letting people down, I think. If I'm being honest, of plain old committing to something I'm afraid to do."

"So what if you do fail? What if you do let someone down?"

"I don't want to. That's the point."

"Then that's a dumb point. Everybody fails, and everybody lets other people down all the time. That's called being human. You can't get away from it."

Calico flipped a few eggs. "It probably doesn't even matter now. Pines hasn't called. He most likely doesn't even want me anymore because of what I said about Bones."

"That's a fat lie, and you know it. Besides, the phones are out, so how do you know if he's tried or not?"

"But what *about* Bones? I can't. I just don't know how . . ."

"Give me a break. Yes you do know. Even with all the tick marks on your stupid list, you've always known. You're just good at lying to yourself."

Calico reached into her back pocket and pulled out her notebook. She shook her head. "Do you know how many cons I've written down about that kid?"

"I can imagine. I bet dozens."

"Up to this point, thirty-eight cons, and every single one of them is valid. You know how many pros?"

"How many?"

"Zero."

"Zero?"

"Zero. Nada."

"Give me that thing."

Calico handed it to Cozy. "Why? Don't you throw it away."

"I'm not going to throw it away. I'm going to add to your list." She grabbed the pen next to the kitchen phone.

"In what column?"

"Which do you think? Pro, of course."

"What can you possibly add? Believe me, I've wracked my brain."

Cozy wrote, then handed the notebook back. "I can add this."

Calico looked at the page. Eggs sizzled on the griddle. "That he needs me."

"Exactly."

"I'm not sure this is fair."

"Fair or not, it sounds to me like the scale is completely weighted to one side."

Calico stared at the book. "You know what? You're right. I've been stupid."

"Definitely. But who hasn't? The question is what you're going to do about it."

CHAPTER FORTY-SEVEN

A WAVE OF FATIGUE WASHED over Calico as she and Cozy served breakfast and poured coffee. The room filled with that kind of quiet relief that always seems to come after storms, both physical and spiritual. Even Nelson Black kept his thoughts to himself.

They all ate in silence, low wind and occasional light rain pattering against the window. After a while, food gone, Rufus drained the last of his coffee and stood. "Thanks. That hit the spot."

"You're welcome," Calico said.

"You leaving, then?" Sal said.

"I'm gonna head back to the room." He pulled his cell out and checked it. "This thing's still not working, but maybe that's a good thing. I think I'm going to write Nora a letter. A long one. Letters are better. I can take my time and say what I want to say without screwing it up. At least I hope. Maybe I'll even mail it. I doubt it'll do any good, but I need to do it. Even if she never reads it. I'm thinking I might write one to the kid too."

"Is this the kid who doesn't exist?" Nelson said.

"The very one. I don't expect you to understand."

"I think that's beautiful, Rufus," Cozy said. "And I think you should mail it. I have a feeling you might be surprised."

"Yeah?"

"I really do."

"You people are a living, breathing soap opera." Nelson grinned. "I love every second of it."

Rufus held out his hand to Sal. "I'm sorry, Sal. Are we good?"

Sal took the offered hand. "You're sorry for what? Thinking you'd take the whole stash? I was gonna do the same thing. Why do you think I had the gun in the first place?"

"I know you were. I'm still sorry, man. Not only for that, though. I talked about your insecurity, but really it was all mine. You're not stupid."

Sal shook his head. "You kidding? Safe to say I ain't winning any Nobel Prize for my intellect. And you were right. I've never read a real book."

Rufus laughed. "That's true. I know you haven't."

"Maybe I will, though. I think I'll start with a David August."

"Excellent choice. At least it's as good a place as any."

"I figured if you've met a dude, you might as well read his books." Sal stood. "I'll go back with you. You might have read some books, but I seen you with the ladies. You're gonna need some help with that letter."

"Uh-huh. And you're an expert on love?"

"I'm from Brooklyn."

"You say that as if it explains something."

"What do you mean? It explains everything. You want help or not?"

"Yeah, man. Come on, then."

"I been thinking. I still think I could rope one of them horses."

"I imagine you could."

"Want to help?"

"Not on your life."

"I'll let you know if there's any change with the phones or the road," Calico said.

Rufus nodded, then looked back at Jimmy. "Thanks, man. I don't really know what else to say."

Jimmy shrugged. "The box is the box. You're the one who stepped up."

"There gonna be music tonight?"

Jimmy smiled. “There’s always music, Rufus. You just gotta listen.”

When the two were gone, Calico started cleaning up. “You should go get some sleep, Cozy. I’ll take care of this.”

“I can help. Aren’t you tired?”

“I’m exhausted, but I want to do it. Get some sleep. Consider it an order from your boss.”

Cozy smiled. “I think I’ll go out on the pool deck and watch the sun come over the mountains first. I love the dawn after a storm.”

“Sounds nice.”

“Also sounds a little lonely, doesn’t it, Burt?” Jimmy said.

Burt shifted in his seat. “I’ll admit I wouldn’t mind seeing a nice sunrise. It’s been a while. You mind if I tag along, Cozy?”

She smiled. “I was wondering if you’d ever get around to asking me something like that.”

Calico watched as Burt stood and set his hat on his head. “Give me just a second. Something I need to do first.” He walked over to Jimmy and the piano and the box. “What do you think, amigo?”

Jimmy smiled and started to play. “I think you know what I think.”

“I ain’t saying I’ll forget. And I know I’ll still grieve from time to time. I ain’t saying goodbye to the memories—or goodbye at all, for that matter. At least not goodbye forever. It’s just that I need to get on with saying hello to what comes next. And I think what comes next could be pretty dang special.”

“Ivy knows that, Burt. I’m sure of it.”

Burt reached into his pocket, pulled out the gold band, kissed it once, and tossed it into the box.

Then he shut the lid.

CHAPTER FORTY-EIGHT

"And then there were four," Nelson said as the door swung shut behind Cozy and Burt.

Calico slid onto a barstool. "Don't you get tired, Jimmy?"

Jimmy paused his song. "Sure I get tired. But the song's not over." He started again.

"Another cryptic quote from Jimmy La Roux. Now we can all sleep in peace," Nelson said.

"Seems to me like you've been the one doing all the talking." Jimmy didn't miss a note when he glanced at Nelson. Calico figured he never did.

She watched as Bones pulled himself out of his booth, made his way to the bar, and poured a cup of coffee. Calico picked up a sugar jar from a table and slid it to him. He dumped in a heaping spoonful and stirred.

Had Bones heard his story too? But he was a kid, the mess in his life so far not his fault. Of course he'd heard; Bones never missed a thing. Still, she didn't want to stir the waters asking unnecessary questions. Some moments were just too fragile.

"One spoon? Cutting down?" Calico said.

"I guess."

"That's a very grown-up decision."

Bones sipped the brew.

Nelson straightened and stretched. "All right, you've got me, Jimmy.

I'm scratching my head. Come on. How'd you do it? Just us here. I've seen hypnosis. I've seen the best. But the whole room at once? It was truly amazing."

"You'd really give five million dollars for the box, wouldn't you?" Jimmy said.

"Sure. I've got five million dollars, but I don't have the box. Are you saying you'll sell? Have I finally reached your price?"

Jimmy stopped playing. "Nelson, my friend, you haven't even come close."

Nelson shook his head and smiled. "I'll have it. You know that. Somehow I'll have it."

"Thing is you have no idea what that even means."

"I'm willing to find out."

"It's a good practice not to wish for things you don't understand."

Irritation flashed across Nelson's face. "What I don't understand is you. Your smugness isn't nearly as endearing as you think it is. You're small-minded. I'm offering five million dollars for a box. Really. What's the matter with you? I've given you the courtesy—undeserved, I might add—of treating you as a professional. As an equal, even. Yet you continue to condescend. I'm getting tired of playing nice, Jimmy. I hope that's something *you'll* understand."

"I think it's time we all got some sleep," Calico said.

Nelson turned to her. "Pretty Calico, do mind your own business."

"Mr. Black, what happens at this motel *is* my business."

Nelson sighed. "You know, the problem with you people is that you're all small. And your smallness blinds you. Don't you know that past that parking lot out there no one in the world cares about your little kingdom? Yet you act as if this dump is the whole universe. It's pathetic. It really is."

"Don't talk to her like that," Bones said.

Nelson raised an eyebrow in Bones's direction. "Well, well, look at this. Is this loyalty I hear? Maybe our Bones is human after all. Bravo, Bones. Although you really should think hard about where this loyalty of yours lies. You know she doesn't care about you."

"That's not true," Calico said. "I do care about him."

"Do you? Maybe. As an employee, possibly. Someone to sweep your walks and clean your pool. But really, let's not go overboard."

"Bones is more than an employee. He's family."

"Family? You have a strange way of showing it."

Calico glanced at Bones. "Maybe I do. Or have. But he's family. *My* family."

Nelson arched a brow and smiled. "I may cry. I really might."

"Go get some sleep, Bones," Calico said. "You look dead on your feet."

"I'm cool."

"Go on. Get some rest. We'll have a lot to do later."

Bones looked at Black, then back at Calico.

"I'm fine," Calico said. "Go. I'm serious."

"Yeah, okay."

"Bon voyage, Captain Shackleton," Nelson said. "Do watch out for icebergs."

Bones ignored this as he left through the kitchen door.

"You might as well go too, Nelson," Jimmy said. "Neither of us still here care much about your show."

"My show's not over. You should know. You have a starring role. We've still got acts ahead of us. As many as it takes." Nelson started for the lounge door. "So we'll simply call this an intermission."

"Whatever you say."

"You're getting it, Jimmy. It *is* whatever I say." With a last wink at Calico, the illusionist let the door swing shut behind him.

Calico looked at Jimmy. "I think the guy will explode if he doesn't get his hands on your box."

"He's been after it a long time."

"Five million dollars? That's crazy."

"It's sure a big number on the computer screen."

"You really won't think about selling it? Even for five million?"

Jimmy played a chord. "What was the end of your story, Calico? You haven't said."

Calico walked over and leaned on the piano. "Come on. How did you do it, Jimmy? And don't tell me it was all the box."

"You really got a thing against the box, don't you?" He leaned forward and lifted the box's lid. "How about you? You got anything you'd like to say goodbye to?"

"There's no such thing as do-overs except in kids' games. I'm not Cozy."

"But maybe there's such a thing as forgiveness."

"If there is, I haven't stumbled across it yet."

"Sure you have. You stumble across it everywhere you turn. Accepting is the hard part."

Calico sighed. "You have no idea how I've messed things up."

"So? Un-mess them."

"With Pines?"

"From what I gather, that's probably a good place a start."

"And Bones . . ."

"That kid is in a world of hurt. And you just called him family, or did you forget?"

"Maybe I did, but I'm not a mom."

"I don't see anyone around here expecting you to be. Bones might not know it, but he needs you in the worst way."

"Even if I believed you, I'd still mess the whole thing up. It's what I do."

Jimmy laughed. "Of course you'll mess the whole thing up. But at least this time you won't be messing it up alone."

"I've been alone a long time."

"Yeah? Sounds to me like it's high time to not be."

"You're like Cozy. You make it sound so easy, but it's not." Calico pulled the notebook from her pocket and stared at it.

"Put it in, Calico. Take a chance on second chances."

She shook her head. "What if I just go out and get another one?"

"Put it in."

She turned to the Bones page. Showed it to Jimmy.

"Put it in," he said.

"Look. Thirty-eight cons and one pro. That's thirty-eight reasons I shouldn't."

"And two reasons you should."

"One. You just saw it. Bones needs somebody. That's all that's on the pro side. What if that somebody isn't me?"

"You forgot another one on the pro side. It ain't only Bones. You need somebody too. That makes two." Jimmy's fingers ran down the keys.

"You really think so?"

"Put it in, Calico."

She smiled. "Are you going to charge me five bucks?"

"Not for this. Never. You want to get rid of the past? That's one thing that's always free."

"Here goes nothing, then."

Jimmy's fingers stopped. His eyes fixed on her, blue and milk. "No, Calico, here goes everything."

"You sure?"

"I am."

Calico put the notebook into the box.

And shut the lid.

CHAPTER FORTY-NINE

BONES WAS SURE HE'D SLEEP like a dead man, but he didn't. The night played over and over in his mind. Sal's gun, Rufus's knife—all like a scene out of some wild movie.

And he hadn't told anyone he'd heard his own story as August read. Calico might ask questions he didn't want to answer.

The craziest part, out of all the absurdly implausible events, was that one thing stood out above all the rest. The woman had stood up to Black for him. She'd called him family. She'd had his back. Maybe not in a big way, but it was enough. And against the famous Nelson Black. He couldn't get over it, replayed her words in his head a hundred times.

And now here he was lying on his cot like a chump, feeling things he never should be feeling. She'd said the word *family*. Now he wanted to work harder. To get up and go sweep the stupid sidewalk just to surprise her.

Maybe, for the first time, he belonged.

He stared at the Honda. He could get on it right now. Fire it up. The highway was still out there, still speaking and whispering. But then again, it wasn't going anywhere. Maybe, at least for a while, the Venus might not be so bad. Besides, the roads were washed out, so there was that. Better to hang around and see what happened.

He pulled a book from his stack. Nothing heavy. A heist story about a jazz band and a painting and an eccentric millionaire with a yacht who wanted to blow up a Nazi sub. It wasn't bad, but three chapters in, his eyes got heavy.

He woke hours later, feeling restless. He'd dreamed about Nazis and paintings and a millionaire. Then the millionaire became Nelson Black, who started shooting holes in the hull of the yacht with Sal's pistol.

The shop was dim, but he didn't turn on the light. He washed up and pulled on some cleaner clothes, then stuck Jimmy's unlit cig on his lip and stepped outside to see what the evening had. The sky was low, pressing, still heavy with cloud but no rain.

A slight rustle behind him. He turned to find the cactus wren giving him the eye through the cholla thorns. He'd almost forgotten about the little bird.

He took the cig, holding it between his middle and index fingers like Jimmy did while he sipped his coffee. The memory of his dream was fading now, quickly, as dreams most often do, replaced with last night's memories. Calico would need him soon. There would be setting up and helping in the lounge—and Juan wasn't here. Before that he'd go down and sweep the sidewalk and clean the pool. Even with the cover on, it was probably a mess after the storm.

He saw him then, Black, sitting on a rock, his back against the shop. "Where did you come from?" Bones said.

"You really need to ask?"

"You want something?"

"You have quite the view from here. It really is amazing. I've never been a fan of the desert. Or the outdoors in general, as a rule. But looking at this I can almost see the attraction."

"I'm not stealing the box. I decided."

Black sighed. "I was afraid that might be the next thing to come out of your mouth. I wish you'd reconsider."

"I won't."

"You might."

"Nah."

"Bones, you'll find loyalty is a funny thing. It's like sand. It shifts and moves. You think someone is on your side, think you're part of something. But believe me, it can all be gone in a second." He made a small wiggling gesture with the fingers of one hand. "Like smoke on the wind from one of Jimmy's incessant cigarettes."

"I'm not stealing the box."

"Jimmy's unreasonable. If he'd only take the five million, I wouldn't even need you to steal it. Five million is a fortune."

"Jimmy doesn't care about money. I don't think it's for sale at any price."

"You said everything has a price."

"I think I was wrong about that."

"She'll let you down, you know. They always do."

"I'll take my chances."

Another sigh. "I see it in your eyes. Even in your body language. You're . . . ugh, content. Content is hard to work with."

"I just think I might stick around a while, that's all."

"I see. So what you're saying is you won't be needing a Harley Davidson."

"I got the Honda running. Jimmy got me a coil."

"Oh joy."

"I gotta go."

"I'm curious, Bones. What was your story? What did you hear last night?"

Bones hesitated. "Stories can change."

"Can they?"

"Yeah. Because people can change."

"No, people never change. They've been the same since they first drew breath, and they always will be. That's what makes them so easy."

"I still gotta go."

"Uh-huh. Bye, then. If you change your mind, I'm in room thirteen." He gazed down at the back of the motel. "But you already know that."

CHAPTER FIFTY

THE RAIN HAD BROUGHT ANTS, a long line of them hurrying back and forth along the sidewalk at the base of the wall. Calico would have to get on that before they found their way into the rooms. But this was the desert. Insects and bugs were all part of the package.

Lady Venus still sat dark by the highway in the gathering dusk. It troubled Calico. Maybe the sign had been struck by lightning during the rage. But it didn't look damaged, just dark. If there was a serious issue, it would cost a fortune to fix. Hardly anybody worked on neon on a large scale anymore.

She jumped when her cell phone rang in the pocket of her jeans. She'd checked the thing a hundred times, but she must have missed the service coming back up. She looked at the screen. Juan, not Pines. She pushed her disappointment to the side.

"Hey," she said.

"You all still alive out there?"

"I'm not sure. I made breakfast this morning myself, so we might find some casualties when we check the rooms."

"Oh boy. How was last night? Any damage? You all just hole up?"

"Everything is in one piece. Lady Venus won't come on, though."

"Uh-oh. That's not good."

"Tell me about it. We were all in the lounge all night, believe it or not."

"All? As in all?"

"Yup."

"How was that?"

"That, my friend, is a very, very long conversation."

"With that group, I imagine it might be. But you're okay?"

"I'm good. I really am. You hear anything about the washouts?"

"They got crews out working. Might be passable by tomorrow morning, they say. Got dozers grading out temporary roads. Won't be pretty for a while, but at least you won't be stuck. And I can come to work then."

"I'd think you'd want to sit on a lawn chair enjoying a few days off."

"No way, Jose. All the things Miranda has me doing around here? I need to come back to the Venus to get a break."

"Good for her. Do your chores and make her happy."

"She's married to me. How could she ever not be happy?"

"See you when you can get here."

"You got it, boss. Try not to poison anybody."

"Cozy's cooking tonight."

"I feel better already."

Her phone rang again as she was putting it back in her pocket. She looked at the screen. Took a deep breath. "Where have you been?"

"Hi to you too."

"Do you know how worried I've been, Pines?"

"Sorry. I had to head back into the hills. Way back. We got the guy, though."

"The one killing the cows?"

"A real serious piece of work. I can't wait to tell you about it."

"So you're coming home?"

"Leaving tonight, I hope. Soon as the paperwork is cleared up. And unfortunately, there's a lot."

"I'm sorry, Pines. I'm really so sorry."

"Paperwork's not that bad."

"You know what I'm talking about."

"Look. I had a lot of time to think about it. It's not fair of me to ask—"

"October seventeenth for our wedding." Calico looked down at her engagement ring. "Are you busy October seventeenth?"

"You're serious?"

"One hundred percent. We can do it sooner, if you want. I want to get married, Pines."

"You don't know how happy that makes me."

"I'd be greatly disappointed if it didn't, and that's not a joke. I was worried when I didn't hear from you."

"It would take a lot more than a bad phone conversation to buck me off. You should know that."

"I do, but I still couldn't help worrying."

"I'm sorry. I would have called if I could. We had to leave in a rush, and by the time I had time to even think, there was absolutely no service where I was."

"I understand. I'd hoped it was something like that."

"About Bones. I'll get ahold of CPS as soon as I get back."

"Good. You can tell them he isn't going anywhere. He's staying with us."

"What?"

"You want me, you take Bones too. We come as a package. And I think we need to make this part permanent."

A pause. "Adoption? I was hoping . . . What exactly happened in the last few days?"

"Tell you the truth, I'm still trying to figure it out myself. The short version is I let a lot of things go. In fact, they disappeared. I can't explain it yet, but I feel so different."

"This sounds like quite a story."

"If you only knew how true that statement was. The point is we get to write the end together. What you need to focus on now is groomsmen."

"I don't need groomsmen. Jake will be best man, but we can keep it small. Like you wanted."

"No way, Pines. If we're really getting married, we have to find a place for Bones. That's a deal breaker."

Pines laughed. "And you think he'd make a good groomsman? Can you picture Bones in a tux?"

"No, but I can't picture you in a tux either."

"That's a good point. We can at least clean him up."

"I'll take care of that. Don't worry."

"October seventeenth."

"It's a Saturday. I want to do it here, on the pool deck, under the Lady."

"That's how I always pictured it."

"Come home now, okay?"

She could almost see his crooked-toothed grin.

"I'm on my way."

▼

If there was one thing Bones hated, it was feeling stupid. Stupid was for other people. Loud people, visible people, unidimensional people. Not for him.

But he felt stupid now. How could he have let down his guard? He *never* let his guard down. He'd let himself feel hope. However brief, he'd felt it. The worst thing a guy could do. His short life had taught him hope never failed to disappoint. This was the first ironclad rule of the universe. The second was people always let you down. Black said she would. He'd been so stupid. And so wrong.

She'd stood up for him this morning. And he'd been dumb enough to think things had changed.

Of course, things hadn't changed. Black was right. People *never* changed. They might talk a good game, but the only person you could trust was yourself.

He'd heard her plain as day. Just as he started to round the corner of the motel. *No way, Pines. If we're really getting married, we have to find a place for Bones. That's a deal breaker.* Whatever, neither one of them would have to worry about getting rid of him, because he'd be long gone.

Tomorrow. He'd leave tomorrow.

There was just something he had to do first. Something he'd regret if he didn't. Something he'd practically already done. After all, he'd heard David August read all about it right out loud.

Jimmy had it coming. Jimmy had led him to believe it was okay to hope. Okay to start trusting.

Jimmy had lied.

The only question now was how to do it. How do you become invisible to a guy who never fails to see you? It didn't matter. He'd find a way. He was Bones. He always found a way.

CHAPTER FIFTY-ONE

Cozy turned out to be a pretty good cook. Chicken piccata, something Bones had never heard of. Calico had him help serve, then told him to take a break and eat. But he said he wasn't hungry. In fact, that's about all he said all night. From his booth in the corner, he caught her looking his way several times, concern on her face. But he ignored her. He was here to focus on one thing and one thing only.

Jimmy played his stupid blues. Crazy that Bones had liked Jimmy's music until now. Tonight the notes made him want to tear his own ears off. Jimmy never even looked at him, but he knew Bones was there. Bones could feel it. The box sat on the piano like always. That was the problem. Jimmy was never more than three feet away from the thing. Even when he took a smoke break, which he'd already done once tonight.

Sal and Rufus sat at the bar, Rufus talking nonstop about his ex-wife he'd talked to on the phone that morning after all. From the look on his face, if the roads didn't open soon, the guy was gonna skip the car and run to California. Sal was still talking about roping wild horses. Cozy was with Burt at a table. Burt was smiling, which, Bones realized, he'd never seen the cowboy do before. David August was nowhere to be seen, though Cozy had taken the author a plate of food earlier.

Bones had to shake his head. Stupid, dumb unidimensionals. All of them.

Nelson Black occupied a table by the wall. He had his chair kicked back, his feet propped up on another. Bones didn't have to look over to feel the illusionist's eyes on him. Neither did he feel any compulsion to tell him he'd changed his mind about taking the box. Black already knew. He always knew.

And so the night went. Jimmy playing, Cozy splitting her time between singing and Burt. Calico manning the bar and throwing furtive glances in Bones's direction. Black being Black.

And Bones wracking his brain for a way to get Jimmy away from the box long enough to take the thing, give it to Black, and then get down the road far enough that no one would ever find him or even want to.

And it had to be by tomorrow.

▼

Funny thing was, in the end Bones didn't have to plan at all. Jimmy practically handed the box to him. Not at night in the dark, so no need to even go invisible. His chance came with a rattle of pipes as Jimmy headed out of the parking lot this morning.

Without his pack.

Bones had come down from the shop to start his day, still trying to come up with a plan to steal the box. Calico was outside cleaning her apartment windows.

"Where's he going?" Bones said.

"They got the temporary roads passable this morning. All he said was that he had to run to Tucson. He left just in time for you to clean his room. Cozy's starting down at the other end. If you need me, I'll come help when I'm done here."

"You want me to clean Jimmy's room?" The enormity of the situation and opportunity was sinking in.

"Yes, I want you to clean Jimmy's room. Bones, is something wrong?"

"No."

"Listen. I want to sit down and talk to you tonight, okay? We need to discuss some things."

"Yeah, cool, whatever." He'd heard the same words from more than one foster. Knew what was coming.

"Pines is on his way back."

"Okay."

"Are you mad at me?"

"I can't be mad at you. You're the boss."

"You know better than that."

"I should start cleaning."

"You can talk to me, you know."

"I'll do the sidewalk and the pool when the rooms are done."

She looked at him for a few seconds. "All right. But we talk tonight after dinner. Good?"

He retrieved a cleaning cart from the office and started down the sidewalk. At Jimmy's room he used the passkey and pushed the door open. Not much to do. Jimmy didn't make much of a splash.

He swiped some surfaces with a dustcloth before making the bed and cleaning the bathroom. Then it was time.

It was almost too easy. He started the vacuum and left it running. The pack was on the floor next to the door. He pulled the box out and set it on the bed. Nothing happened. This surprised him a little. He'd half expected the thing to glow red, or start smoking, or talk to him or something. Stupid.

He pulled four full Kleenex boxes out of the cart and forced them into a pillowcase. Stacked two high and side by side, they formed a rectangle roughly the same size as the metal box. He put them in Jimmy's pack, latched it, and set it back by the door. It wouldn't fool anybody for long, maybe not at all. But if it bought him even a little time, it would be worth it. Who knew? Maybe Jimmy wouldn't check the pack at all until tomorrow.

Bones figured the vacuum would buy him at least ten minutes. Plenty of time. He put Jimmy's box into another pillowcase.

The back window opened smoothly, and the screen came off with an easy push. He was through within three seconds, up the hill to his shop in another forty-five. It took only a few more seconds to stash the box into the cavity beneath the loose floorboard. By the time he was back down the hill and back through the window, he'd been gone two minutes, tops. Breathing hard, he rolled the vacuum across the carpet a few times to simulate a reasonable pass, then packed the cart and moved on to the next room.

Cozy was already there. "Hey, kid. Just in time to help me make the bed."

"Okay."

"Are you all right? You're sweating."

"It's hot."

"Not that hot."

"I'm good."

It was everything Bones could do to hold it together through the day. Sweeping the sidewalk and cleaning the pool early afternoon, he swore he heard Jimmy's bike coming every thirty seconds. He'd also decided he didn't trust Black to give him the Harley just because he had the box. Better to hold it for ransom. But no way he'd take the thing with him. Safe under the floor of the shop, no one would find it without clear instruction. You could look right at that board and never suspect anything was different about it.

Then he'd call the number on the card in a few days, and once he had the new Harley, he'd tell Black where to find the object of his weird obsession. But he sure as heck wouldn't tell the magician anything until he'd delivered on his end of the deal.

It was close to seven by the time he was back in the shop. Still no Jimmy. So far, so good. He gathered what cash he had, picked out several books he didn't want to leave behind and put them in two backpacks along with the chips and a few cans of root beer he'd stashed under the floorboard, then tossed in his percolator. He added some of the clothes he didn't want to leave behind, then clipped the packs together, slung them across his back fender, and strapped them down with a couple of bungee cords.

Bike ready, he went to the back of the shop and lifted the loose board.

The metal gleamed in the low light.

It was done, then. Nothing left between him and the highway. Nothing left to do. No one to say goodbye to. Just him and his bike and the sky and the future. He was Shackleton.

He opened the shop door and wheeled the Honda out.

CHAPTER FIFTY-TWO

Bones set his unlit cig on his bottom lip and looked out across the valley toward the purple Chiricahuas. The sunset was massive tonight. Towering orange-gold that seemed to take up half the sky. Piles of leftover storm clouds twisted into weird and fantastic shapes. How strange that this was the last time he'd see this view. But there'd be other places and other sunsets. He'd see things even more amazing than this.

In fact, he told himself, he'd see things so amazing he'd forget all about the sunsets from the Venus. He'd forget Jimmy and Calico and Early. He'd even forget Gomez Gomez and how sad he'd felt watching his friend's ashes swirl up into the wind. He told himself he'd forget everything. He knew deep down he was lying, but he did it just the same.

He turned the Honda's key, and the bike purred to life. A sound he'd waited for—for so long—and here it was. He twisted the throttle a fraction, let out the clutch, and the bike jumped forward with an impatient lurch. *This is it.* He worked both brakes as he rode the steep trail from the shop down toward the motel. He was doing it, man. He was really doing it. In five minutes he'd be gone like he was never here.

He hadn't thought he'd feel nervous when the time came, but he did. He felt something else too. More than one something. He felt mad. He felt sad. He felt cheated though he didn't know why. Nobody had ever promised him anything.

More than anything, he still felt stupid. Stupid for trusting someone other than himself. Stupid for thinking he ever *could* trust someone other than himself. In the end, that's all there was to it. Everyone was out for themselves.

Cool. Whatever. I'd say see you later, but it would be a lie. All you'll see is dust. I'll see a horizon, and after that the whole world. I'll see a million sunsets better than this.

He took the long way around the motel, past the kitchen and around the lounge. The Honda's pipes rattled the walls. He was like a fighter jet doing a final flyby. Let 'em all know Bones was here and now Bones is gone.

He saw Jimmy's Harley as he came around the lounge. He hadn't heard him come back. Then Jimmy himself, leaning against the wall smoking one of his dumb cigarettes. Whatever. On impulse, Bones took the cig from his own lip and flipped it toward the biker as he passed. He wouldn't owe anybody anything. Not even a stupid cigarette. Not anymore. He hit the gas, and the Honda spat gravel.

The parking lot blurred as he flew over it. He was free, man. This was what it was all about right here. Freedom. This was what it had always been about. Everything else had been a distraction. Everything and every*one.* Jimmy, Cozy, Juan, Calico, even Gomez Gomez—all a distraction. Not one of them had ever had his back. Not really. And he needed none of them. He wouldn't look back. Not ever.

He swung around a ladder truck with a couple of guys on it going over Lady Venus. Then there it was, the highway and everything it led to. The scene got blurry. He rubbed his eyes with the hard heel of his hand and told himself it wasn't tears, only the speed and the wind. He'd get some sunglasses at the first town down the road. He downshifted and felt the bike surge.

A mile, two. Okay, maybe they were tears, but who cared? Who was here to see? He was alone, and that was what he wanted. He caught movement in his rearview mirror, but with the tears and the vibration, he couldn't tell what it was. More throttle, more speed. That would be his way of life from now on.

Except the shape in the mirror didn't get smaller. It got bigger. Then he could hear it, even over the sound of his own engine, the unmistakable roar of a Harley Davidson.

No way. Bones gave the Honda every bit of throttle it had. He watched the speedometer climb from fifty to sixty to eighty, then ninety. It topped out at ninety-two. Still, the shape in the rearview grew.

Then it was on him, then beside him. He couldn't make out any details through his tears. Then a great, loud roar, and the thing was in front of him. He saw a red brake light and slowed, then slowed more as the Harley forced him to decelerate. Slower and slower until he had to drop his feet for balance and come to a stop. In that instant, fifteen years of anger breached his internal dam. He shouted at the sky and punched his gas tank.

Stinking Jimmy. Why couldn't he just let him go?

And then someone was in front of him.

Not Jimmy. Jimmy still sat on the Harley.

Calico.

Bones wiped his eyes again. He hit the kill switch on the handlebars, and the Honda's motor went quiet. Out in the sage a cactus wren sang and another answered.

"What are you doing out here?" he said.

"I should ask you the same thing."

"You rode on the back of the Harley?"

"You think my car would have caught you? What are you doing, Bones?"

"I'm riding. What do you think?"

"Are you crying?"

"No. I was going fast."

"All right. Now go fast again. In the other direction. We'll deal with the fact you don't even have a license later."

"I'm leaving."

"Without saying goodbye?"

"I don't know."

"Turn around and go back to the motel."

"You can't tell me what to do."

"I just did."

"I told you. I'm leaving."

"No, you're not."

He reached for the key, but her hand beat him to it. She pulled it out of the ignition.

"Give that to me," he said.

"No."

"Why not?"

"Because I don't want you to leave, Bones."

"Why not?"

"Because I'll miss you."

"No you won't. You won't even notice. If you did notice, it would be a relief."

"I know you think you're invisible. You think I don't see you. But I've got news for you. I see you every second of every day. You don't hide from me, Bones. You never have. Maybe I hid from myself, but that's over now."

"You could hire a lot of guys out there."

"I don't mean I'll miss an employee. I mean I'll miss *you*. I care about you."

"You don't have to say that."

"Yeah, I do, because it's true. Like it or not, it's true, okay? Look. Neither one of us is perfect. We both know that. But we can mess up this life together. You don't have to be alone. If you stay, I don't have to be alone either."

"You won't be alone. You'll have Early."

"Yeah, I will, but I want you to be here too."

"What are you talking about? What about what you said on the phone?"

"What phone? What in the world are you talking about?"

"Man, I thought you were on my side. I almost bought into the whole thing. But then you told Early he had to find a place for me. Don't say you didn't, because I heard you."

She stared at him for a beat or two. "In the *wedding*, you idiot. I told Pines we had to find a place for you in our *wedding*."

"The wedding?"

She held out the key. "Turn that thing around and go back."

The Harley turned over. Jimmy wheeled around and pulled up next to them. "You gonna need a ride?" he said to Calico.

She looked at Bones.

Bones sighed. "She can ride back with me."

"You sure?"

"Yeah."

Jimmy shook out a cig and passed it to Bones. "I think you accidentally dropped yours."

Bones took it. "Yeah, I might have."

Calico climbed onto the back of the Honda as Bones fired it up.

"Go slow," she said.

"Why? You just went like a hundred on Jimmy's Harley."

"That was enough for me. I want to at least live long enough to eat dinner. Juan's back, and he's made carne asada tacos."

"I wonder if he'll make me a burger."

"Maybe, but I'll tell you what. You're going to eat a salad first."

"What?"

"You heard me. I'm making it myself, and you're going to eat every last bite. I'll make one tomorrow too. And if you ever try to leave again, I'll ground you for the rest of your life. Got it?"

"Yeah, I got it." He throttled, careful not to go too fast. He turned on his headlight and rolled through the fading gold.

He rode home.

Weird. Nothing looked blurry now.

CHAPTER FIFTY-THREE

Calico actually did make Bones a salad. And she actually did make him eat it, right there at the bar. Tomatoes and onions and beets and Thousand Island dressing. It wasn't bad except for the beets.

Bones asked Juan for a burger, but the cook told him he could eat carne asada like everyone else. Bones pretended to grumble but secretly kind of liked being lumped in with everyone else.

He was part of something.

Not until he was halfway through his third taco did he remember the box. How could he have forgotten the stinking box? His heart jumped to his throat. Where was Jimmy? Maybe the biker's absence was a good sign. If he knew the box was missing, he'd surely be raising the roof about it.

His mind spun. Assuming Jimmy hadn't noticed the loss yet, there had to be a way to fix this. Maybe there was still time. There had to be time. What would Jimmy think? What would Calico do if she knew Bones had stolen the box? He waited, heart still in his throat. When Calico walked over and started typing on the computer's keyboard, he saw his chance. He slid off his barstool, eyes on the kitchen door. He could have the box in his hands in minutes. But how could he get it back into Jimmy's pack? One thing at a time. He'd find a way. He had to.

He heard the lounge door swing open behind him, and he forced himself to turn. Jimmy La Roux walked in.

With the pack slung over his shoulder.

"Where do you think you're going?" Calico said.

Bones pulled himself present. "Huh?"

"Your dishes and silverware. Take them into the kitchen. You can wash them later, after we clear tables."

"Yeah, okay." Bones kept an eye on the pack, moving slow while he cleared his things from the bar.

"There a problem?" Calico said.

"No." Plate and utensils in hand, Bones pushed through the kitchen door. Juan was washing a pot at the sink and didn't look up. Bones considered. He could be out the back door, up the hill to the shop, and back with the box within two minutes. Then all he'd have to do was distract Jimmy somehow while he made the switch. But how could he distract Jimmy?

One thing at a time.

He was through the kitchen and halfway out the back door when his feet stopped. He looked up at the shop and the pine-topped mountains behind it. The moon was a sliver, hanging beneath a black pile of clouds. Stars bright, as if the storm had given them a good rest. He could do it. He knew he could. He could pull it off. No one would ever know what he'd done.

But he would.

Why did that bother him? It never would have before. But these people were different now. They weren't pawns in a game. They weren't unidimensionals. They were . . . family. He turned around slowly, torn.

Juan was looking at him. "Something wrong, amigo?"

"Yeah, usually."

"Wrong can be fixed, eh?"

"I doubt this can."

But he knew what he had to do. He wouldn't lie to them anymore. What would Calico do? What would she think? Maybe she'd even decide she'd made a mistake making him stay.

Then he heard the piano.

And his heart sank.

Jimmy knew. C'mon, Jimmy *always* knew. How could he ever have thought he could fool the guy? And soon Calico would know too. He hadn't even had the chance to come clean.

He pushed open the door to the lounge. Calico's eyes were on him.

"I took it." he said.

"Took what?"

"The box. I thought you didn't want me here. I thought a lot of things. But even if they were true, I never should have done it."

Calico looked toward the stage, and Bones followed her gaze. The box glinted on the piano.

He looked back at Calico.

"I have a pretty good view of the back hill from my apartment, you know."

"You saw me?"

"And that spot under the floorboard in the shop is kind of an open secret. The old owners told me about it when I was first looking at the place."

"You took it back?"

"I helped. But I had a feeling you'd wind up doing the right thing."

"What if I hadn't?"

"I'm your family, Bones. Get used to it. I told you we'd mess up things. But we're in it together. Got it?"

"Yeah, I got it. But I should tell Jimmy."

"You think he doesn't know? Now help clear the tables so Cozy can sing."

Bones smiled. It felt strange on his face.

CHAPTER FIFTY-FOUR

It was like no one wanted to check out. They were all there except for David August, whom Bones hadn't seen since the storm. Juan was manning the bar, and Calico still shared Bones's booth. She'd had the talk with him she'd mentioned. A talk like none Bones had ever known. Then again, he'd never had a family before.

With the highway passable, the Great Nowak was back with his crew, sucking up to Nelson Black, who was pestering Jimmy about the box. Jimmy, deep in the blues, did a good job of ignoring the guy.

"Five million bucks?" the Great Nowak was saying to Black. "And he's not taking it?"

"Won't budge. Jimmy's what they call a man of principle, aren't you, Jimmy?"

Jimmy said nothing.

"Yeah, but five million bucks. You gonna go higher?" Nowak said.

Black cast an evil eye at the question. "If I was, do you suppose I'd discuss it here in front of the man I'm trying to make the deal with?"

"Yeah, but how long are you gonna try? You've been here . . . what? A week or more?"

"Great Nowak, my friend and esteemed contemporary, I'll keep trying until I get the box. Although I do have an appearance at the MGM Grand in Lost Wages next week, so I hope it doesn't take much longer. If it does, I suppose I'll catch Mr. La Roux down the road. It's become a bit of a ritual, to tell you the truth."

"MGM, huh?"

"Nice place. Ever played there?"

"You know, I can't say that I have."

"If you ever do get the offer, make sure they have the crab salad in the green room. The crab salad is out of this world."

This seemed to please the Great Nowak immensely. "You know, I will. Thanks for the advice."

"My pleasure. How's the wife?"

"Recovering nicely. Thanks for asking."

▼

Later in the evening, all conversation stopped, every eye on the figure standing in the lounge door. David August but not David August. His eyes were bright, determined. Not the watery, bloodshot things Bones had seen before. The man's khakis were clean, and he'd made a reasonable attempt to iron his shirt. He held a full bottle of Bacardí in one hand and his ever-present briefcase in the other. He wore no gun. He looked neither right nor left as he crossed the room to Jimmy at the piano.

"Evening, David," Jimmy said.

"It goes in the box, and then it's gone forever. Right?"

"That's right."

August opened the box and dropped the bottle in with a thud. "I need a new story."

"You're in luck. New stories happen to be the special this week."

August set the briefcase on the piano, worked the combination, and opened it. He took out the manuscript. "This thing has haunted me for years."

"Has it?"

The author thumbed the pages one last time and dropped the pile into the box. "Gone forever."

"I have a feeling you'll write something a whole lot better."

"I have a feeling I will too." He shut the lid, then opened it and grinned. "I really do think I will." He closed the briefcase, then crossed the room and set it on the bar in front of Rufus and Sal. "Juan, you have any coffee going?"

"You bet."

Sal pointed at the case. "What's this?"

"I have to tell you a secret, boys. I used you."

"You what?"

"The novel I really want to write? Not the one about pirates. It's about a couple of wannabe hard cases I met at the El Faro Beach Club bar." He glanced at Burt. "Burt, you'll be vindicated to know I was channeling my inner Elmore Leonard."

Burt laughed and lifted his coffee cup.

"You used us?" Rufus said.

"I did. I wanted to get in my head how you'd talk, how you'd act, when you thought you were right next to the big score. I never expected you to bring a gun, though. Not even a knife."

"You used us," Rufus said again.

"I did."

"For a David August novel."

"The very thing."

"Dave, that's the single greatest thing I've ever heard."

"You're welcome, Rufus."

"Rufus? Not Russell?"

"Rufus."

"So what now?" Sal said. "Are you giving us two million bucks for our service?"

David laughed. "Lord, no. I'm not that generous. But there's a pretty chunk in there to get you down the road. Consider it a thank-you."

Sal opened the case and thumbed through the bills. "This ain't a bad thank-you, Rufus. Check it out."

"Dave," Rufus said. "I don't even know what to say. Man, I can't believe you considered us as characters for an actual novel."

"We are what you call colorful, though. Remember?" Sal said.

"You certainly are," August said.

"I suppose the story's over," Rufus said. "What with us shunning our wicked ways and all?"

August laughed. "Are you kidding? You follow a story where it goes. How about this for a storyline? A defalcator surfer who winds up wanting to make good and an obnoxious Brooklyn gangster who actually ropes a wild horse. Literary gold. I'll get the money back on the advance alone, not to mention the film rights."

"Defalcator?" Rufus said.

"It means bandit, criminal, crook," Sal said.

Rufus stared at his friend, then laughed. "You don't know what a conquistador is but you know defalcator?"

"It's all about context, man."

"Yeah, I guess it is."

Sal leaned forward a little, his eyes bright. "So, Dave, I'm gonna start a ranch. And Burt's gonna help me. You want to write about that?"

"That's just the stuff. An almost mobster lassos a wild horse and starts a ranch."

"Ropes, not lassos. Right, Burt?"

"On the money," Burt said.

August smiled. "I'll make a note. And I hope you don't mind me tagging along for a while to take notes. My ex-wives will tell you I'm an acquired taste."

The phone behind the bar rang, and Juan answered. "Calico, it's for you. The sign guys."

Calico slid out of the booth and walked over. "Hello?" Her eyebrows drew together as she listened for a few seconds. "Uh-huh. You're sure about that? That's solid?" Another few seconds. "Is there any wiggle room on that? Okay. I see. No, hold off for now, and I'll let you know."

"What did he say?" Cozy said as soon as Calico ended the call.

"He thinks it might have been lightning. Along with weather and a whole lot of years. They're talking about a hundred and twenty-five thousand dollars to make her like new again."

"That much?" Juan said. "Seems like you could buy a dozen brand-new signs for that."

"But there's only one Venus."

"It just so happens Rufus and I are a little flush at the moment," Sal said. "We'll kick in."

"Absolutely." No hesitation from Rufus.

"Not on your life," August said. "I'll cover it. After all, with what I'm saving on liquor, it'll be pocket change."

"You're all very kind, but I can't take your money. No way."

The piano stopped mid-song, and all eyes turned to the stage.

"No argument," Rufus said. "We'll help."

Jimmy took out a cigarette, stuck it on his lip but didn't light it. "How much is a house in Ventura these days, Rufus? I'd guess a bit more than is in that case."

"Probably," Rufus said. "Still . . ."

"And horse ranches can't be cheap."

"That ranch can wait," Sal said.

"What are you trying to say, Jimmy?" Rufus said.

Jimmy fingered a note or two, then looked at Black. "It's just a box, Nelson. I been telling you for years."

Black stood with a rush. "Are you serious, Jimmy? Five million. I'll write you a check right now."

Another note. "A hundred twenty-five thousand, wired to Calico's account. I don't take checks from illusionists, no offense."

"What? That's all you want?"

"I believe that's a hundred thousand more than your very first, original offer. In the end, I'm pretty proud of my negotiating skills."

Black narrowed an eye. "What's the catch?"

"Catch is it's just an old box, man. Is it yes or no? Decide before I change my mind."

"A resounding yes." Black pulled out his phone. "I'll have the money wired immediately. Calico, I just need your pertinent information."

Calico looked at Jimmy. "You can't do it. I won't let you."

"Not your choice. It's my box. At least for the next couple of minutes."

"At least take the five million," Bones said.

Jimmy lifted a shoulder. "David said it pretty well. Money like that, a guy's arm is bound to get tired. Don't take much gas to fill up a Harley. Calico, give Nelson your routing number and get the Lady Venus some love. She deserves it, and so do you. I wanna see you both shining the next time I come this way."

"But the box," Calico said. "I won't do it."

"Yeah, you will." Jimmy started to play. A growling blues shuffle. He smiled and winked. "It's nonnegotiable. Give him the number."

"Jimmy, are you sure?"

"A hundred and twenty-five thousand percent."

CHAPTER FIFTY-FIVE

Bones sat on the dresser in room fourteen watching Jimmy pull his few things together. "Five million dollars. You know how many Harleys you could buy with five million dollars?"

"I already have a Harley that suits me fine."

"I don't."

"You'll get there someday. You'll buy it yourself."

"Maybe. But I think I'm actually cool where I am right now."

"Bones-with-the-unspeakable-last name, you have stumbled upon the great secret of life."

"I think my last name might be Pines pretty soon. That's what Calico says."

"I'm happy for you."

"The thing is . . ."

"What?"

"Last night I wanted to put something in the box."

Jimmy looked up at this. He straightened. "Yeah?"

"Yeah. But then Nelson couldn't get out of there with it fast enough, and Calico said he checked out before sunrise this morning."

"He might have thought I'd change my mind. He's been after that thing for a long, long time. What were you gonna put in the box?"

"Well, I heard my story too, and it ended with me alone. I thought that was fine, but now I don't."

"Stories change."

Bones held up the key to the Honda. "I know. Still, I was gonna put this in."

"Your key? No joke?"

"All that bike really meant for me was getting out of here. But now . . . You think they'll make me wear a tux for the wedding?"

"I doubt it. And you can have a bike without wanting to ride to the edge of the world, you know."

"I know. But I wanted to change my ending like everybody else."

"It looks like it's changed to me. Sometimes it happens like that. Now you know you're loved."

"But I want to *do* something. Something to earn it. Or pay it back."

"You think you can earn love?"

"You know what I mean."

Jimmy sighed. "You mean you wanted to make a gesture."

"Yeah."

"All right. Tell you what. Toss the key into that ice bucket there."

"What?"

"You heard me. Toss it in."

"It doesn't count. It's not the box."

"You said yourself it's just a gesture. That's what you wanted. Toss it in. You'll feel good."

Bones rolled his eyes, lifted the lid off the bucket, and tossed the key in. "I feel the same."

"You gotta put the lid on."

Bones did.

"Now take it off.

Bones lifted the lid and reached in for the key. "Wait. How did you do that?"

"Feel better?"

"Seriously, man, how? What about the box?"

"I don't know how many times I have to say it. That was just an old metal box. That's it."

"I still don't understand. Black really bought a plain old box?"

"I tried to tell him."

"Dude, he's gonna blow a gasket."

"Ain't life fun?"

Jimmy lifted his pack to his shoulder and headed out the door. Bones followed. They stood for a minute watching a crew work on the Venus sign.

"That was cool what you did for Calico," Bones said.

"Yeah, but it was for me too. I'd be sad if the Lady wasn't waving me in when I get back this way."

"You'll be back, then?"

"What do you think this is, that old movie *Shane*? I'm not riding off into the sunset. I just got a gig for a few weeks up in Coeur d'Alene, that's all. I should have left this morning, but that Juan makes some menudo good enough to make a man wait, right? You oughta try it."

"Never. When will you be back, then?"

"Ah, I don't imagine it'll be long. Can't stay away from the Lady. You take care of yourself, huh?"

"Yeah."

Jimmy threw a leg over the Harley, then reached into the pocket of his denim shirt, fished something out, and flipped it to Bones. It was the Honda key.

"How did . . ."

Jimmy snuffed his cig out on the palm of his hand, flicked it out onto the gravel, then winked. He hit the throttle, and a minute later he'd disappeared down the highway, the sound of pipes fading.

Bones put the key in his pocket. Then he whistled one of Jimmy's blues tunes through his teeth as he looked out over the valley. It was one of those wide Arizona afternoons. The quiet kind, where tall piles of pillowy clouds pull their shadows across a valley floor, everything sand and sage and sunlight and sharp angles. Where the sky is so deep it feels endless, and hawks dip and circle on the updrafts and never get tired.

He stuck his unlit cig on his bottom lip, picked up the broom leaning against the wall . . .

And started sweeping stardust off the sidewalk.